Grace Restored Series, Book 4:

Summer Secrets

C.J. Peterson

Texas Sisters Press, LLC

This book is dedicated to my loving husband and dear family who love and support me. You all mean more to me than you will ever know. Thank you! I love you!

A portion of the proceeds will be donated to Hope's Door, whose mission is to offer intervention and prevention services to individuals and families affected by domestic violence and to provide education programs that enhance the community's capacity to respond. To learn more about them, check out their web page: http://www.hopesdoorinc.org/

To learn more about C.J. Peterson, you can find her online at:
http://cjpetersonwrites.com/
'While the stories are fiction, the journey is real!'

C.J. Peterson

Summary

Summer Secrets is the fourth book in the Grace Restored Series, which follows the life of Katie MacKenna. Struggling after a tumultuous year of loss and being targeted by an unknown person who calls himself 'The Hunter,' Nick decided she needed a break and took her to his home in Australia. Katie was hoping to leave Joey Rossi and Cristian Gombeda behind for some rest and relaxation, but things are far from relaxing in Australia. She thought she knew Nick, but upon their arrival she learns about his identical twin brother, Nate, who she had no idea even existed. How many more secrets are contained within Australia's borders? Is Nick really who she thinks he is? What else will she discover during this season? What has become of the situation regarding Joey Rossi and Cristian Gombeda?

Matthew 10:26-28

[26] "So have no fear of them, for nothing is covered that will not be revealed, or hidden that will not be known. [27] What I tell you in the dark, say in the light, and what you hear whispered, proclaim on the housetops. [28] And do not fear those who kill the body but cannot kill the soul. Rather fear him who can destroy both soul and body in hell.

Table of Contents

C.J. Peterson

Preface

Scenes from Book 3 of the Grace Restored Series:

SPRING SHADOWS

"Mornin', y'all!" Katie said with a smile on her face. Both she and Nick were the only two who knew it was a forced smile. After the conversation they had in the car about her frustrations in wanting to quit, she didn't want anyone's pity.

"Hey, Katie!" Emma got up from her desk and gave her a hug, closely followed by everyone else in the office that she knew. "You're looking *much* better these days."

"Thanks." Katie blushed. "Still working on the recovery portion, but this vacation should do us both some good," she said, giving Nick's hand a squeeze.

"The full six weeks?" Seth asked. Nick nodded in response. "Good. We'll miss you, but this is a much deserved vacation."

"Are you saying we will be without your slaughtered vernacular for a whole six weeks?" a guy sitting at one of the new desks in a three-piece suit asked. To Katie, he seemed haughty from the start, and she instantly didn't care for him.

"Katie, I would like to introduce you to one of our latest acquisitions. He's still on a trial basis, though you wouldn't know it by his bold arrogance. Katie MacKenna, this is Eugene Kennedy," Nick introduced them.

As Katie shook his hand, Eugene explained, "Yes, I am Eugene Kennedy of the Kennedy family. This is only a brief stopping point before achieving my aspirations to attain a position in the real office."

Katie looked to Nick for an explanation. "The DC office," Nick clarified.

"And, he only *thinks* he's a Kennedy, but he's actually a distant relative, four times removed. I, however, *am* a relative of Lyndon B. Johnson. Chad Johnson, at your service," Chad introduced himself, taking the shot at Eugene, as he bent in half to kiss Katie's hand.

"A southern boy?" Katie asked.

"Texas. Born and bred." Chad nodded. Chad seemed more relaxed and laid back. He stood around six foot, with light brown hair, and dark brown eyes. His southern charm definitely endeared him more to her than Eugene's arrogance.

"How are you related to LBJ?"

"My great-great-grandmother was his sister."

"Oh! So you really *are* related to him?"

"Oh yeah."

"That has helped him to get to where he's going," Seth explained. "He's getting fast-tracked through here on his way to potentially the Secret Service or CIA."

"Yeah. I haven't decided which one yet," Chad added.

"Kennedy, on the other hand – "

"I *am* a Kennedy," Eugene cut Nick off. "I only need to narrow the exact route through the family tree."

"He's been too busy chasing other goals," Seth jumped back into the conversation. "Agent Kennedy *is* cocky, but he has a right to be. You see, he's a Harvard graduate, who went into the Air Force Special Operations group after graduation. His background includes sniper."

"Yes, unfortunately he *does* have a right to brag there. He's a great shot," Nick agreed. "Unfortunately, his vision deteriorated due to being in the desert so long, and they pulled him from his position."

"Much to my dismay," Eugene added. The six-foot-two, twenty-nine-year-old, had short, dark-brown hair and blue eyes. "So, I joined the FBI."

"Only because the CIA wouldn't take him," Todd said from his desk where he was doing research on his computer.

"Ya know, ya keep that up and it may discourage me from goin' to the CIA," Chad pointed out.

"Here's hoping," Todd commented. "We'd like to keep you. However, if you go to the Secret Service, at least we'll know you're moving up, instead of moving down."

"Ouch!" Katie chuckled. "Don't like the CIA much. Do you?"

Todd shook his head. "Not so much."

"They think they're better than us," Nick explained.

"Then in that case, Agent Kennedy *is* in the wrong agency," Katie quipped.

"Your first impression has much to be desired," Eugene pointed out. "I have achieved much success in my exploits. I am aware of your adventures, and am surprised that your intellect is still intact and balanced. Any accolades you receive, seem to be at the expense of others, yet your fortitude to continue intrigues me. Does it not concern you that you pose a danger to those around you?"

Katie narrowed her eyes at him as she crossed her arms. Feeling that Katie was a volcano about to blow, Nick wrapped his arm around her shoulders to hold her in place, while he covered her mouth with his other hand.

Seth finagled his way between Katie and Eugene. Getting into Eugene's face, he demanded, "Where do you get off talking to her like that?"

"I've read the reports. I'm aware of the continuous endangerment that seems to surround her. I'm not comfortable in the least at the idea of having her be a colleague of mine."

When Katie went to jump at him, Nick had to wrap both of his arms around her to hold her back. Standing her ground, she responded to Eugene with an icy tone, "Your irrational judgment of me is offensive and absurd. My past and current status is none of your concern. I am a formidable opponent on any field, despite being a target on several occasions. I know who I am and my limitations. I know *where* I came from and know *Who* has my future. You, however, shame your pseudo family supposedly routed in the Kennedy clan! Your only attribute seems to be that you can fire a weapon with extreme accuracy. However, if you cannot gain the favor of your fellow compatriots, then you, sir, are a lost cause and a liability. Get off your high horse, and come down to the real world, or you're in trouble!"

His eyes momentarily popped wide-open before he listened with intrigue. "The phraseology in which you form your argument intrigues me."

"You use big words, thinking no one else knows them. Hate to break it to you, Sparky, but this bunch is bright. You may think you're talking over them, but in reality, knowing them, they're talking circles around you."

"My, my! Your temperament has much to be desired as well." He then asked Nick, "Has she always been this bellicose?"

"Don't know what ya mean?"

"He means to say that I'm disagreeable and have a temper," Katie translated.

"Her hostility is gauged by those around her," Seth pointed out. "It's justified ninety-nine point nine percent of the time. If you want to fit in here, you'd better do a much better job of appreciating the skills and assets of those around you."

"Some are a little easier than others," he said under his breath.

"She's a feisty little filly, but I like her," Chad said, going back over to his desk. "Seems to be able to hold her own with even a pompous, arrogant, mule."

"Are you calling me a donkey?" Eugene asked, appalled.

"No." Chad glared at him, as he clarified, "Due to the ladies present, I'm not going to use the term I would like. I'm too much of a gentleman to offend them. When they're gone, I'll let you know *exactly* how I feel about your display."

"I'm not afraid of you," Eugene said, crossing his arms in a huff.

"You should be." Chad got up from his desk and stood toe-to-toe with Eugene. Looking him in the eyes, he said, "I've wrestled pigs with more manners and better breeding than you. Taking you down will be a pleasure and a treat."

"You wouldn't dare!"

"Try me," he said, and left for the printer.

"Well, that was fun," Dakota huffed. "A word of advice, friend?" he offered to Eugene, as he crossed his ankles on his desk and rested his hands behind his head.

"Do I *want* to know?"

"I would heed the advice and take notes," Todd advised. "He's been around for quite a while."

"What is it?" Eugene asked, impatiently.

"I know who trained her. There's a reason the big guy's holding her back."

"What do you mean?"

"You think her tongue is sharp? I, personally, wouldn't want to go into a hand-to-hand match with that young lady you just insulted. The one holding her back is the one who trained her. He's about the only one in here who can beat her."

Eugene slowly turned toward Katie in shock. "Her? She's lanky at best."

"It's not how much muscles ya have, mate," Nick reminded him. "It's how you use them."

*   *   *

"I cannot believe it's taken so long for us to get here," Katie said as they began their decent into Cairns, Australia, after their stopover in Sydney.

"It's worth the trip. I promise you."

"I'm sure. I'm excited, yet nervous to meet your family."

"Wanna know the interesting part of this trip?"

"What?"

"My mum and dad don't know."

"What do you mean they don't know?" Katie asked, horrified. "Aren't we going to their house?"

"Yep. Nana and Pop know, but not Mum or Dad."

"You can't be serious!" Katie said, panic setting in.

"It's been ten years. Trust me. They'll just be happy we're here."

"You're just going to have us drop in after ten years without warning?"

"It's a good secret. There is such a thing as good secrets."

*   *   *

They pulled up to what Katie would consider a cottage type home, situated on the beach. "Nice."

"It's small, but it's all they need," he said, getting out of the vehicle.

The tiny, beachfront cottage was wrapped with white wood siding and light blue shutters. Located on an acre of land, the three-bedroom, two-bathroom home had a nautical feel to it, and she couldn't wait to see what the inside looked like. Taking a deep breath of the air, she exclaimed, "Love the smell of the ocean."

Nick pulled their suitcases from the trunk. "Mum and Dad do too, but I would much rather be on the station." He paid their taxi driver before they headed toward the front door.

When he knocked on the door, it flew open in a matter of seconds. Squealing in excitement, his mom threw her arms around his neck and screamed, "Nicky!"

"G'day, Mum," he said with a grin ear to ear. Then he gestured to Katie, as he said, "Mum, I'd like ya t' meet my girlfriend, Katie MacKenna."

"Ohhhh!" she gushed as she hugged Katie. "She's a looker! Good onya, Nicky!" At first, Katie froze, not expecting the hug, but quickly recovered and returned the hug. "Let me take a good look at ya both." She stood back and crossed her arms as she shook her head. "Yer lookin' a bit on the slim side." She turned Nick to the side, examining him. "Tsk! Tsk! Tsk! Nana's gonna fill ya till yer full ten times over!"

"We're goin' to the station?" he asked, pleasantly surprised.

"Actually, Nana told us you were comin'," she said with a grin. "She wanted us t' come out to the station, but I objected until she fessed up. Yer a sneaky lil' buggar. Ya almost got away with it. We have a barbie t'night t' welcome ya back, and then head out t' the station on Monday, givin' us Sunday t' rest."

"Great!" He grinned.

"C'mon in. Yer ol' man is in the house."

He raised an eyebrow. "Too lazy t' answer the door?"

"Na. He thought maybe you were Nate. He's not happy with that ocker lately."

"Nate?" Katie questioned.

"My brother. He's a drongo of the worst kind."

"He's the reason Nicky went to the States to begin with. I'm just so glad yer here," she said with tears in her eyes. She hugged him again, not wanting to let him go.

"It's okay, Mum. I get it. It put me in a better position in life."

"But, we haven't seen ya in forever."

He hugged her back as he kissed her head. "I'm here now. Please enjoy this time we have."

"How long are ya here for?"

"About five and a half weeks."

"Nice!" she said, wiping the tears off her face. "Let's go."

"Is, uh, Nate comin' over?" Nick asked, glancing at Katie.

"If he does, she'll be shark bait," they heard a voice from the dining room.

"Hey, ol' man!" Nick smiled, happy to see his dad.

"Wait. What do you mean, shark bait?" Katie asked.

"The bush ranger likes the sheilas. Yer a looker, an' don't think it's gonna escape his eyes. And, the fact that she's with you?" His dad shook his head and sighed. "Yeah, that just sweetens the pot."

"I don't understand."

"Whenever the boys got together, there has always been trouble. Now, Nicky's always been a good boy."

"Yes, the golden haired son of the two of us," Nate said, leaning on the wall next to the kitchen from where he entered the front of the house.

Nick's head snapped up at the sound of his brother's voice. "Nate."

Katie looked from Nate, to Nick, wide-eyed. The only difference Katie could see was that Nick was about two inches taller than Nate. "Oh, dear heaven!" Katie said, stunned.

"Well, she's a beauty, brother. Did ya bring me a treat from the good ol' U.S. of A.?" he asked, resting his arm over Katie's shoulder.

Katie pushed his arm off and moved closer to Nick. She felt violated, even though he barely touched her. Still in shock by their appearance, she struggled to find something to tell them apart. If he was as dangerous as he seemed, she would need to be able to tell which one was which, or she could be in trouble!

Chapter 1

Summer in Paradise?

"Keep yer hands off, mate," Nick snapped, wrapping his arm protectively around Katie as he glared at his identical twin brother, Nate. "She's not for you. She wouldn't even pee on you if you were on fire. She's very intuitive when it comes to reading people."

"Nicky!" His mom smacked his arm. "Such language!"

"Oh, no. You've gone an' upset Mum. Now who's the bad son?" Nate chuckled. "You've been here all of five minutes an' you've already buggared up? That must be a record for you."

"Shove off!" Nick shot, taking a step toward his brother.

"Boys, boys, don't get yer brumbies in a bunch. Have a seat. Let's talk it out. Paige, wanna get us somethin' t' drink? Take Katie with ya," his dad, Zack, said. "She doesn't need t' hear this. Come t' think of it, we'll go t' the backyard so she doesn't have to. Way t' make a first impression, Nate."

"Nothin' I did," he objected while Zack shoved them out the door.

When they were out of earshot, Paige mentioned, "There's a set of twins in each generation. In his father's case, the boys are fraternal, but they're a lot alike. In the case of Nicky and Nate, they're identical, but couldn't be more opposite if they tried."

"I can't believe how much they look alike. I'm really struggling to find something different about them."

"It's in the eyes, love. The anger got a hold of Nate early. We sent Nicky away so it wouldn't get him too. That's my only regret in life," she said as they went to the kitchen. "Would ya mind gettin' the glasses from that cupboard t' yer left?" Paige asked, pulling the lemonade and beer from the fridge. "I assume yer gonna want the lemonade?"

"Oh, yes please. I don't drink."

"I knew ya looked like a good girl." Paige smiled. "Just two glasses. The boys are gonna want these." She lifted the beer to the counter.

"Um, Nick doesn't drink anymore either."

"Oh! Didn't know that. Okay." She shrugged. "Then pull out a glass for him too. He's gonna need it," she said, nodding toward the window where they could see Nate and Nick yelling at each other, while Zack leaned against a tree with his arms crossed, keeping a close eye on them. "He doesn't know what t' do with 'em. This is not how we wanted Nicky's homecoming t' be. Maybe at the barbie he'll relax."

"Bar-b-que?" Katie asked.

"Yes. We're gonna have t' teach you some new terms, or yer gonna miss half the conversations…especially when we get t' the station. Nana doesn't take mercy on anyone. She's a tough ol' bird. Tough as they come."

Katie watched her pouring the drinks before she asked, "Please don't take this the wrong way, but you look tired. Would you like me to take these outside?"

"Oh, sweetie, I couldn't take it wrong. I *am* tired. But, no worries, I'll take them out." She patted Katie's hand.

Katie cocked her head to the side, watching her. "With all due respect, is there something Nick doesn't know about you?"

Paige froze at her words. Gently setting the pitcher of lemonade on the counter, she slowly looked up at Katie. "How do you know?"

"My mother died of leukemia when I was seven. I know what someone looks like who has gone through chemo. Is that the reason Nana had to tell you Nick was coming? Was it because you were too tired from chemo to go to the station?"

"Amazing." Paige shook her head. "Yes, that's why. And, no, Nicky doesn't know."

"Does Nate?"

"No one in the family knows except Zack. We've been keeping it from them in hopes of remission."

"What is it?"

"Breast cancer."

"How bad?"

"Not too bad for the moment. Please don't tell Nicky."

"I won't, but please don't wait until the last minute. That wouldn't be fair to him."

"I'll tell him if it gets really bad," she promised. "He really likes ya, ya know? He's never brought a girl here."

"Thank you." Katie smiled. "I like him too. He's such a sweetheart."

"Very protective, though. However, using my powers of observation, I'm thinkin' you don't need protectin'."

"What do you mean?"

"Ya look strong. What do ya do for a livin'?"

"I'm a police officer."

"Yeah. He doesn't like wimpy girls. Well, he used to, but now he's lookin' for substance over looks…not that ya don't have both by the look a' ya," she said with a wink and a smile. "C'mon, looks like Zack may need that beer already. Nicky may even reconsider an' want one when he's finished with that conversation."

*   *   *

That afternoon, while the guys argued and got things settled between them, Katie went down to the beach. She spent the time in prayer, surrounded by the serenity of the ocean. Tuning out the yelling, she watched the wondrous nature that surrounded her.

"Be careful of the sun, love. This is the perfect time of year t' come this way. Being the dry season, the humidity is low, and the breezes are frequent," Paige said, sitting on the beach next to her. She passed her a glass of lemonade. "You'll burn in a tic if yer not aware, though."

"Speaking of which, you shouldn't be in the sun either," Katie said before she took a sip of the refreshing lemonade. "Wow! This is great!"

"Thank you. I'll tell ya what. If ya come back with me, I'll get out of the sun."

"Deal." Katie got up, brushing off the sand. "This place is gorgeous. I know why y'all live here."

"Lived here all our married life. If we were t' attempt t' buy this place now, we wouldn't be able t' afford it."

"I'll bet!"

"But that Nicky? He'd much rather be sweatin' in the sun, working with his hands. I shoulda let 'im stay on the station, but I didn't think that was far enough," she said as they slowly walked back to the house.

Katie pocketed a couple pretty shells, as they continued on their way back. "Far enough from what?"

"From the anger."

"Not sure what you mean."

"I'll tell ya about it later. Right now, we gotta separate those boys."

"Yes, ma'am."

"Oh, no reason for such formalities, love. Just call me Paige."

"Not sure if it's in me to call you that."

"Ya got two choices, love. You can call me Paige or Mum. Choice is yours."

Katie smiled, shaking her head. "Sorry, it's a sign of respect."

"I get that, but ya got two choices, Buckley's and none," she said with a twinkle in her eye.

"What does that mean?"

"It's Paige or Mum."

"All right," Katie agreed, knowing she would more than likely do her best not to call her by name until she was sure of where she stood. Paige seemed open and real. While she appreciated it, it seemed a little out of place to her.

"Fine! But you bloody well better not lay another finger on her or I'll have your guts for garters!" Nick growled as he stood less than six inches from Nate's face. They were still in the backyard with Zack in the middle of them.

"Well, he's madder than a cut snake!" Paige looked at him, wide-eyed. "Wonder what 'e said?"

"Don't think I wanna know," Katie mumbled. "I'm not used to seeing him this angry."

"That's why we sent 'im away. When Nate's not around, Nicky's in a much better mood."

"I see."

Walking over to Katie and his mom, Nick took Katie's hand, as he said, "Katie, let's go for a walk. I need t' get out of here."

"Tell ya what. In the interest of family relations, I'll go so you can get t' know yer parents again. I'll be back for the barbie. Wouldn't miss it for the world," Nate said, and spun on his heal before leaving out through the backyard fence.

"Okayyy, what did I miss?" Katie asked, nervously tucking her hair behind her ear.

"Well, that was quite a welcome home," Zack said, as the group headed back into the house. "That bloke's gonna get 'imself nicked if 'e's not careful."

"He's been in the cooler more than once," Paige mentioned over her shoulder while heading into the kitchen.

"And, he'll be in there again. That boy's gonna be the death a' me." Zack sighed, shaking his head.

Paige poked her head around the kitchen doorway for a moment. "At least ya got one good son," she said, and disappeared back into the kitchen.

"Well, have a seat, Katie. Seems with as angry at Nicky got, that we need t' get t' know ya."

"What do you mean by that?" Katie asked, taking her seat at the table.

"He's only that protective of those 'e holds close t' him. I have a feelin' he brought ya here t' meet us," Zack said, glancing at Nick before turning back to Katie. "His inner circle is extremely small, an' I promise ya he hasn't brought a single lady home with 'im before you. So, tell me about yourself, love. I have a feelin' we're goin' t' be family sometime in the near future," Zack said with a satisfied grin.

"You've turned into a cheeky lil' buggar in your old age, haven't ya, ol' man?" Nick teased.

"And, your language has completely changed," Katie said. "I'm having some trouble following the conversations."

"No worries. We'll teach ya. As far as you, boy, you've gotten more brazen in yer old age," Zack added, lightheartedly chastising him.

"Just lettin' ya know I missed ya."

"Wouldn't have ya any other way. Now," he turned back to Katie, "tell me about yourself, love."

"Well," she cleared her throat, "I'm a police officer with the Cleveland Police Department."

"Only for another year or so," Nick pointed out. "After that, she's headed to Quantico."

"Yer gonna be a fed?" Zack asked, amazed.

Katie nodded. "Yes, sir. Nick's been training me for more than three years."

"Well, then, you shouldn't have any trouble. Keep those skills handy if Nate's around."

"Kind of surprised to hear you speak about your son like that."

"He's always been a bit of an ocker."

"Not a good guy," Nick explained. "I'll do my best to keep up with the translations for you."

"I appreciate it," Katie said. Then she turned back to Zack and asked, "Now, considering that I had no idea Nick even *had* a brother," she glanced at Nick, whose face flushed in embarrassment before she looked back to his dad, "What can you tell me about Nate?"

"Not surprisin' ya didn't know about Nate. There are days I'd like t' forget him myself." His dad chuckled, easing Nick's anxiety. "Ya see, they may be twins, but they're nothin' alike. Basically, everything ya know about Nicky, apply the mirror opposite to 'is brother. Now, I know 'e's my son, but the anger got 'im early, takin' 'im from me too soon."

"What does that mean?"

"It means there's a curse put on this family from generations back. Ya see, while the last three generations were born Aussies, the generation prior was Irish through an' through. As the story goes, a witch cast a spell on our clan when my mum's father killed her son. Now, those were dark days in our clan's history, but it has unfortunately stuck with our family, an' in each generation the anger attacks an' stays with a male member."

"Except for your generation," Nick said.

"Oh no. Even you don't know of our brother, Jasper."

"*What*? *Who*?" Nick looked at him in shock. "I'm sorry, Katie, I had no idea of any of this."

"It's true. He doesn't," his dad defended him, seeing the shock on both of their faces. "We hid it from 'im in order to do our best to save 'im. Ya see, Jasper didn't make it outta his teen years. He died shortly before his nineteenth birthday. We're not even able to utter his name around Mum, or she'll skin us alive. She's done 'er best t' bury it, but it's still there, an' yer old enough now to understand."

Nick couldn't believe what he was hearing. *How could he have an uncle he didn't know about? Where did this curse come from, and why wasn't he told about it before now?* "I don't – I don't have a clue what you're talkin' about."

"Of course not, Nicky," Paige said, coming into the dining room with a tray of cold cuts, bread, and a bowl of chips. "We didn't want ya t' know. Last time you were here, you were just a boy at seventeen, but now yer a man. We also needed t' tell ya face-to-face. This is not something you explain over the phone. Sorry you have t' hear it as well," Paige apologized to Katie.

"It's okay, really. It's just something I've never heard," Katie explained, wondering what else she didn't know about Nick and his family.

"By the look a' ya, yer Irish as well?" Paige asked, taking her seat.

"Yes, ma'am," Katie said.

"Then you are familiar with the dark side of life in Ireland in the ol' days?"

"Yes, ma'am."

"Then you should understand that what we are sayin' is entirely true."

"It could be, but it's something I've never heard of first-hand. I always thought that stuff was a myth."

"Where there's light, there's dark. Do not be mistaken. You have no clue of the things going on around you," a man said, leaning on the wall next to their sliding screen door that led out to the beach.

"Ethan! C'mon in," Zack said, getting up from the table and opening the door, giving Ethan a hug. "Nicky, Katie, this is one of my mates, Ethan Carson. He's, uh…." He looked to Ethan for help.

As he shook hands with Katie and Nick, Ethan explained, "I am with a group known as A.N.G.E.L. –"

Katie studied him only for a moment before she cut him off, "Why are you here?"

"What do you mean?" he asked, confused.

"You're strong…in a good way. I don't know exactly what you do, but the room lightened up when you came in," Katie said, her body on edge at everything she had run into since landing.

Ethan shook his head as he crossed his arms. "Hawk warned me of the possibility, but I didn't think it was true."

"What was true?" Katie asked. She felt on edge, yet he had a strange familiarity to him. "Who are you?"

"Katie!" Nick looked at her, surprised by her sudden assertiveness.

"What are you involved in?" Katie demanded from Ethan.

"Wow! She's good!" Ethan said, as he sat down at the table with the others. "I'll address that in a moment," he said to Katie. Then he turned to Nick and explained, "While you are well grounded, young Katie here is in tune with the inner person."

"She is a good judge of character," Nick agreed.

"It's more than that. Whether she knows it or not, she can tell if a person is one of His, seeking, or have committed to the other side."

"You're a bit cryptic there, mate. Can you be more specific?"

Ethan sighed, shaking his head with a chuckle. "Ohhh, Hawk's gonna owe me big for this one. The little buggar knew what he was sending me into."

"*Meaning*?" Nick demanded, on edge himself. "Look, we've not had a good start here, and frankly you're not helpin'."

"Certain gifts are handed out by the Spirit. Katie's is discernment and wisdom."

"I'm still in the room," Katie reminded him, her voice cold.

"I know. I'm settling his spirit first," he apologized to Katie. When he turned back to Nick, he explained, "Certain individuals in this world are part of a bigger group, with a much bigger job than even yours as an agent."

Nick sat back in his chair and crossed his arms. While his father was familiar with this man, he was not. And what he was telling him, was bordering on disturbing.

"A.N.G.E.L. stands for Available to Nurture God's Eternal Love. If someone claims to be an A.N.G.E.L., they have to tell you what it stands for. That's our code," Ethan explained. "Now, while the Spirit was given to each of us who are His, a smaller contingent operates in the shadows, going where we are sent in order to help those of the Lord's who need us the most. Sometimes it's a matter of providing food, delivering a message, or even something as big as saving their lives. The reason I'm here is because I was sent to warn you that you are both in danger."

"Explain," Nick snapped. "My patience is running thin at best, Carson."

Ethan took a deep breath before he disclosed his true intention for being there. "Your father and I have crossed paths many times over the past several years regarding his family."

"Careful, that's *my* family you're talking about," Nick warned.

"Exactly. We're the reason you were sent away."

"I don't understand."

"Sins of the father can be passed down, even unto the fourth generation. This goes two ways, though. Good virtues and faith can be passed down as well. Your family has done its best to fight a darkness that has attached itself to you. Now for you," he said to Katie, shutting Nick down before he could object. "You cannot tell me that you didn't feel the darkness from Nate."

"I did," Katie admitted.

"And you cannot tell me that you didn't feel the light from me. You said as much."

"I did," Katie agreed, still weary.

"You're in danger here, just as much as you're in danger back home. You have more than one target on you that you need to be aware of. Hawk sent me to you to remind you to be on guard. There are other A.N.G.E.L.s around who are looking out for you as best as possible, but you," he turned back to Nick, "need to stay vigilant as well."

"He's tellin' ya the truth," Zack jumped into the conversation. "While I love my son, Nate's not a good man. He's out to destroy you," he warned Nick.

"Why?" Nick asked, shocked.

"Because he knows what your future holds," Ethan explained. "He knows just how important you are going to be for His service."

"Whose service?"

"The Lord's. While it took you a while to trust Him, He has always had a plan for you and your future generations."

"Okay. So if we take your message to heart, what are we supposed to do about it?"

"Be on your toes. If another A.N.G.E.L. comes to you, listen without question to what they tell you to do. There are many of us, and we grow stronger in numbers every year. For a while we were dwindling, but as His message spreads, our numbers grow. Some are strategically placed, knowing what's coming."

"This is just too much!" Nick threw his napkin. "I bring her here t' rest an' meet the family, an' this is what I get? I have half a mind to take 'er home immediately."

"No!" Katie, Ethan, and his parents objected at the same time.

"Why not?"

"Because we're supposed to be here," Katie said, resting her hand on Nick's. "Whether we're comfortable or not, we're supposed to be here. Whatever Nate's plan is, we now have a head's up and can stay on our toes. This is a known factor. If we were to go back home, we have no idea who is leaving those messages for me, or where Joey Rossi is at the moment. That's an unknown factor."

"Well, *you* seem so smart and knowledgeable," Nick said sarcastically to Ethan. "Who's after her in the States?"

"I only know what I need to know, and that's not what I need to know," Ethan said calmly, noting Nick's size and the anger he exuded.

Nick stood from the table. "Stuff this for a game of soldiers!"

Katie jumped up and grabbed Nick's arm as he went to leave out the screen door. When he turned toward her, she said, "You've only been here for a few hours, and anger's already pouring from every muscle in your body. I feel this man can be trusted. If you trust my judgment at all, then please sit back down and let's figure out how to get you protected."

"*You're* the one who needs protecting."

"And you can't do that if you're already lost," Katie pointed out.

Knowing she was right, he sat back down at the table. Still unsure, but trusting Katie, he asked Ethan, "What do we need to do?"

*   *   *

"I just get tired of being on edge every minute. I wanted us to relax, not be in the middle of things here," Nick admitted to Katie as they worked in the kitchen to get ready for the cookout that night. "I don't mind doing this type of thing, but I know Nate's going to be here as well."

"So will Ethan and his friends," Katie said. "We need to trust them. I have a feeling we'll need them in the future."

"Unfortunately, I have a feeling you're right." He sighed. "I can't wait until we're in a plane, in the air with nothing around us that's trying to hurt you."

"If I remember correctly, he said that Nate was trying to destroy *you*," she corrected him.

"It's you I'm more concerned about."

"Nick, you are not super-human. You're not exempt from getting hurt or killed. I remember you being in the ICU, and I don't want a repeat of that. How would you feel if I was unconscious for over a week?"

"I would be a mess."

"Then please be concerned with yourself as much as you're concerned with me. We're together. We're a pair. If anything happened to you, you have no idea what it would do to me. Please take care of yourself?"

"If ya don't take care a' yerself, you can't take care a' her," Paige explained as she popped into the kitchen to grab the completed salads, and disappeared out to the backyard once again.

Nick looked after her. "She's been running around like a chook being chased by a weasel. I feel bad."

"Chook?" Katie questioned.

"A chook is a chicken."

"Yeah, she's been running around. She loves you and wants your party to be fun."

"Oh, this isn't just for me. It's for them as well." He smirked. "Don't let them fool you. They have a barbie as often as possible."

"They don't seem the partying type."

"They're not the partying type, but they enjoy their friends and family."

Nate stumbled into the kitchen. "G'day, brother!"

"Yer half off yer face already!" Nick shook his head, disgusted. "Get outta here before Mum sees you!"

"Oh no. If I miss my brother's party, I'll never hear the end of it. And, I wouldn't miss a moment with this beauty," he said, draping his arm over Katie's shoulder.

"Keep your hands to yourself," Katie snapped, shoving him away.

He grabbed her chin, pulling her to him and growled, "I'll take whatever I want, *when* I want."

Nick snatched his hand and flipped it behind Nate's back as he slammed him against the wall. "Touch her again, and I'll make you regret ever being born."

"Already regret that, mate."

"I am *not* your mate! It's bad enough I have to be your brother."

"Nicky! Let 'im go!" Paige shouted.

"Yeah, *Nicky*, let me go. Yer wrinklin' my clothes."

"Mum, make him leave," Nick growled, "or this won't end well."

"Nate, I think you should go," Zack said, stepping into the house when he heard the commotion.

"Ethan an' his friends are here, mate," another friend of Zack's said, poking his head into the kitchen. "Oh, bloody hell! Do I need t' call the coppers?"

"Nope. Nate's goin'," Zack said firmly.

When Nick released him, Nate stumbled out of the house, mumbling to himself.

"Bloody ocker!" Zack growled in anger. "Why does 'e have t' come here half off his face?"

"Now, boys, let's just enjoy the party now that he's gone," Paige said, doing her best to keep her own emotions under control.

Zack shook his head as he crossed his arms. "He brings the anger with him an' it spreads like a plague. Best keep yerself in check, Nicky. If yer not careful, he'll push ya, and then he wins."

"If he touches Katie again, he won't win. He'll be dead."

"Come talk with me, mate," Ethan said, appearing at the doorway. "My friends an' I need t' have a chat with you."

"You keep an eye on her. Understand?" Nick warned his dad.

"I will," he agreed.

When Nick left the room, Katie let out the breath of air she had been holding since Nate grabbed her. Dropping onto a stool in the kitchen, she held her head with her hands as she braced her elbows on the counter. "I don't…I don't even know what to say."

"It's not yer fault, love." Zack rested his hand on her shoulder. "They've been fightin' since birth."

"They were even fightin' in the womb," Paige pointed out.

"About as bad as Jacob an' Esau, eh?" Zack chuckled, hoping to lighten the mood.

Katie looked up at him with tears in her eyes. "I don't find anything about this funny. I'm sorry if you're used to it, but this has been intense at best. I wish we could just relax."

"We will, love. He's gone for the night, an' we head t' the station the day after tomorrow. Once we're in the middle of the Outback, I promise ya that nothin' will happen t' ya there."

Katie sighed. "Sure, famous last words."

*   *   *

Katie was exhausted by nine that night, but the party was still going full swing. "I don't mean to be rude," Katie said to Nick, "but I'm exhausted."

"That's okay, love." Nick hugged her. "Go ahead an' go to bed. I'll tell Mum an' Dad. After the travelling, the events a' t'day, an' jet lag, pretty sure they'll understand."

"Thank you. I love you," she said, and gave him a kiss.

"Love you too. Now, go get some sleep," he said, gently patting her on the behind before she went into the house.

When she went to her room, she downloaded pictures she had taken over the last few days of travelling onto her computer. She knew her friends were waiting to see pictures of their trip. As she uploaded them to her social media page, she couldn't help but think of the events of the last few days…several months for that matter. *How did Ethan know about the person leaving her notes? Would he and his friends really be able to help them?*

She knew she could trust them, and after she finished with her page, she did her devotions, and thanked the Lord for His continued protection and love.

*   *   *

He had been friends with Riccardo, Ethan, and Seb on social media, and was thrilled to see when Katie finally connected with them as well. While he wouldn't comment, he could keep a close eye on her from the safety of his own home.

He flipped through the photos she uploaded from their trip, and excitedly printed some of the pictures of just her. He cringed when he saw the ones with Nick in them. It made him sick to see that she was with him.

He would bide his time until just the right moment. Then he would reveal himself to her once again.

Chapter 2

Summer Daze

Katie was startled awake with a hand over her mouth. "Shhhh," she heard hissed.

"Nick?" Katie asked, with his hand muffling her voice.

"Afraid not, love," Nate sneered.

For a split second, Katie froze in fear as he towered above her. Her instincts kicked in, and she slammed her leg into his, knocking him off her. "NICK!" she screamed as loud as she could, but the party outside drowned out any noise she could generate.

Climbing off the bed to get away, she was caught from behind by Nate as he leapt across the bed, knocking her to the ground, and a struggle ensued.

*   *   *

Danny Hawk, the leader of the A.N.G.E.L.s suddenly perked up mid-sentence.

"Sir?" Ethan asked, noting Hawk's shift.

Danny looked toward the house and yelled, "Nick, get to Katie!"

Nick and his friends ran for the house. They burst into Katie's room to find Nate on top of her, trying to tear off her clothes. Struggling beneath him, Katie screamed.

Nick grabbed Nate and threw him across the room into the other men who pulled the struggling and yelling Nate from the room. He then snagged the blanket off the bed and wrapped Katie in it as he held her. "I want to kill him, but you need me more. I'm letting them take care of him, because I made you a promise."

Nodding was her only response as she shook in pure terror. She could still feel his hands all over her, even though he was nowhere in the room.

"Katie?" Paige asked, quietly coming into the room. She got on her knees next to Nick and Katie, and gently brushed Katie's hair out of her face. "Are ya in there, love?"

Katie only stared ahead of her, blinded and deaf to whatever was going on around her. To her, everything seemed muffled and moved in slow motion. It seemed like she was living a bad nightmare.

"Did he…?" Paige's question hung in the air. When Nick shook his head, Paige sighed in relief and said, "Thank the Lord."

Nick did his best to control the anger that raged within him as he said, "If I ever see him again, I *will* kill him. I'm tellin' you right now!"

"Nicky, don't say that."

"If Danny Hawk didn't warn us, he would have raped her, and who knows what else. She's saving herself for marriage, Mum. Do you understand what that means?"

"Yes," she said, sitting back against the wall, wrapping her arms around her knees. After a moment, Paige asked, "What are your intentions with Katie? Now," she held up her hand to stop Nick's objections, "I know your past. I know how you used to be. I also know Katie's a good girl, and according to Ethan Carson, she's a valuable asset to the Lord. Is she just another stepping stone or are you serious about her?"

"Mum!" He looked at her, stunned, as he held Katie, making sure she felt protected even though he felt like he let her down.

"She's gettin' deeper into this mess, an' I need to know whether t' put her on a plane for her safety or protect her as one a' my own."

"Protect her as one of your own," he said, making his intentions clear.

"'Nuff said. We leave in the mornin' for Serenity Wells," she said, effectively ending the conversation as she got off the ground. "The constable will want t' speak with her. They'll have t' do it at the station though. There are more eyes there t' watch out for anyone."

"She won't be able to talk. I know her. She's terrified at the moment. The constable can do his best, but look at her, Mum. She's not in there."

Kat Parker, one from Hawk's unit, lightly knocked on the door.

"Well, I'll leave ya to it. If ya need me, ya know where t' find me. I'm gonna go clean up this mess," Paige said, excusing herself before she left the room.

Nick nodded for Kat to come into the room. She was about thirty-seven years old, and stood all of five-foot-five. Her thin frame and dark-brown hair set off her kind green eyes. Nick knew, though, while she looked passive, each member of

Hawk's group was a force to be reckoned with, and he knew Kat was no exception.

"I woulda done the same if I found 'im," she said, kneeling on the floor next to them. "Yer dad is gettin' taken in as well. He beat 'im up pretty good before they could pull 'im off. I doubt he'll be charged, though," she explained. "Nate, on the other hand, will be chilling in the cooler for quite a while. Ya don't need t' be worrin' about 'im for a long time."

"Thank you," Nick said appreciatively. "I don't think he'd still be walking around if I'd gotten a hold of him."

"While I don't doubt that, I believe that's why we're here."

"I don't think I'll be able to get her to talk."

"Probably not," she said, tucking a portion of Katie's hair behind her ear. "She's in shock. Rest assured, though, she's been there before an' pulled through. She can do it again. I'll go get a damp cloth to clean up her wounds."

"Thank you," Nick said, as Kat went to the bathroom.

When she returned, he watched Kat gently clean the scratches on Katie's face and arms. When she finished, she covered Katie back up and set the cloth on the floor. Placing her hands on each side of Katie's head, Kat quietly prayed, inviting the Spirit to come in and take over. She understood that He was the only one who could reach her.

*   *   *

The next morning they loaded the car and headed out to the station. Nick's heart broke as he sat in the back seat with Katie. She hadn't said a word, and seemed to be operating in a daze.

Even in the morning when she ate breakfast, she didn't seem fazed by anything said or done around her.

Before they left, Hawk told Nick one of his men was at the station. He said he was there due to the activity in the area, mainly stemming from an adjacent property to the station that they couldn't gain access to, so they chose to view it from the next station over.

Nick took comfort in knowing one of Hawk's men was there, but he was still on edge. He wanted to make sure Nana and Pop met Katie, though. They were important to him, and he especially wanted to know Nana's thoughts on Katie. With Katie not in her best frame of mind, he half wondered if it was a good idea anymore. Part of him wanted to get her back to the states, but in the mood she was in, he knew she didn't stand a chance with whoever was hunting her there.

This brought to mind more thoughts and concerns. His unit did their best to track down any leads in regards to Joey Rossi or Cristian Gombeda, but they hit only dead ends. Whichever one was hunting her back home, they knew how to cover their tracks. He prayed for some sense of clarity concerning the situation back home, and peace and calmness on the station. Knowing his grandparents and their workers, though, he knew that would be a stretch.

*   *   *

Driving down the dusty road, Katie saw in the distance the entrance to two stations. One had a sign that read: Akoonah Station – the station Katie heard Ethan speaking about. The other was the station Nick's grandparents owned: Serenity Wells Station. After the last few days, she wasn't sure what was going to happen, but she knew even as distant as she felt, that

Jesus was still walking beside her, and she would hold onto that until she could see the light of hope once again.

*   *   *

The sun hung high in the sky as they pulled up to the two-story homestead. Multiple structures dotted the landscape, which included two massive barns, a long bunkhouse, and a myriad of areas fenced off from each other, containing sheep, cattle, and horses.

"Serenity Wells has been in Nana's family since they set foot in Australia. Her maiden name is Sullivan. This has been the first generation where the Locke name is synonymous with Serenity Wells and not Sullivan," Nick explained, as they unloaded the car. "*Despite* the best efforts of the elements and some bush rangers through the years, it's productive and doing very well."

Katie only nodded in response as she took in all of the scenery. It was beautiful, and if she hadn't experienced what she did the night before, she would be free to enjoy it.

"Nicky!" a short older lady, with long silver hair that was pulled back in a braid came running out of the main house with her arms open wide. "Where the bloody hell have ya been, boy?" she demanded as she tightly hugged him.

"Working. Sorry I haven't been able t' come back before now. I brought someone I'd like ya t' meet," he said, pulling the silent Katie over to him. "Nana, this is Katie MacKenna."

After she hugged Katie, Nana rested her hands on her shoulders and looked at her eyes. "She's not there. What happened?" she demanded from Zack and Paige.

"Nate," Zack said. "As a matter of fact, just got outta the cooler myself this mornin' 'cause of it."

"*What happened?*" she asked, more sternly.

"Is that…please tell me that's Nicky and not Nate?" a young man about Nick's age asked, as he came from the barn.

"Pete!" Nick's face lit up when he saw his childhood friend.

"Nick!" he shouted, running the last few steps and hugged Nick. "Hey, mate! Where ya been?" he asked, taking a step back. "An', who's the sheila?"

"Katie, this is one a' my mates Pete. Buri is his pop, an' the one I told ya about that taught me t' play the didgeridoo."

Katie nodded in response as she shook Pete's hand.

Nana crossed her arms in a huff. "I'm not a patient woman anyway, but yer not helpin'. She looks like a broken pack a' biscuits!"

"Nate went on a bender before the barbie last night, arrivin' lookin' like the dog's breakkie, so we sent 'im away," Zack explained. "Between that an' the barney that wasn't fit for young or old that he and Nicky got into when they arrived yesterday, he thought he'd take it out on Katie here."

"*What* did he do?" Nana demanded, the iciness of her tone not lost on anyone.

"He attacked her after she went t' bed," Zack admitted.

"Crikey!" Pete exclaimed. "An' he's still alive?"

"Not if I see 'im again," Nick said, anger visibly evident in his entire body.

"Nicky, we need t' take a walk." Nana looped her arm through Nick's. "I'll get t' know Katie when we get back, but I need t' have a yack w' ya."

As they walked away, panic filled Katie. She was being left alone, and had yet to figure out what was said from the point of their arrival on the station.

"You look as nervous as a long-tailed cat in a room full a' rockin' chairs," Pete remarked to Katie.

Tears brimmed her eyes, as she felt lost, scared, and anxious at the same time.

"I think the two of us will take a walk as well. C'mon, love." Paige looped her arm through Katie's. "Pete, can ya give Zack a hand in gettin' the bags upstairs?"

"Of course," Pete said, and helped Zack. As the two girls walked one way, and Nana and Nick walked the other, Pete commented to Zack, "Looks like you've had your hands full."

"You have no idea, mate."

*   *   *

"Katie, I know yer a good girl. I also have seen that yer a strong young lady. I'll do my best through this conversation t' keep out the Aussie lingo, but I feel you need t' talk some a' this out. Yer lost, love," she said, sitting down on a bench that overlooked the station. "I'm sorry. I can't walk around anymore."

"I know." Katie sighed as she sat down beside Paige. Taking Paige's hand in hers, Katie admitted, "I'm terrified."

"I'll bet! Besides the obvious, what else is there?"

Katie gulped. Trust for her was difficult at best.

"C'mon. Pretty sure we're going t' be family sometime in the future. It won't go anywhere. I trusted you with my biggest secret."

"I know. I guess with everything that's happened so far, I'm afraid to find out what else is coming our way," she admitted. "All y'all seem very open and friendly, but –"

"I get it. While we speak English, it still has many foreign terms. I can only imagine yer frustration at some of the conversations."

"It's not easy. And now that Nick's off with Nana, I feel lost," she admitted, looking down at her fingers.

Paige lifted her chin so she was looking at her. "You don't need to worry about a thing out here. We'll look out for you. Out here, there's a reason they call it Serenity Wells. You can relax out here. Now, the blokes around the station? You'll figure 'em out. It may take a bit, so I need ya t' clear yer head or they'll get t' ya."

"What do you mean?"

"Love," she rested her hand on Katie's knee, "the blokes at this station will bend over backwards an' give their life for ya if they think yer worth it. If not, such as in Nate's case, you don't 'ave a prayer in the world. You 'ave a tender heart, an' I know you'll win them over, but ya gotta give 'em a chance. Ya got a couple strikes against ya, though."

"Meaning?" Katie asked, her heart rate picking up.

"Well, first off, yer a shelia. Yer Nick's, so that'll help, but yer still a shelia, an' a good lookin' one at that. The second strike against ya is that yer a yank."

"I'm not a northerner," Katie objected. "I currently live in Ohio, but I'm a southerner."

"Not this far south," Paige explained. "Look, a yank is a yank. Ya may hear the term 'seppo.' When you do, it's rhyming slang. Seppo or septic tank is rhyming slang for yank."

"That doesn't make sense." Katie shook her head, confused.

"There will be a lot that won't make sense, and we'll do our best as a family to head that off, as well as keep ya informed."

"I appreciate that."

"Now we need t' talk about last night."

"I don't –"

"Ya need t' talk about it, love. You an' Nicky both are gonna have t' talk this out, so ya might as well start with me because ya know it won't go anywhere."

Katie shook her head and crossed her arms, hugging herself.

Paige slowly pulled her arms apart and held both of her hands. "You haven't had a mum for as long as you can remember. Seven is a very young age t' lose yer mum. Please let me step in that spot for this moment an' help ya through this? What did he do?"

Katie shook her head.

"What did my son do t' ya, love?" Paige rubbed Katie's arms.

"He, um…." Katie shuddered as a few scenes passed through her mind. "He ripped at me, touching me, grabbing me in places…please don't make me do this," she begged, her body trembling.

"Did he rape you?"

"No." She shook her head. "I thought at first he was Nick, but then…he wasn't," she said, quietly.

Resting her hand on the side of Katie's face, Paige said, "An' he never will be. I'm sorry that happened t' ya. Even worse, that it happened t' ya in our home, where yer supposed t' be safe. Please give us another shot at protectin' you."

When Katie nodded, Paige hugged her and held her until she cried it out.

*   *   *

"What do you wanna talk about?" Nick asked when he and Nana had been walking around for over five minutes in silence.

"Haven't seen ya in over ten years, an' when I do, ya bring a lady who's been attacked by my other grandson. That all happened within a day of ya bein' here. Think we may need t' talk. The anger is pourin' from every fiber in you."

"Of course it is!" Nick snapped. "That bloody yabbo attacked my woman!"

"Nicky!"

"Nick! My name's Nick!"

"Watch yer tone with me!" Nana glared at him. "I realize yer angry, an' why, but you will still speak to me with respect."

"Nana, there's no disrespect intended toward you. It's that dingo you call a grandson. He snuck into her room an' attacked her. If we weren't alerted, he would have raped or…or worse."

Nana let out a low whistle. "What a way t' be welcomed t' the country."

"I wanted to bring 'er here t' allow her a chance t' breathe. She's bein' hunted back home. That girl is stronger than she seems, but even strong people sometimes need help."

"I understand."

"I don't think ya do," Nick explained. "This person, whoever he is, has sent people t' kill her. He's almost blown her up, an' even invaded her home on more than one occasion…an' we live in a secure building. We've narrowed it down t' two people, but they both have gone under. I brought her here, thinkin' maybe, *just maybe*, she could breathe an' be cut a break."

"She's on Serenity now. She'll be protected."

"She'll have t' be for a bit. I have t' have the time t' break through the wall she threw up last night. Frankly, I don't blame her either. She was attacked by a man with *my* face! Do you understand how messed up that is? My *twin brother* attacked the woman I'm intending t' marry!"

"You're *what*?" Nana looked at him, stunned.

"I'm going t' ask her t' marry me. I haven't had the guts t' do it yet."

"You're afraid of her? Then you aren't ready."

"Yes, I am ready, but it's *her* that's not ready. She's got a whirlwind flying around her right now, an' this *certainly* didn't help!"

"I'm sure it didn't."

"Got any brilliant advice now?" Nick crossed his arms in a huff.

"No," she said quietly. "You've got a lot going on, but I want ya t' release it t'day for the time yer here."

"Nana, I already know about the curse." As soon as he said it, the color drained from Nana's face. "I also know about Jasper."

"Do *not* say that name in my presence!"

"Why not? He was my uncle. Of course, I had no idea he even existed until yesterday. How many more secrets are there, Nana? How can I function if I keep getting blindsided? How am I supposed to fight somethin' that I know nothin' about? It's like trying to navigate a minefield without a map!"

"Calm yer brumbies, mate."

"No! I *will not* calm down! I need t' know what's going on here!"

Nana watched as Katie and Paige had slowly made their way up to her and Nick, without Nick hearing her. Touching Nick's shoulder, Katie asked, "Can we talk?"

He spun around in shock at not hearing her. "How did you do that?"

"Nick, there's a lot going on and we need to talk. Please?"

"C'mon, love, we gotta get supper goin' or those blokes in the field are gonna have *us* for dinner," Nana said, ushering Paige back to the main house.

Katie hugged Nick. At first he held back, not wanting the anger to suffocate her, until he finally gave in and held her. "I love you," he said, barely a whisper. "I'm so sorry about last night."

"It's not your fault. Look, things are going on around us that we can't control. We both need a break. Let's use this time to find out more about each other. I can work through Nate's actions with Stacey when I get back to Cleveland."

"She's going t' have her work cut out for her. Your attacker had my face."

"But not your heart," Katie reminded him. "I know the difference as soon as you open your mouth, or at your touch, that it's you."

"Do you mind if I kiss you?"

"Why do you need to ask?" she questioned, looking into his eyes. Seeing the pain, hurt, and anger churning in them, she reached up and touched the side of his face. "You are my love. I need you to be the strong man I know you to be. I need you to fight this anger for both of us."

"I need *you*," he said and leaned down, cupping her face in his hands and kissed her. With each second, the anger melted away. As he intertwined his fingers in her hair, the hurt buried itself for the moment.

When they took a step back, the pain floated away. Looking in his eyes, she admitted, "I need you too,"

"Yer gonna have a new set of trials here on the station."

"I know. But I also know you and your family will look out for me. Your mom explained about 'seppo' and the perception of the men regarding women."

"That's only the half of it."

"Nick, things are never going to be perfect, no matter how much we want them to, but I know as long as you're with me, I can make it through."

"Thank you."

"Ya know, it's kind of cute how your accent has gotten thicker since we've gotten here." She smiled, running her finger around his chin. "It definitely works for you."

"Really?" He grinned, dimples in full view. "How's that?"

"Time will tell, but I think being in the country has already calmed you quite a bit. You're right. You are a country boy."

*　　*　　*

As Nick showed Katie around the station, Nick was greeted with delight, while Katie got an awkward feeling from the guys. Knowing they were checking her out made her feel like a piece of meat. Knowing even more the disdain that they held for 'yanks' made her cringe on the inside.

"What does 'Akoonah' mean?" Katie asked on their way to the barns.

"Where'd ya see that?" Nick asked, confused.

"It's the station across the street from here. Isn't that the station Ethan Carson was talking about yesterday?"

"Yep. It's Aboriginal for 'flowing water.'"

"How is that bad?"

"It's not. It's what's flowing from it that's bad. That place has evil flowing from every corner of it. I'm glad the only place the two stations touch is at the north field."

"What's up there?"

"It's one of the pastures used for cattle. They rotate the pastures."

"I see."

"Now, over here are the sheep paddocks," he said, directing her to a section that had several fenced in areas, containing at least twenty to thirty sheep apiece. "They get sheared twice a year."

"They're cute."

"Yeah, but not when they get messy…an' they stink. We're going t' head to one of my favorite places before we head back t' the main house. Once I get you back in front of Nana, now that you're more yourself, she may not let you outta her sight."

"Why not?"

"Because she's going t' want to get a good idea of who it is that holds her grandson's heart," he said, squeezing her shoulders.

Katie blushed as they walked into the barn.

"Pete!" Nick called. "Hey, mate, where ya hidin'?"

"Over here," they heard Pete's voice from one of the stables.

"Whatcha doin'?" Nick asked, leaning on the door of the stable.

"Cleaning the last of the stables for the day. This one is Star's stable."

"Got it. Is Jumbunna still here?"

"Yep. Your horse is over on the other side. He's the third one from the left as you face it."

"Good," Nick said, relieved.

"He's got a good ten years left in him. He was only five when ya left."

"Just glad he's here," Nick said, pulling Katie with him to the other side of the barn.

"Whoa! He's big!" Katie remarked when she saw the beautiful, chestnut brown Australian Stock Horse that had white on his hooves. "He's a gorgeous horse!"

"Nana gave him t' me a couple years before I left," Nick explained, rubbing the horse's nose. "You're a beaut, aren't ya? Bet ya don't remember me."

"Has she ridden before?" Pete asked, walking over to the pair.

"Nope," Katie answered.

"Hmm, I'm thinking maybe Star will be your best bet. She's our mildest, most laid back horse."

"For what?" Katie asked, heart racing. "You think I'm gonna get on one of these things?" she asked, horrified. "You've lost your mind!"

Seeing the whites of her eyes and hearing the startle in her voice, Pete couldn't help but burst out in laughter. "Yer on a station. A' course yer gonna ride at some point. Chances are, it'll be tomorrow before ya do."

"I'm starting not to like you," Katie said, crossing her arms with a smirk.

"That's okay." He placed his hand on her shoulder. "I already know I like you. Just be on yer toes around here. Unfortunately, others may not have the same impression of ya that I do."

"What impression is that?" Katie asked, curious.

"You seem like a good person."

"Ohhh, you don't know the half of it," Nick jumped into the conversation, as he fed his horse a carrot. "She's a police officer, training for Quantico more than likely within a year or so."

"Really?" Pete asked, impressed.

Katie nodded.

"Sorry, but ya don't look like ya could pull the skin off a custard."

Katie raised an eyebrow in question.

"This may be a conversation for later," Nick said, wiping his hands off on his jeans. "She's had enough challenges since we've been here t' last her a while."

"I heard."

Changing the subject, Katie asked, "What does Jumbunna mean? Pretty sure that's not your standard horse name."

"It's Aboriginal. It means to talk together," Nick explained. "Pete's dad, Buri, helped me name him when Nana gave him to me."

"Nick was a friendly bloke growin' up, but he only let people get so close. I think Nate had somethin' t' do with that," Pete pointed out.

Nick groaned. "Please don't remind me of him. I just got myself t' a good place."

"Sorry, mate."

Just then, they heard the dinner bell being rung from the front porch.

"That's Nana. If we don't get there quickly, we'll hear it from her," Pete said, washing his hands in the sink of the tack room. "We still need to wash our hands in the sink of the kitchen. That's her way of making sure *everyone's* hands are clean for dinner. We may stink, but our hands are clean." Pete grinned, drying his hands off on the towel. "C'mon. Let's go."

On the way to the house, Katie noticed the looks of the guys, and got a sick feeling in her stomach. Praying in her head for strength, she hoped with every bone in her body that she would 'pass' the family test. She loved Nick with all her heart, and couldn't imagine life without him.

"Who's the shelia?" a guy asked, who was also about Nick's age. He had reddish-brown hair, and dark brown eyes.

"Flynn, this is Katie," Nick introduced him to her.

He looked her up and down. "She's a beaut. Ya picked a good one."

"Keep to yerself, or I'll knock yer block off," Nick warned.

"Yeah. Right." He grinned, dimples in view, as he shoved his hands in his pockets.

"He's already gone rounds with Nate. I wouldn't push it," Pete warned.

"Nate? Really? How's my cousin doin' these days?"

In a split second, Nick released Katie's hand, and spun around, grabbing Flynn by the collar of his shirt. He got into his face, as he said, "He *attacked* Katie. Don't make me take out my anger for that lout out on you."

Raising his hands in surrender, Flynn said, "No worries, mate. I didn't know." When Nick released him, Nick retook Katie's hand, and started back toward the house. Flynn added under his breath, "Wouldn't mind takin' a crack at her myself."

Katie shoved Nick toward Pete to hold him back before she walked over to Flynn. Crossing her arms in front of her, she challenged him. "Go ahead. I could use a little release of tension myself."

Hearing her words, Nick got loose of Pete and stood there, watching in amusement, knowing if he needed to, he would jump in.

"Why are you not comin' after me? What? Yer now lettin' a woman handle your battles for ya? Have ya gone soft in yer old age?" Flynn snapped, looking from Nick to Katie. "I could snap 'er in half."

"Ha!" Nick laughed.

"What do ya mean?"

"I know who trained her, mate. Go ahead. Make my day," Nick said, resting his elbow on Pete's shoulder. "This should be fun."

As a crowd gathered, Flynn turned back to Katie and asked, "What's he goin' on about?"

"I've had a lot going on lately. I could use a good punching bag," she explained.

'Oooo's' and various other comments were heard from around the men gathering around them.

"I can't hit a girl. My ol' man would have my head."

"Are you scared?" Katie challenged.

The murmurs got louder among the men around them.

He chuckled. "Of you? Not on your best day."

Katie walked around him, sizing him up. "You don't look like much. You seem to have a bigger mouth than you do muscles. Is that your strongest muscle? Your mouth? This'll be easy."

Flynn rolled his eyes. "We're not allowed to fight on the station."

Katie laughed. "Now you're using your grandmother as an excuse. Ohhh, this should be good."

"She doesn't allow fightin' on the station."

"So, you're chickening out? Am I hearing right? You're walking away?"

"I have to," he quietly admitted, kicking dirt with the toe of his boot.

"Fine." Katie clapped his shoulder. "If you're choosing to walk away from scrawny, little ol' me, allow me to enlighten you on how good of a choice that was. You see, not only am I currently a police officer, but a spectacular special agent in the FBI has also trained me for over three years. Wanna take a wild guess on who that was?"

Flynn slowly looked from Katie, toward Nick. When Nick nodded, with a grin on his face, Flynn sighed, shaking his head. "Fine. Let's get t' dinner before Nana has our head."

"That was fun," Katie commented as they finished their walk to the main house.

"Yeah. I wasn't sure if you were going t' have t' show him or not," Nick admitted. "Nana would have a fit, but before this is over, I have a feeling your talents are going t' have t' be seen at some point.'

"She's really that good?" Pete asked, on the other side of Nick.

"She is. I've trained her very well, an' didn't take any mercy on her durin' that training either."

"He didn't," Katie added. She heard the comments Flynn had to endure on the walk back to the house, and knew it would come back around eventually. The testosterone levels at the station were high and she knew a challenge like that would not go unanswered.

*   *   *

After washing their hands, the family, along with the thirty ranch hands, gathered around a long, wood table, done in a picnic-style in the dining room. This style allowed everyone to fit around the table, yet gave the feeling of closeness without being too close.

After grace was said, Nana started the food around the table. "So, Katie, what do you think of Serenity Wells?" she asked.

"I think it's beautiful," she said, plopping a scoop of mashed potatoes onto her plate before passing them to Nick. "I'm fascinated with the animals."

"Don't they have them in the States?" one of the guys, who Katie later learned was nicknamed 'Barwon' due to his big mouth, asked.

"They do," she said, hesitantly, surprised by the assertiveness of the group. "We currently live in the city."

"Have you ever seen or worked with sheep?" Pop, whose real name was Tommy, asked.

"Afraid not," she admitted.

"What about horses? Have you ever ridden a horse?" Flynn asked.

"Afraid that's a no as well."

"Just what *do* you do in that big city of yours?" Barwon asked.

"I'm currently a police officer."

"Currently? Meaning you're not going to be an officer for long? Did ya get fired?" Flynn asked.

"Nope. She's going t' Quantico in a year or so," Nick jumped into the conversation.

"Really?" the massive Barwon asked, impressed. He was not your average Aboriginal. Standing around six-six, bulky was a mild term for him.

"Yes, sir."

"Sir? I like that! She called me sir! You can call me his nibs," he said with a smile and a wink.

"Not likely," Nick said under his breath.

"What's that mean?"

"It means that you're not likely t' be the boss anytime soon."

"The ol' man an' lady will only be around here for so long," Barwon pointed out.

"Then it goes to my dad or Uncle Adam. Where do you get off sayin' it's goin' t' you?"

"Never said it's comin' t' me. However, pretty sure Flynn's gonna need a second in command."

"Not you."

"That's rich comin' from a kid who just popped in here after ten years."

Nick stood and slammed his hands on the table. "Considering the disrespect you've used in regards t' Katie, you should count yerself lucky that Nana's sittin' there, or this would be an entirely different conversation."

"Don't know what ya mean, mate?"

"I heard the comments. Pretty sure she did too. We're not deaf."

"You bring a bloody seppo on this station, an' expect us just t' welcome her with open arms?" Barwon stood, matching Nick's stance.

"I have half a mind t' kick you into next Tuesday!" Nick growled.

"As if you could," Barwon challenged.

Nana took a spoon full of mashed potatoes and aimed it at the wall between the two men. Letting it loose, it splatted against the wall. When everyone turned toward her, she simply stated, "We're eatin'," before she went back to her plate.

"Yes, ma'am," both Nick and Barwon said, retaking their seats.

Katie couldn't help but note the way the men respected Nana. What she said was unquestionably done without hesitation. Katie decided befriending Nana would definitely be high on her list if this was going to be a relaxing trip at all.

Chapter 3

Summer Splash

The next morning, Katie sat upright in her bed when the ringing of a bell startled her out of a sound sleep. Groggy, she quickly got dressed and ran a brush through her hair.

As she was brushing her teeth, Nick popped his head into the bathroom. "Better hurry. Nana doesn't take kindly t' people being late for meals."

"What ungodly hour is this?" Katie grumbled.

"Six. She's been up for over an hour. Have t' warn you, so you have a head's up, she's a mornin' person."

Katie only groaned in response as she dropped her head.

"I'll see if I can find some caffeine around the station," Nick said with a chuckle.

"Some peanut butter toast and orange juice would be perfect."

"Not likely here. Milk, eggs, steak, an' bread will be more what we're lookin' at. I *may* be able t' find some coffee."

Glaring at him with her eyes narrowed, Katie explained, "I've had a rough night. I had quite a few nightmares. Humor this early is not appreciated."

"Oh, I'm not jokin' about the coffee, milk, eggs, steak, an' bread. This is an operating station. Light meals are definitely *not* on the menu. The men need their protein an' calories. Sorry, babe, welcome t' station living."

Taking a deep breath to control her emotions, she asked, "Is there any way I can have the light version of that?"

"Well, she does scramble the eggs, so I would take the scrambled eggs and bread. That should be light enough."

"I don't know if I'm up to facing those guys today."

"Sorry, love. They're family. They're at every meal."

"They're Neanderthals."

"I know. You need t' sharpen those skills of humbling these guys. I have faith in you that you can handle it. You were even able to humble me several times, along with the educated Agents Walker and Kennedy. A couple of bush rangers should be no problem."

She hesitated a moment before she asked, "Why is it everything is a battle for me? Why can't something just be easy for once?"

Wrapping his arms around her, he pulled her to his body and kissed her head. "We're easy."

"Now. We were a struggle in the beginning."

"And, once you get through this initiation, they'll love you just as much as I do."

"Here's hoping."

*   *   *

Thankfully, much to Katie's delight, the men were not morning people either. Coffee was passed around, but she declined, mentioning to Nick that it looked like jet fuel.

After they got their assignments and dispersed to their jobs, Nana asked Nick, "So, what are you plannin' on doin' t'day?"

"Well, I was going t' ask if you needed any help anywhere in particular?"

"Good question," she said, sitting back in her seat. "Katie, would you like to help me in the kitchen?"

Nick just about choked on the sip of coffee he took. "I'm sorry. You want *what*?"

"Does she not cook?"

"*She* is once again in the room," Katie snapped. "And, yes, I do cook some, but, sorry to say that list is short."

"Well, then," Nana said, pleased, "There's no time like the present! Yer gonna help in the kitchen, while Nicky, why don't ya go find Pete? He may need a hand in the barn."

"Sounds good," Nick agreed.

"Paige, why don't you an' Zack just relax on the porch for the mornin'. Yer lookin' a little tired."

"I am. Thank you," she said sheepishly.

For the first time, Nick got a good look at his mom. "Mum, are you okay?"

"Yeah. Why?"

"Because she's right. You *do* look tired."

Katie tapped Paige on her foot as a signal for her to tell Nick.

"I'm fine. Just with all of the excitement over the last week, an' a portion of that bein' bad, it's finally caught up t' me."

Katie kicked her a little harder, making sure she got the hint.

Resting her hand on Katie's, Paige explained, "I'm okay. There's just a lot going on around me lately."

"Like?" Nick pressed.

Noting Nana's satisfied look, Katie had an inkling that Nana knew more than she was telling.

"Just with finally seein' you, the attack, an' comin' out here…well, things have piled on. Let's just take the morning t' relax an' see how I feel this afternoon."

"Right oh," Nick said, standing. "Love you all." He gave Katie, Nana, and his mom each a kiss on the cheek before he bolted for the barn.

Paige sighed as the screen door closed. "He's a good boy. I'm glad we sent him away. He's made somethin' of himself, an' I couldn't be prouder."

"Then why are you lying to him?" Katie snapped.

Paige looked at Katie, wide-eyed.

"She's right. I know somethin's up with you, but I don't know what," Nana said. "Yer keepin' somethin' from all of us."

"I'll tell you when the time is right."

"I said you were lookin' tired in front of Nicky, so he could pull it outta you," Nana explained. "I *know* somethin's wrong. Why won't you tell me?"

"On that note, I'm outta here. You comin', Zack?" Pop asked, hoping to leave the situation to the ladies.

Zack got up and followed him out. "Without hesitation."

After a moment of awkward silence, Katie asked, "What are we doing for lunch?"

"Not so fast." Nana shook her head. "We're not finished here."

"Don't know what yer talkin' about, *Charlotte*," Paige said, using Nana's real name.

"I could leave the two of you alone," Katie offered.

"Nope. You sit right there," Nana ordered. "I have a feelin' you know more than yer sayin' as well."

"She's not going t' say anythin'," Paige defended her. "She knows, but told me she won't tell."

"A secret among family could be a dangerous thing."

"Yer controlling an' meddling ways have gotten more information than ya should have *ever* had," Paige said angrily. "You went around me an' got my son sent away from me an' it wasn't even his fault!"

"Paige!" Nana said, appalled by her outburst.

"No! You control the information goin' in an' outta this family. You have for years!" Paige was bordering on tears as she continued, "Just because you lost Jasper –"

"Do *not* say that name around me!" Nana spat.

"He was your son!"

"Who just about killed your husband!" Nana shot. When Katie gasped, Nana swore and said, "You infuriate me at times, Paige. I love ya t' death, but the family secrets don't need t' be put on Katie's ears. She's not family."

"She will be."

"I will….*what*?" Katie asked, stunned.

"My son loves you with all his heart," Paige explained. "Anyone with a set of eyes an' a brain knows the two of you were meant for each other."

"Don't change the subject!" Nana growled.

"This family has a lot of secrets, Charlotte," Paige said, a little more in control of her emotions. "At some point, Nicky needs t' know about all of them."

"Not yet."

"Who do you *really* think is gonna take over this station?" Paige challenged.

"What do ya mean?"

"Zack an' Adam are good guys, but they're not leaders. Flynn's been here all his life, but he's not strong enough t' lead this station either. You an' I both know Nicky's the one who should be takin' this station over."

"Agreed."

"An' he needs t' know everything…an' I mean *everything*," Paige said sternly. "How can he fight, if he doesn't know what he's fightin'? Yer the only one who knows it all. Yer the only one who can tell 'im how t' fight this."

"Fight what?" Katie asked. "The anger?"

"It's not just anger. It's a curse," Nana clarified.

"How do you fight a curse?"

"With everything you have."

Shaking her head, Paige corrected, "With all the *family* you have."

"Agreed. Now, we got some men who are gonna be hungry about noon if we don't get cookin'."

"Not so fast," Paige said as Nana went to get up.

Slowly sitting back down, Nana impatiently hinted, "Yer gettin' brave, there, Paige."

"Might as well. If yer gonna shoot me, I might as well make it worth it."

Katie looked at the two women, wishing with every fiber of her being that she were anywhere but there.

"What is it?"

"Since you opened yer big mouth, you need t' know that I have breast cancer."

"*Knew* there was somethin' goin' on. Crikey, Paige! Why didn't you tell us?" Nana asked, angry. She swore again. "I *knew* you were hidin' somethin', but I never thought it was this big."

"Watch yer mouth, Charlotte."

"Quit callin' me Charlotte!" Nana snapped.

"I do it t' get yer attention."

"Obviously." She sighed. "How bad is it?"

"Currently in remission."

"Does Nicky know?"

"No."

"Nate?"

"No."

"Then, how did *you* know?" Nana asked Katie.

"Because my mother died of leukemia, and I know what a person looks like who's going through chemo. There are a few telltale signs."

"I see. When did you find out?"

"She called me on it the first day she met me," Paige explained.

"Braver than I thought you were."

"She was attacked less than twelve hours before you met her. If yer judging 'er on when you first met her, then yer missin' the mark," Paige pointed out.

"I pride myself on my judge of character."

"Then ya may wanna reassess this one."

"Excuse me," Katie piped up. "I am *right here*," she said, irritated. "Y'all have done nothing but talk around me. Look, I get that y'all are in an argument, but I don't get why *I'm* here."

"Because I wanna know what you know," Nana said simply.

"Then you may want to ask *me* and not Paige."

Nana smiled, pleasantly surprised. "Brazen. I actually think I may like ya after all."

"Good."

"Good, *what*?"

"Now that you have a better understanding of where we stand, how about we compare notes. I *do* feel that Nick should be here, though. I don't feel right about talking about him or his family without him here."

Nana shook her head. "It'll kill him."

"We don't have secrets," Katie explained. "I kept Paige's because she promised to tell him if it got bad again, but what's been hinted at here…" she shook her head, "he needs to know."

"No," Nana said, sternly.

"Yes," Katie challenged, the anger slowly churning within her. "He's a grown man who lays his life on the line daily for his country. Do you not think he can handle family history? Really?"

"I don't know that he's ready."

"The man is frequently in fire-fights with guns!" Katie snapped. "He's not some young kid." She stood. "I'm going to the barn. I'm also going to fill him in on what I've already heard…unless you would like me to bring him back so you can do it. I don't, and *won't* keep anything from him. He's a big boy. Trust me. He'll be shocked, but he can handle it. He'll take the information, process it, adjust his thinking, and go forward. That's how he operates."

Nana stood, bracing her hands on the table. "Are you tellin' me how t' manage an' talk t' my grandson?"

"I'm telling you to give him some credit. He's not a teenager. You said yourself that he should be the one to take over the station. How can he handle the station if he doesn't have all the information? Secrets can cause a lot of damage. I *will not* jeopardize our relationship for *your* pride."

"How *dare* you!" Nana snapped, glaring at her.

"How dare *you*! You seem to be a controlling individual. While your heart is in the right place, I question your judgment on what you're keeping secret."

"You don't know me well enough to judge me!" she said, stunned by her audacity.

"Wanna bet?" Katie challenged.

Paige couldn't believe her eyes. *Was Katie really challenging Nana? No one challenged her and came out the other end of the argument a victor.*

Crossing her arms, Nana sarcastically said, "By all means, enlighten me. I'll take notes while yer at it."

"Then listen carefully," Katie started. Nana's eyes momentarily showed the shock she felt as Katie continued,

"You are a strong woman, who has had to carry a lot. It shows on your face and stature. You're family's past has worn on you more than you know. You also don't put up with anyone breaking rules. I'd be willing to wager a bet that you've had to prove that over the years only a few times to make your point. These men know you mean what you say. They don't challenge you. The only reason I'm challenging you right now is because I know your grandson very well." Katie walked over to her. Standing in front of Nana, she rested her hands on her shoulders. "But you are also a tenderhearted person, who hasn't had the opportunity to show that side of you too often. *You* are the one who runs this station, not Pop. You are strong, but as Nick once told me, even strong people need help. You're hard on these guys, because you love them so much. I have a feeling you would give yourself for any one of them."

She nodded in agreement. "I would. They're my boys."

"How am I doing so far?"

"I have t' admit that yer doin' good."

"Then, also know that in your protection of others, it's eaten you up inside. You're running around trying to keep this station running, while trying to hide all of those secrets, and keep everything covered. It's made you hard. Your heart is jaded. I know, because I've been there. If you can let your family help you carry that weight, it will make you feel lighter on the inside, and you can be more focused on running this station…which is your passion."

"How do you know all of this about me? I didn't see you for all of an hour yesterday."

"I study people."

"Ready to do yer reassessment yet?" Paige challenged Nana, satisfied Katie had proven her point.

Nana studied Katie for a few minutes, walking around her, sizing her up. "Yer strong. My grandson doesn't like wimpy women. You've lived a hard life as well. I can see it in yer eyes."

"I have a feelin' Nicky found a young lady who has a good blend of both of our qualities," Paige pointed out.

"I would have t' agree. We'll need t' work on 'er cooking skills, though."

"Please, and thank you!" Katie said, relieved. Then she added, "*After* we bring Nick in here and fill him in."

"Stubborn too," Paige quipped.

Nana smirked. "That would be from *you*."

* * *

"So, let me see if I'm understanding what you're telling me," Nick said, finally catching his breath. "Yer tellin' me that Jasper," when he said his name, Nana cringed, but Nick pushed on, "got so angry with Dad that he went t' kill him, and *you* shot him so he wouldn't?" he asked Nana, who nodded. "Is that why you won't let anyone talk about him?"

"This curse has taken over for four generations at this point," Nana explained. "In doing so, we've lost at least one male per generation…except yours. In sending you away, I believe we saved yer life."

"From Nate?"

"Exactly."

"Is there more to this? Who else have we lost, and how?"

"In yer dad's generation, it was Jasper. He wanted to kill yer dad, because he was jealous of both boys. The three boys were having target practice in the north field when Jasper turned on the twins. Hitting Adam first in the shoulder, Adam got away and got help, while Jasper aimed his gun at Zack." Nana sighed. "I got there first. Jasper had Zack on his knees, with his hands in the air. He had the gun to Zack's head. When he cocked his gun, I shot Jasper in the head. Had I been a moment later, Zack wouldn't be alive." She took a moment, but not wanting to answer any more questions on that story, she jumped into the rest of the generations, "In my generation, my brother Aiden was killed in a bar fight. His anger triggered others around him, and the fight got outta hand. In my father's generation, the original generation that got the curse, my father's brother, Liam, killed the witch's son in the clan wars."

"How can she fault him specifically?" Nick asked, stunned.

"Because she needed someone t' blame. Since Liam was the one who took her son, she demanded payment of blood in return."

"How can you believe this stuff really exists? It all sounds circumstantial at best. In Jasper's case, was there a mental issue we don't know about?"

"No. He was born with the anger in him. Having two older twin brothers, he got sidestepped when it came to attention. Then, if I remember right, her name was Briana, decided that Jasper didn't even come close to Zack, so he lost it. Jasper liked Briana for years."

"But, to shoot yer brother over a girl?"

"Yers attacked Katie over a girl," Nana pointed out. "He could have done worse had you not stopped him."

"Your disagreement with Nate is over a girl?" Katie asked, stunned.

"That was a last straw thing," Nick said, shaking his head, dismissing the conversation.

"And Briana was the last straw for Jasper. Yer right, Katie could very well had been killed by Nate the other day," Nana pointed out.

"If it wasn't for Hawk and his people, she would have been," Zack added.

Nick shook his head and crossed his arms in a huff. "This is insane."

"Not necessarily," Katie jumped into the conversation. "You said the north field is adjacent to the station Hawk and Carson were concerned about, right?"

Nick shook his head, confused. "Right."

"You said the station's name means flowing water. You told me that flowing water isn't bad, it's the evil that's flowing from it. What if, when Nana's family settled here, the anger flowed over to the station across the way? What if the north field is the battleground, so to speak? That's where Jasper went to kill the twins, right?"

"Right."

"What if?"

"There, and the stable as well," Nana said.

"What happened in the stables?" Nick asked, not really sure he wanted to know.

"Aiden almost killed me. It was a fight that..." Nana stopped short.

"That what?" Nick asked.

"The fight started in the north field when I caught him making out with the neighbor's daughter. He threatened to kill me if I told, because our families didn't get along at all." She sighed. "I ran back to the barn to get my horse because Dad was in the east field. He slammed me into the stable wall with his hands around my throat. The story goes after he choked me unconscious, he made a beeline for the bar…which is where the bar fight escalated and he was killed. Ya know," Nana said, considering Katie's theory, "you may have a point about the north field."

"Technically it's the station across the way," Katie pointed out. "The fact that the north field is the only portion that touches their property is where it bleeds over."

"How do we combat that?"

"We don't. We're aware of it," Nick said, processing all the information he was given. "I'll get up early in the morning and go pray over the field. That needs to be done each day."

Nana shook her head. "I dunno about that."

"Nana, one of Hawk's people is here. I'll be willing to wager a bet that he's either already doing it, or is more than willing to do it."

"Who?"

"Shawn O'Brien."

"The red head up watching the cattle in the south field?" Nana asked.

Pop nodded. "I think that's where he is."

"Well," Nana sighed, "guess I'd rather have 'im here helpin' out than not. All right. If you can talk t' him an' see if he'd be willin' to do it, I don't have a problem." She let out a slow breath of air. "I guess I don't get this God thing. How is some myth supposed to stop a curse?"

"God's not a myth!" Nick said, stunned, while Katie just sat there with her mouth open.

"Close yer mouth or the blowies may fly in," Nana mentioned.

"Flies," Nick said to Katie before he turned back to Nana. "I can't believe you think He's a myth! God *is* real. He's stronger than anything this world can dish out. I cannot tell you how disturbing that statement was to hear."

"I guess. I dunno. I only go to church for Easter an' Christmas. I know I'm supposed to, so I do," Nana explained.

"But, you don't know *Him*," Katie pointed out. "God is about relationship. You can't know Him if you don't study His word. You can't even begin to understand Him without having a relationship and trusting Him."

She shrugged. "Have t' take yer word for it."

"Oh, Nana." Nick dropped his head onto his hands. "Is there a church near here?"

"Yep. It's about thirty K down the road."

Katie looked at Nick in question, so he explained, "Thirty kilometers. That's about eighteen and a half miles away."

She nodded in understanding. "Got it. Do you want to go on Sunday?"

"I think we should," Nick agreed. Then he looked to Nana, "I would like you and Pop, and Mum and Dad t' go with us."

"I don't know."

"For me?"

She sighed in frustration. "Fine. We'll go."

"We will too," Paige agreed, grabbing Zack's hand.

Zack stood. "I'll see if I can get Adam and Flynn t' go too," he said and left for the field, taking Pop with him.

"Yer takin' a break on the porch with somethin' t' drink," Nana ordered Paige.

"Grumpy in yer old age?" Paige shot, as she got up and got a glass of lemonade before heading toward the rocking chair on the porch.

"Yeah, well, you would be too if you had t' deal with these boys on a daily basis," she quipped.

"But you love them," Paige said, and left for the porch.

When she was gone, Nana turned to Nick and said, "You know this station will be yours next."

"Who says I want it?" Nick asked, taken aback. "I have a life in the States."

She shook her head. "Nicky, you're the only one strong enough t' take this over. I'll worry for the station if it's in anyone else's hands."

"What about Adam? Or Flynn? Both of them have grown up on the station."

Nana went over and sat down next to Nick. Setting her hands on his shoulders, she turned him toward her. "Nicky, you know in yer heart this is where you belong."

Looking from Katie to Nana in confusion and desperation, he admitted, "I know, but I have a life already. Katie's goin' t' be goin' t' Quantico within a year. You can't expect me t' just drop everything an' come runnin'."

"I'm not gettin' any younger."

"I realize that, but I *have* a life. An' who says Katie wants t' come live here?"

"Wait. What?" Katie asked, stunned. "This is a conversation between the two of you."

"No. You know how important you are to me. You can't seriously think in the long term that we're not going t' be together. This is somethin' that *does* concern you."

"Nick, please don't put me in the middle of this. You know how much I love you," she said, and stood. Placing her hands on his head, she leaned down and kissed his cheek. "Know that I will follow you wherever you go. Wherever you are, to me, is home," she said, and left for the porch.

"Are you guys going riding?" Paige asked when she walked outside.

Sitting down on the other rocking chair, Katie shook her head. "Doubt it. The conversation's kind of heavy in there."

"What's going on?"

"Nana's talking to Nick about the station."

"Oh really? How's that going?"

"He's concerned with his world back home."

"Is that his only concern?"

"No," she admitted. "He wasn't sure about me wanting to be here either."

"What did you tell him?"

"I told him that I love him, and that I would follow him wherever he wants to go. To me, wherever he is, that's home."

"Good answer. You're very wise for your age."

"So they tell me."

The front door burst open as Nick came out. "Let's go riding. I need a ride."

"Everything okay?" Paige asked in concern.

"I just need a ride. C'mon, Katie," he said, and grabbed her hand.

Katie practically had to run to keep up with him. "What's going on?"

"I have a lot on my mind."

Katie pulled back on his hand and he spun toward her. "What's going on?"

"I just need to take a ride."

"If you take a ride, and take me with you, you'd better remember that I've never been on a horse before and I'm scared."

Putting his hands on his hips, he growled in frustration.

"Maybe you should take a ride on your own."

Stress written all over him, he confessed, "I need t' talk to you about some things, an' I don't want anyone listenin'. I know yer scared, but you can ride Star."

"I've-never-ridden-before," she reiterated sternly. "I know you're used to them, but I'm not. The idea of you riding to get rid of anxious energy and me having to follow really terrifies me. You have no idea how much you're scaring me."

"I'll be gentle. I promise. Trust me."

Sighing, she crossed her arms and agreed, "If you can't trust the FBI, who can you trust?"

He chuckled and hugged her. "I love you."

*   *   *

The horses saddled, Katie felt the horse move under her, which unnerved her. "I'm scared."

"But you're doing it," Nick encouraged. "You're facing your fears."

"Okay, to go left, pull the reigns this way." Pete showed her. "To go right, you pull this way. Then to stop, just pull back. Star's our calmest horse. She'll listen to you. She could even find her way back on her own if ya get lost. Just tell her t' go home."

"Got it." Katie nodded, still unsure.

"It'll be a piece a' cake. Just relax an' follow Nick's horse, an' Bob's yer uncle."

When Katie raised an eyebrow at him, he burst out in laughter, which made Star shift under her. "Okay, not helping," she said nervously.

"Just breathe, Katie. This'll be easy. It'll help distract me," Nick pointed out. "Ready?"

"Ready as I'll ever be," she said under her breath.

"Keep in mind that even though this is the dry season, we do still get rains once an' a while," Pete warned.

"Great," Katie huffed.

"Doubt it'll happen, just givin' ya warnin'. Have a good ride," he said before they rode out into the station.

Nick led her past the main house back into where the brush was thicker. A good portion of the station had been cleared, except maybe a hundred or so of the acres. Riding for quite a while, Katie wondered just how big the station actually was.

*   *   *

After riding Star for over forty-five minutes, Katie finally felt comfortable on her. Pete was right. She listened very well. While it was still unnerving feeling Star under her, Katie was getting used to it. In her nervous state, she talked to Star quite a bit.

Finally, much to Katie's relief, Nick stopped and got down. He tied Jumbunna to a tree, and then talked Katie down from Star while he held Star's reigns. After tying Star to another tree, he led Katie over to a set of boulders, so they could sit down and talk.

"What's going on in there, handsome?" Katie asked, brushing the hair out of his face after several moments of silence. "I can see and feel the anxiety. The anger is still hanging in there, but I think it's coming out in the form of frustration."

"It is frustratin'. My family seems t' think they can dictate how I spend the rest of my life."

"What do *you* want to do?"

He sighed, shaking his head. "I honestly don't know. I've always thought I would be an agent."

"Diane was forty-two when she left. What's she doing now?"

"Honestly? I don't really know."

"What would *you* do if you had to retire at forty-two?"

"Hmm. Never really thought about it."

"Maybe *that's* what you should be thinking about. You told me before that you're a country boy at heart. Your mom's told me just how much you loved being on the station when you were younger. What does the station mean to you?"

"It means everything t' me. It's my family's history. It's…t' me, being here is t' be free. I love workin' with my hands. The banter with the guys is refreshing. I enjoy hangin' with Pete. We've been mates since we were in nappies."

"So, the problem is?"

"I have a life in Cleveland. I'm an FBI agent. I hope to someday be your husband."

"You can't be my husband here?"

"Do *you* want to be here?"

"I want to be where you are."

"That's sweet, but this isn't just living here. It's a lifestyle. I don't think you fully understand what you're askin' for in volunteering t' live here."

"Do you know how much I love you?"

"Yes."

"How much?"

"With all your heart…same as I love you."

"If I wanted to move back to Oklahoma, would you do it?"

"Depends on why you want t' move back."

"What if my dad had cancer and I wanted to be there with him?"

"Since he's changed, I don't have a problem with it."

"But, you're an FBI agent."

"I would transfer t' Oklahoma." He shrugged. "If it's that important t' you…ohhhhh," he groaned, knowing where she was going with the conversation. "If it's important to me, it's important t' you."

Katie smiled and nudged him. "Knew you were a smart one."

"I have my moments." He nodded in understanding. "I feel really stupid."

"Why? For being chivalrous? For wanting to take my feelings into consideration? Look," she put her hand on his knee, "I want to finish some things back home before any decisions are made, but know that I will leave it up to you when or *if* we come back here."

"I appreciate that, but I want it t' be a decision between the two of us."

"Fair enough," she agreed. "So, what are you going to tell your grandmother?"

"Nana'll understand. She'll want t' keep in close communication, though."

"Good thing you have a good phone plan."

"I knew communication with my family was a must. I can't do that on a regular plan. It's worth the extra money t' me."

"So, when you make decisions, they basically follow with what's important to you?"

"Not necessarily," he countered. "I also apply logic and prayer t' the bigger decisions."

"Good idea. Then I guess we pray about it until we get an answer from God."

"I'm thinkin' that's a brilliant idea. I knew I liked ya for a reason," he teased her. A drop of rain hit his head. "Hmmm, we should head back t' the station," he remarked as the rain picked up pace. "Pete said there could be random storms."

Getting up off the rocks, Nick untied Star first and helped Katie up on her horse. After he got on Jumbunna, they headed toward the station. They only got several feet when they saw a flash near the main house or barn. The thunder cracked so loudly, the rumble shook the ground. Both horses bucked. While Nick could keep his horse under control, Katie couldn't hold Star and she bucked Katie off. When Katie fell, she hit her head on a rock. As soon as she bucked her, Star ran for the stables.

Jumping off his horse, he tied it to a tree before Nick ran over to Katie. "Katie, honey, can you open your eyes?" Nick asked, lightly tapping her face, with no response. "C'mon, hon, I don't wanna leave you here t' go get help. It's not entirely safe out here. I can't move you, though, until you're conscious enough t' tell me if yer hurt."

Not getting a response, Nick took a good look around to make sure there were no creatures around that could put her life in further jeopardy before he went for his horse. At that moment, another bolt of lightning crackled across the sky and Jumbunna pulled so hard on his reigns that he almost got loose before Nick could grab them. He calmed the horse enough to get on him and rode toward the station as quickly as he could.

"Pete!" Nick yelled as soon as he crossed the threshold of the barn.

"Nick?" Pete furrowed his brow as he came out of Star's stall. "Where's Katie? Star came in a little bit ago without her."

"Is your horse saddled?"

"Yes. Where's Katie?"

"She needs help."

"You run and tell Nana an' I'll meet ya at the house," Pete said, making a beeline for his horse's stall.

Nick turned Jumbunna, and headed for the main house. When he was almost there, something made him look toward the north field. That's when he saw what looked like a man on a black horse, jump the fence, heading out across the station.

"Nana!" Nick yelled, not getting down.

"What are ya shoutin' about?" Nana demanded, drying her hands on a towel.

"Katie's hurt in the bush, an' some bush ranger just jumped the fence an' rode into the station, headed in the direction I left Katie in."

"Let's go," Pete said, with a backpack on as he rode. His horse was a beautiful black horse, with white hooves.

"Go! Go!" Nana shooed them. "I'll alert the others about the rider."

Nick and Pete took off, full speed into the brush. They rode up to where Nick left Katie to find her still there, much to Nick's relief. His concern, though, was that she wasn't moving, as a matter of fact, she hadn't moved at all.

"What happened?" Pete asked, dismounting.

"When the lightning struck the first time, Star bucked Katie off an' she hit her head on the rock. I almost lost Jumbunna on the second strike."

Pete lightly tapped her cheek. "Katie? Can you wake up for me?"

Katie moaned, as her head went side to side.

"Please, love, wake up?" Nick pleaded.

It took her a few moments before her eyes fluttered open. Looking up, Nick saw the bewilderment in her eyes. "What's going on?" she groaned.

"Star bucked you," Pete explained. "Does anything besides yer head hurt?"

Nodding in response, she struggled to keep her eyes open.

"Can you move all of your extremities?"

Making sure she could move everything, she nodded.

"Can you slowly sit up for me?" he asked. Both men, on either side of her, helped her sit up. "There ya go. How do you feel?"

"Um, ohhhh," she groaned, holding her head.

Hearing a noise to his right, Nick looked and smacked Pete to look as well. When they did, another flash of lightning in the distance lit up the sky, except for the silhouette of a horse and rider. The horse whinnied and kicked up its front legs before they rode on.

"You saw that, right?" Nick checked, for his own piece of mind.

"Yes. Let's get Katie back t' the house as soon as possible. Whoever that was made the hair on the back of my neck stand on end."

"Agreed," Nick said, heading for his horse. When he was up, Pete hoisted Katie up in front of Nick, who wrapped his arm tightly around her before he took off for the house, closely followed by Pete on his own horse.

By the time they reached the main house, Katie was unconscious once again. The blood mixed with the rain, stained her clothing.

"Bloody hell!" Nana exclaimed when Nick passed her down to Barwon. "Is she hurt anywhere else?"

"From what I could tell, the main damage is her head. She may need stitches," Pete explained as he tied his horse to the porch. "Has Dad started the tea yet?"

"Yep." Nana nodded. "I called him in t' start it as soon as you blokes left. Take 'er up t' her room, Barwon. Paige an' I will get her wet clothes off an' dry her off. Then you two can go up," she said, following Barwon into the house.

"Yes, ma'am," Pete and Nick said.

"Sorry, mate, no horse or rider on the station," Flynn said, riding up to the house. "Did you blokes find Katie?"

"Yes. She's on her way upstairs. She's unconscious. We saw 'im in the brush," Nick pointed out. "He would have already cleared the station by the time you guys started looking."

"Sorry just the same. We didn't even see 'im out in the station. I checked with the others."

"We both saw him," Pete said sternly. "Whoever or whatever he is, he was, in fact, on the station."

"Right oh," Flynn said under his breath. "The others are securing their areas before coming in. With this rain, they want t' make sure the animals don't lose their minds."

"Good idea."

*   *   *

The women dried off and put clean clothes on the unconscious Katie before letting Pete and Nick into the room. Pete got her conscious enough to have her drink the tea his dad made for her, and then let it take over until she went back to sleep.

"She'll sleep off any fever that may come about, but when she wakes, she'll be terribly sick," Pete explained.

"Should she be sleeping with a head injury?" Nick asked.

"I gave her a minimal dose, enough that I should be able t' wake her every hour."

"Every hour? That's gonna be a long night."

"Right, but if I can't wake her, then we have a problem."

"Got it."

"I had t' put three stitches in the back of her head, but her hair hides it very well."

"Good. Was she awake when you did it?"

"Nope. I had Nana help me when she went t' sleep so she wouldn't feel it. Good news is that she actually bled out."

"How is that good?"

"If she didn't bleed, she would definitely have t' go to the hospital. At that point, she would have probably been bleeding on the inside…not good."

"I see."

"No worries, mate. Not like we haven't run across this type a' injury before. She'll be apples in no time."

"Here's praying!"

*   *   *

Groggy, Katie got up to go to the bathroom. When she finished, she looked in the mirror and saw all the blood in her hair, so she got in the shower, not knowing there were stitches in her head. That didn't matter, though, because less than a minute into her shower, she was overcome with nausea so badly, that she barely shut the shower off and got wrapped in a towel before she lunged for the toilet and proceeded to throw up. This went on for three solid minutes. Her head pounding ferociously, she curled up on the floor of the bathroom, not wanting to move.

That's when she heard a light knock on the door before it slowly opened. "Hey, love, how are you feelin'?" Nick asked, grabbing another towel to make sure her private parts were all covered. "I heard someone throwing up an' noticed your door was open an' you weren't in bed. I made the assumption it was you who was throwing up."

She only nodded in response.

"Want me t' help you back t' bed?"

Since she nodded again, he gingerly scooped her up off the floor and carried her back to her room. "Here's a small trash can in case you get sick again," he said, placing the tiny trashcan against the wall on the other side of the bed.

Katie passed the wet towels to him as she was under the covers. "Here."

"Want your pajamas?"

"New ones would be nice, if you wouldn't mind?" she asked, rolling toward the wall. "My head is pounding."

"I'll bet. Hang on a sec," he said, and left the room. He hung the towels before getting her a fresh pair of pajama pants, a t-shirt, and a clean pair of underwear. "Okay. I'm going t' go get Pete t' check you out. Be back in a few. In the meantime, go ahead and get dressed. Take it slowly, though, huh?"

She only nodded, so he closed the door behind him before taking off down the stairs and out the door for the bunkhouse. "Pete?" Nick whispered, lightly shaking him. "Pete?"

"What? Huh?" Pete sat up, startled out of a sound sleep. He groaned. "What time is it, mate?"

"It's around two in the mornin', but Katie woke up. She threw up big time. She was in the shower, is that gonna effect the stitches?"

"No. Bet her head's poundin', though."

"Oh yeah. Wanna check 'er out before I let 'er go back t' sleep? She was lookin' pretty groggy."

"Yeah," he said, climbing out of bed as quietly as he could. Despite the fact that the men knew what happened to Katie, and that Pete was the one caring for her, he got sworn at multiple times for making noise before he was out the door. "Crikey! Grumpy lil' buggars in there," Pete said, closing the door behind him.

"That bad?" Nick chuckled as they crossed the station toward the main house.

"Yeah. That's a crew I wouldn't wanna wake up on their best day."

"Yeah, but they're good blokes."

"They have their moments," Pete said, tongue-in-cheek.

They made their way quietly up the stairs to Katie's room, which was the first door on the left, across from the bathroom. In the five-bedroom home, Nana and Pop had a room, Paige and Zack had a room, Adam had his own room, while Flynn and Nick shared a room, and Katie had her own room.

"I left the lamp on because it was dimmer than the bedroom light," Nick explained as they entered her room.

"Um?" Pete questioned, looking at the empty bed.

"Throwing up again," Katie said, coming back into the room after brushing her teeth.

"Hold a sec," Pete said as she went to get back in bed. "Before ya lay down I wanna see. Close yer eyes," he told her before asking Nick, "Can you turn on the overhead light?"

When Nick turned on the light, Pete got a good look at the stitches before sending her to bed. Nick turned off the overhead light as she snuggled under the covers.

"I've got a stronger tea already made downstairs. You have a fever an' this'll knock it outta ya," Pete said, and left for the kitchen.

"I hope it doesn't have the same effect that the other one had. My head is pounding beyond belief!" Katie complained.

"How are you feeling otherwise?" Nick asked.

"My head is overriding everything at this point."

"Okay, I want ya t' drink this as fast as ya can," Pete said, bringing in a mug of tea a few moments later. "It doesn't smell or taste the best, but it'll knock that fever outta ya. Pretty sure you're good t' go in sleeping for quite a bit. I'm satisfied anyway."

"Well, I trust you," Nick said, resting his elbow on Pete's shoulder.

"Ewww!" Katie shuddered. "What's in this? It smells and tastes horrid!"

"Just drink it an' quit whinging!" Pete laughed.

Katie raised an eyebrow. "What's that?"

"That means whining." Nick chuckled. "And, she usually doesn't. I've had that tea before an' gotta tell ya that I whinged too."

"All right." She sighed before she chugged the tea. Shuddering again, she handed the cup back to Pete, who disappeared out the door for the kitchen.

"Okay, you need t' get some rest," Nick said, tucking her in. "Be warned that this tea is strong. It has some side effects."

"Now you tell me," she groaned. "Oh!" she said, her legs falling asleep. "My body is feeling funky."

"No worries. It's supposed to."

Katie giggled. "You know, you're kinda cute."

Cocking his head to the side, he asked, "Are you okay?"

She only giggled in response, feeling giddy, almost drunk. "Ya know, I've never drank before, but I'll bet this is what it feels like. My head is swimming and my body feels funny."

"Then it's workin'," Pete said, coming back into the room. "When you wake, grab that trash can right there in your bed. Pretty sure you won't make it to the bathroom this time."

"Am I fixin' to get terribly sick again? My head was pounding so hard after last time."

"No worries. There is one more side effect, so Nick, keep an ear out for her, huh?" Pete warned.

"How long will she be sleepin' for?" Nick asked.

"Oh, at least ten t' twelve hours, easy. Sweet dreams, Katie," he said, and left.

"Ohhh, Niii-iiick?" Katie giggled.

Nick looked at her wide-eyed. "Are you okay?"

"Yep. And, you're *really* cute," she said, running her fingers down his chin, resting her hand on the side of his face.

He blushed, with a grin. "Oh boy."

"Aww! How adorable! Ya know…come here." She pulled him closer to her. As he got closer, her arms suddenly dropped to the bed. "I, umm, what's going on?" she asked, confused.

"Medicine in the tea is taking effect. Just rest, sweetheart," he said, as her eyes closed and her head fell to the side.

Tucking the blankets around her, he kissed her cheek before he left her in the room, sound asleep.

Chapter 4

Summer to Remember

Katie woke up in her dorm room on the University of Oklahoma campus. Disoriented, she stumbled to the bathroom to take a shower and wake up. The silence around her was almost irritating, as she hoped to get some idea of why she was there and not in Australia with Nick.

After her shower, she got dressed and went out onto the campus. The bright sunshine and stillness in the air told her it was summertime.

"Morning, Katie!" a girl ran up to her and hugged her.

"Hey!" Katie said with a fake smile, hoping to remember who the girl was and why she hugged Katie.

"Are you and Ryan going to the party tonight at Ty's?"

"Um, more than likely." *What was going on? Party at Ty's house? Why would she go with Ryan? What happened to Nick?* "Um, pardon me, but I think I slept too hard. Do you know where Ryan or Ty are at the moment?"

"Duh! They're in class. Speaking of which, why aren't you? Your final exam is today."

"I don't know."

She touched the side of Katie's face. "You have a bit of a fever. Why don't you go back to your room? I'll get you some soup and let the guys know. You can go to the office later and explain that you had a fever this morning and I'm sure they'll let you take a make-up exam."

"Um, why don't I go with you? If you could go and actually get them though, I'd appreciate it," Katie said, taking the shot at finding someone she actually knew who might know what was going on.

Heading toward one of the buildings, with the girl talking a mile a minute about how cute and sweet both guys were, and how Katie was very lucky to have Ryan as her boyfriend, Katie's headache magnified. To Katie, this was confusing on so many levels. She decided to ride it out and see if there was an end to this nightmare somewhere.

"Katie?" Ryan asked, concerned, stepping out of class. "Gina said you were sick. What are you doing out here?" He placed his hands on either side of her face. "You have a bit of a fever. Why don't you go back to the dorm?"

So, her name was Gina. "I don't want to. I kind of need to talk to you and Ty."

"Tell you what," he said, glancing at his watch, "Why don't you and Gina go to the cafeteria and we'll meet you there after class. We only have about twenty minutes left. We have to wait for everyone to finish their exams before we can leave."

Katie agreed, so she and Gina headed toward the cafeteria. Not sure where 'Gina' fit into all of this, Katie decided to keep her around for a bit.

On the way there, Gina droned on about Ty and Ryan until Katie thought about banging her head against the wall. She was having a hard time wrapping her brain around the idea that she and this girl were best friends.

"So, what do you think?" Gina asked, bringing Katie back into the conversation.

"About what?"

"Katie? Were you even listening?"

"Kind of. I'm a bit disorientated. I don't really understand what's going on here."

"What do you mean? You graduate at the end of this semester and start as a teacher over in West Springs in the fall. What's so confusing? It *would* help if you actually took the exam for your last class, though."

"West Springs High School?"

"No, junior high. Ty has the high school. Are you okay?"

"Kind of. Okay, I'm going to ask you some weird questions, but I need you to stay with me and answer them."

"Of course."

"What's my major?"

"Duh. Art."

"Not art and criminology?"

"Why would you major in criminology?" she asked, confused. "Oh wait! I remember you saying one time you were thinking about that one, but you and Ryan decided to just do the art major, since he didn't want you doing anything in law enforcement."

"I see. And how long have Ryan and I been going out?"

"About six months after y'all got here. Why don't you know this stuff? Did you hit your head?"

Katie felt her head and cringed when she found a lump on the back of her head. "I think so." As Gina checked Katie's head for any more bumps, Katie asked, "How long have we been friends?"

"Are you kidding? We've been roommates since day one. Wow! Maybe we *should* take you to the hospital."

"No. Just a few more questions and I should have a pretty good idea. Why did I pick here and not Cleveland?"

"As in Ohio? Good heavens! From what I know about you, you've never set foot outside of Oklahoma, let alone go to Cleveland, Ohio," she said, retaking her seat opposite Katie.

Dropping her head in her hands, Katie sighed. "Are my dad and Cami still married?"

Gina's face went pale. "Um, no more questions. I think Ty and Ryan need to answer this one."

Glancing up at Gina, Katie demanded, "What happened to my dad?"

"He couldn't handle you not talking to him. And, after Cami left him, he lost it and..." her voice faded. "I'm really sorry, Katie."

As tears formed in Gina's eyes, Katie asked, "When?"

"Last year. That's why you're taking summer classes to finish your degree. You had to take time off. You spiraled pretty badly." She wiped a tear off her face. "You really don't remember this stuff, do you?"

Katie shook her head, feeling the world spin under her feet. Taking a deep breath to clear her mind, she said, "So, let me get this straight. Ryan and I are dating."

"Pretty sure he's going to ask you to marry him soon."

"Are you and Ty together?"

"Only if God is smiling down on me today. He's still enamored with you."

"How does Ryan feel about that?"

"They have an understanding."

"I see. And, my dad? He committed suicide last year?"

"Yes. It was in March. You tend to get grumpy in March anyway, and that didn't help. You had to go home and get the house and things sorted. Me, Ryan, and Ty went with you. That's the reason we all had to take these summer classes to finish. It took us a bit to pull you out of that one."

Shaking her head in disbelief, Katie pushed forward, "So, I've *never* been to Cleveland?"

"Not that I'm aware of."

"And, I'm *not* doing a double major?"

"Nope. It's always been art."

"Is Ty –" Katie was cut off as Ty wheeled into the cafeteria with Ryan.

"Sorry we couldn't come any earlier. We finally asked to leave because you didn't look so good," Ryan explained, giving Katie a kiss on the head before taking his seat beside her, while Ty pulled up to the end of the table in his wheelchair.

"We may have to take her to the ER," Gina mentioned.

"Why?" Ty asked.

"Because of the questions she's been asking about you two and her dad. She didn't even remember that her dad passed away last year." As soon as she said the last part, both Ty and Ryan looked at Katie, wide-eyed.

"Okayyy, did you hit your head?" Ryan asked, and proceeded to run his fingers over her head. When he hit the part where she hit her head, she jumped and groaned. "When did you do that?"

"Don't know. Um, I may need some direction," Katie admitted. "I don't know where my classes are or what I'm taking."

"Really? You only have one final exam left," Ty said, shaking his head. "How bad is the bump?"

"Actually looks like she's already been to the doctor, because there are stitches in her head. I don't understand. When did you go to the doctor?" Ryan asked.

"I don't know." Katie sighed. "Look, just let me go back to my room and figure some things out."

When she stood to leave, Ryan asked, "What if we eat first and then go back to the dorm?"

"No. I need to go for the moment. I have to think," she insisted.

"At least let me escort you?" Ryan offered.

"No. I know my way back."

Before she left, Ryan went to kiss her, and she gave him her cheek. He wasn't happy, but with as confused as she felt, she needed to get a clear head before she did anything else.

By the time she got back to the dorm, she already knew what she would have to do. Taking some time to go to the office to take her exam, it took her a couple of hours, but in the end she was relieved to know that she passed. She also got permission to leave her belongings in her room for a couple of weeks. Of course she had to pay, but it was worth it.

Upon returning to her room, she was relieved that Gina wasn't there, so she checked her bank account balance online and booked a ticket for Cleveland, Ohio, set to leave in a few hours.

After printing her ticket and calling a cab, she set to packing. It was the summer, so she packed jeans, t-shirts, a couple pairs of shorts, and a light jacket. She wasn't sure what she would do when she arrived, but she had to find out what happened up in Cleveland.

*   *   *

The nerves set in as the plane descended into Cleveland. She had more than enough money to keep her floating for a while, as well as her bankcard if needed. From what she could tell, she had gotten the money from graduation. It seems she kept the family home since it was already paid for. This would make sense if she and Ryan were supposed to be getting married, since his parents lived right next door.

Taking a cab to a hotel in an area she knew to be safe, she checked in and got settled. Her stomach was a nervous mess, but she had to know what happened to the people she loved in Cleveland.

The first place she thought to look into was Cook's café. It was around lunchtime, so she headed over there. She had to catch her breath when she saw Dom still behind the counter. *Did he still attack those girls since she wasn't there? Would this visit set the attacks in motion?*

"Welcome to Cook's Corner Café. Have to say I've never seen you here before. Are you new to the area?" Seb asked, walking up behind the counter in front of her to take her order.

"I, um," she nervously cleared her throat, "I'm new. I just got off the plane less than an hour ago."

"Oh! Welcome to our area. How did you hear about us?"

"Through a friend who used to live here. He said to make sure to come here if I ever came in this direction."

"I see. And, does this friend have a name?"

"Nick Locke," she offered, checking to see if he gave a reaction to the name.

"Well, never heard of him, but if he likes the café, have to say he has good taste. So, what can I get you?"

"How about fried chicken, mashed potatoes, and lemonade?"

"Sounds great. I'll be back shortly with your lemonade," he said, taking her menu and setting it behind the counter.

When he was gone, Katie looked around the café. That's when she saw, over in the corner, a booth full of her college friends…including Jillian and Aaron. She gulped. *It was amazing how much things had changed without her there.*

She shuddered when Giovanni walked into the café and sat at the counter near her. "Good afternoon." He offered his hand.

As Katie shook his hand in greeting, she said, "Yes, it is. Do you live around here?"

"Yes. Are you new here?"

"Yep. Just got off the plane. A friend told me to come here if I ever landed in Cleveland."

"Oh? Where are you from?"

"Oklahoma. Do you," she cleared her throat again, "do you go to school here?"

"Unfortunately," he grumbled.

"You don't want to go here?"

"Not really. My dad made me major in accounting. You'd laugh if I told you what I really want to do."

"Oh? What's that?"

"Veterinarian."

"I see. And, why can't you do that?"

"You're not laughing?"

"No. Whatever your dream is, is your dream for a reason. But, why aren't you in school for it?"

"Because my dad made me go for an accounting degree."

"Why?"

"So I could take over the family business."

"Which is?"

"Well," he rubbed the back of his neck nervously, "it's an organizational type business. What is it you do?"

"Art teacher."

"Sounds –"

"What can I get you?" Seb asked Giovanni, coldly, as he set the lemonade in front of Katie.

After Giovanni gave him his order, Seb quickly disappeared. "He doesn't seem to like you," Katie pointed out.

"There are a lot around here who don't care for me."

"Why is that?"

"Because of my father," he said, his eyes turning a deep dark brown, anger churning within them.

"Seems like we're going in circles. How about this…hi, I'm Katie MacKenna," she said, shaking his hand.

He moved to the seat next to hers and countered, "And, I'm Giovanni Rossi."

*   *   *

That afternoon, she and Giovanni walked around the campus and got to know each other better. She could tell he was fascinated with her, but still kept her at a distance. Setting up to meet at the café for dinner that night, Katie headed back to her hotel to get a shower.

Katie knew Ryan, Ty, and Gina would be upset, so she pulled the battery from her phone before she left her dorm in Oklahoma. She didn't want the angry voicemails or texts.

She now knew Jillian and Aaron were still alive. That, to her, was a relief. What scared her, though, was that Dom was still in the café, and Giovanni was still headed toward taking over the Rossi Family. And what broke her heart, was that her dad never found the gift of restored grace God wanted to give him, and he instead chose to take his life.

*   *   *

Katie and Giovanni talked long into the night, leaving the café as it finally closed around eleven. Giovanni dropped Katie off at her hotel, making plans to pick her up for lunch the next day.

Around nine-thirty the next morning, Katie got a knock on her hotel room door. Looking through the peephole, she instantly recognized Seth and Nick. A thrill ran through her body at seeing Nick, but she had to rein it back, knowing at that moment, he had no idea who she was.

Taking a deep breath, she opened the door. "Can I help you?"

"Are you Katie MacKenna?" Seth asked.

"Yes, sir. How can I help you?"

Showing her their badges, she quickly checked them before returning them. "Okay, and why are you here?"

"Two reasons, actually. The first is because you have some concerned friends who have tracked you all the way to Cleveland from Oklahoma," Seth explained.

"And the second is because we would like to talk to you about a proposition," Nick added.

"C'mon in. I'd imagine this is fixin' to be a long conversation. Do you want some coffee?" she asked, gesturing toward the coffee pot in the room.

"Fixin' to?" Nick raised an eyebrow.

"Going to," Katie corrected. Then she asked again, "Do y'all want some coffee?"

"No thank you. Please, have a seat," Seth gestured toward the bed, as he and Nick each took the chairs at the little table in the room.

When she sat down, Nick started, "We noticed that you were with a young man yesterday. Are you going to see him today as well?"

"What's your interest in Giovanni?" Katie asked.

"Are you aware of what his family does?"

She shrugged, playing dumb. "He said it was an organization."

Nick chuckled. "That's a good term for it. His dad is head of the Rossi Crime Family."

"What does this have to do with me?" Katie asked innocently. *This was working out better than she thought it would.*

"Well," Seth cleared his throat, "the Rossi family is a difficult family to get into, and since you two met innocently, it wouldn't be an issue for you to be a friend."

"Well, we're building a friendship. That doesn't mean I'm his friend."

"He doesn't let too many people near him," Nick pointed out. "Are you going to see him again before you leave back for Oklahoma?"

"Who says I'm going back?"

With a stunned look, Nick asked, "Why would you not go back home?"

"There's a lot I don't understand at the moment. I'm trying to figure things out."

"Maybe you should start with getting a hold of your friends and fiancé," Nick pointed out.

"He's not my fiancé. And, how did you guys find me?" Katie asked.

"Well, have to say you didn't make it easy," Seth started. "You bought your ticket to Cleveland with your bank card. Your boyfriend is quite the resourceful young man. The problem was figuring out where you were once you got here.

Since you only used cash, that didn't make it easy, but we were watching Giovanni, and when we saw the two of you together, it made things a lot easier to connect the dots. The question is, what are you doing here? And, how did you just *happen* to run into Giovanni?"

"That's difficult to explain," Katie admitted.

"Try us."

Katie sighed. *Would they really understand?* "I felt the need to come here and see some people."

"Was Giovanni one of them?"

"In a way."

"In *what* way?" Nick pressed.

"I don't know if I can explain it to you. Just know I felt led to come here."

"That doesn't answer our questions."

"I'm afraid I don't have an answer."

Nick sat back in his chair and crossed his arms, frustrated. He huffed. "You just so *happen* to take off and come this way, and just so *happen* to end up running into Giovanni Rossi on your first day here?"

"Well, I ran into a few people here since my arrival," Katie pointed out. "I also met someone named Seb, and now the two of you. That tends to be how things work."

"What time are you meeting with him today?" Seth asked, changing the subject, feeling the tension between Katie and Nick.

"He's picking me up for lunch."

"Moving quickly, aren't ya?" Nick challenged.

"What *exactly* are you insinuating?" Katie snapped, the anger visible in her face as her eyes flashed green and then returned to their natural hazel.

Nick's eyes momentarily popped open before a satisfied grin crossed his face. "So, you like young Rossi."

"As a friend, yes. I don't know him well enough for anything else at the moment."

"You seem quite familiar in surroundings that you've never been to," Nick observed.

"What do you mean?"

"Why did you pick this hotel? It's noticeably close to the campus. You also found the hole-in-the-wall café that is on the outskirts of the campus. People tend not to find it unless they've gone to school there. Now, having said that, we know you've never set foot in Cleveland before now…or have you?"

"I have not."

"Then, can you explain how you know of these places?"

"Nope."

"What are we missing?"

"Not a thing." Katie said adamantly. Getting impatient, she stood. "I need to get ready for lunch. Unless there is anything else, I would like you to go."

"You don't like me, do you?" Nick challenged.

"Nope. You're arrogant and egotistical."

While Seth snickered, Nick's anger was evident, as he demanded, "Where do you get off calling me arrogant and egotistical in one conversation?"

Katie leaned on the table next to him. "Pretty sure you're going to volunteer to be my handler, hoping to get in good with Giovanni. And, unless I miss my guess," she turned to Seth, "You're hoping I'll fall for Nick with his charismatic personality and good looks, so I won't fall for Giovanni."

Stunned, Seth shook his head. "I don't understand."

"Well, allow me to clear something up for you. I don't intend to help either of you. I don't care how much you push. Giovanni will do what he wants to do. If that means leaving his family to become a veterinarian, then so be it. If that means he stays as head of the Rossi Family, then that's his choice. I don't intend to hang around long enough to either help you or fall for him. I have a life back in Oklahoma."

"Then why are you here?"

"Because I had to find a couple of things out."

"Which are?" Nick pressured her again for answers.

"My business, not yours. There's a reason I turned my cell off and have used cash."

"You more than turned it off," Nick pointed out. "You pulled the battery and left it in Oklahoma. The only reason we found you is because you were seen with Giovanni."

"You can leave now. I don't intend to help you at all."

"Fine," Nick said, as he and Seth stood. "If you change your mind –"

"I won't," Katie cut him off. When they left, Katie leaned against the closed door, her heart racing. *What had she done? Why didn't she just stay in Oklahoma where she was put? What drew her to Cleveland in the first place?*

*　*　*

After dinner, Giovanni dropped Katie off at her hotel. She packed up her belongings and bought a ticket for Oklahoma the next morning. *While she didn't want to continue this disaster, could she leave Nick?*

Around nine that night, she got another knock on her door. Looking through the peephole, she groaned when saw Nick by himself. Opening the door, she demanded, "What do *you* want?"

"I think we got off on the wrong foot."

"I'm leaving in the morning."

"Why?"

"Because I'm supposed to."

"Are you?"

"What?"

"We're called to places for a reason," he said, stepping into her room. As she closed the door behind him, he continued, "I've ran our conversation through my mind all day. There are a lot of questions I don't have answers for."

"Who says I'm going to answer them?"

"They're not all necessarily questions from your end," he pointed out.

She crossed her arms in a huff. "What do you mean?"

Stepping closer to her, he placed his hands on her shoulders, and she froze. "Like why I'm so attracted to you."

"Is this some kind of game?"

"No. That's what I've been struggling with all day. When I first saw you, I was immediately drawn to you."

"That's a load of rubbish and you know it."

"No!" he snapped. Turning away from her, he crossed his arms. Sighing, he admitted, "It's like I'm magnetically attracted, to the point that I can't do anything else but think about you."

"Oh wow!" She rolled her eyes. "Does that really work?"

He spun around and grabbed her face, kissing her with an undeniable passion, a passion she felt a thousand times when they kissed.

Katie pushed him away and demanded, "You need to leave. I have a plane to catch in the morning."

"Why? Why are you leaving?"

"I have a life."

"You have more than that here and you know it!"

"Leave!" Katie demanded.

After he left, she had a restless sleep, tossing and turning all night long. By the time she woke the next morning, she was still tossing and turning between regret and relief. *Could she leave things unfinished here? What would happen if she stayed? Should she return back to her neatly packaged life that was waiting for her in Oklahoma or should she risk it all and stay in Cleveland?*

By the time the plane landed in Oklahoma City, she was still tormented on what direction to turn. Walking into the airport, she was met by Ryan, Ty, and Gina. "What are you guys doing here?"

"The FBI office in Cleveland contacted the sheriff, who called us to tell us when you were landing," Ty explained. "Care to share why you pulled a sudden disappearing act?"

"I don't know. I just felt I had to go there."

"Why?" Ryan demanded. "We have it all here. Both of us have jobs and a house. Why would you throw it all away to go to Cleveland of all places? Seriously, Katie, there are times I really don't understand you."

"Katie?" she heard, and spun around to see Nick standing in the airport.

"Who's that?" Ryan demanded.

"Nick? What are you doing here?" Katie asked, stunned.

"I found out what plane you were taking and took the same one. I was in first class, so you wouldn't see me."

"*Who are you?*" Ryan growled.

"Guys, this is Nick Locke, an agent in the FBI office," Katie explained.

"You didn't need to escort her," Ty pointed out. "She's an adult."

"Who makes adult decisions," Gina added. Then she asked, "Why *are* you here?"

"She and I have unfinished business," Nick explained. While Katie's eyes blazed with anger, he continued, "She's helping us with a case, and we need her to finish it."

"Is that the reason you went to Cleveland?" Ryan asked.

"That's cool!" Ty said, his demeanor shifting.

"No. Not cool." Katie crossed her arms. "*Very* not cool!"

"Well," Ryan protectively put his arm around Katie, "maybe we should talk things out over dinner?"

"We actually need to get back to Cleveland," Nick hinted.

"Why?" Gina asked. "She just got back."

"Because we have to get back to the case," Nick pressed.

"Fine," Katie said with a sigh. "When do we leave?"

"In an hour."

"Then we'll eat and then she can go," Ryan insisted.

*   *   *

Before they left, Ryan went to kiss Katie, but once again she gave him her cheek. It took Nick all of fifteen minutes to bring it up, as they sat in first class. "Aren't you supposed to be marrying that Ryan bloke?"

"Yes," Katie groaned, knowing Nick had the entire trip to question her.

"You didn't seem all too friendly with him," he pointed out.

"Ladies and gentlemen," the captain came over the loudspeaker, "we are expecting some rough weather for our trip. When the seatbelt sign comes on, please take note and stay in your seat, only getting up for emergencies. If necessary, we will divert to another airport. I apologize ahead of time for any inconvenience this may cause, but safety is our number one priority."

"Good to know," Nick said under his breath as they buckled their seatbelts.

"Can you finally tell me why you followed me all the way to Oklahoma?"

"I told you, we're connected." He shrugged like it was no big deal. "Now, I'm pretty sure you feel it as well."

"I do," she admitted.

"Then, why would I chance letting you slip away?"

"Who says I like you? Connected and attracted are two different things," she pointed out.

"Well, aren't you the blunt little thing," he chuckled.

"You call it honest."

"You say that with a sense of familiarity."

"Because if we're being honest with each other, I know you Nick Locke."

"Oh really?"

"Yes. I know you're originally from Australia. I know you have a twin brother who hates you, and that's the reason you were sent to live with your grandparents in Jasper, Montana."

Looking at her in wide-eyed horror, he gulped. "How do you know all that?"

"The same way I know your dad, Zack, has a twin brother, Adam. I also know Adam, and his son, Flynn, live on Serenity Wells Station, with your Nana and Pop."

"Okay, you either need to stop, or you need to tell me what in blazes is goin' on here!" He sat up in his seat, on edge.

At that moment, the plane was struck by lightning, catching the right wing on fire. In the chaos that instantly surrounded them, along with the screams of terror, it didn't take long for Katie to see the tornado nearing them out the plane window. As the plane spun, Katie grabbed Nick's hand, and prayed with every bone in her body.

As soon as the tornado neared the plane, they didn't stand a chance. In a last ditch effort, the pilot did his best to get control of the plane and change direction. The gauges spun out of control, leaving the pilot flying blind for a few more precious seconds before they crashed into the ground.

* * *

Katie sat up in her bed with sweat dripping off her body. Wiping her face, she looked around the room, her heart racing out of control. *Where was she?* It took her a moment to realize she was back in the safety of Serenity Wells Station. The screams still echoed in her mind as she looked around the room, the plane crash fresh in her memory.

Lying back on her pillow, she slowed her breathing to control how much her head spun. "It was a nightmare," she assured herself. "A nightmare that felt very real, but a nightmare nonetheless."

At that moment, she heard a knock on her door, and Pete entered carrying a cup of tea.

"Oh no, please. Not another one."

"Katie," he sat on the side of her bed, "yer fever's still pretty high. You need t' drink this t' feel better."

Shaking her head, she pleaded, "Please! You don't understand!"

"Actually, I do. You see, there's unfinished business in your mind that you need to straighten out. This allows you to do it. Now, drink," he insisted, wrapping her hand around the cooled cup of tea.

Sighing, she drank it. Deciding to get it done and over with, she chugged it as quickly as possible.

"There now." He set the empty cup on the nightstand before tucking her in. "It'll only take a moment to take effect. You just relax an' let your concerns guide your dream," he said, running his fingers through her hair as she slowly opened and closed her eyes. "Quit fightin' it, Katie."

"It's scary," she complained.

"I know, but you need t' work through a little bit more. You'll wake up with all questions answered."

"Thank you," she said in relief. Letting the medicine take over, she drifted back to sleep, into yet, another world…

*   *   *

"No, we need to talk," Seb demanded, shoving Katie into her chair as he stood behind her.

"I don't want to talk to you," she crossed her arms in a huff.

"Look, I think there was a misunderstanding, and I want to clear what happened between us earlier tonight down at the dock. I don't like how things ended. How did you get home, by the way?"

"I called Nick."

"Of course you did. The big bad FBI agent to the rescue," he scowled.

"He's a friend."

"Oh, sure," Seb said snidely, as he went around to the front of her. "Do you have feelings for him?"

"As a friend," she countered.

He roughly grabbed her chin, forcing her to look at him, "No, as more than a friend. Admit it. You want him."

"Nope."

Pushing her to the ground by her chin, he then put his knee in her back, while he grabbed her right arm and whipped it behind her back, pulling up. When she screamed in pain, he said, "You *will not* talk to him again. All he wants is to take over your life. He wants to control you."

"No, *you* want to control me!" she screamed.

"Why won't you just let me love you? Why do you make it such a fight?"

Finally getting her left hand under her, she flipped, sending Seb several feet over, allowing her the time to stand. She grabbed her right shoulder in pain. "Because you hurt me. Why would you even *remotely* think I would love you?"

Pushing off the ground, he lunged for Katie, landing squarely on top of her. "You will be mine," he growled in her face.

"No. I won't."

They struggled for several moments, before Katie took the open slot and kneed Seb in his groin. When he rolled over in pain, she ran to her room and locked the door behind her. Grabbing the phone, she quickly dialed Nick's number. When he answered, a relieved, yet terrified Katie responded, "Nick, Seb's trying to kill me! Please help!"

"Are you at the dorm?"

"Yes, he – " she screamed as Seb kicked her bedroom door in, and she dropped the phone in shock.

"Katie?" Nick yelled into the phone.

Seb pulled the phone from the wall, throwing it into the hall, as Katie backed away from him. Tripping over the bed, she fell backwards, and he jumped on top of her. "There, that's better."

"Get-off-me!" she screamed as she kicked and squirmed under him.

Backhanding her across the face, he growled, "Shut up! You and I are made for each other! Don't you understand what you mean to me?"

"Obviously nothing if you treat me this way. Now, get off me!"

"No," he said, and grabbed her throat, cutting off her air.

Struggling to push his hand away, she kicked her legs. "Stop!"

"You and I *need* to talk, and we're going to talk."

"Not if you…I can't breathe!"

Releasing her throat, he bent down and forcefully kissed her, while he held her hands down on the bed.

After a moment, Katie opened her eyes, to see Seb flying through the air, out into the hallway. Relieved to see Nick standing there, and the lights of police vehicles flashing as the cars were down in front of the dorm, she knew she was safe.

*   *   *

Nick accompanied Katie down to Oklahoma for her friend's graduation. When they returned, Nick was once again called out on the night of the rehearsal dinner for Stacey and Scott's wedding. The next evening, he showed up in time to make sure Katie was protected from Seb, but even then, he felt slightly out of place as Katie and Lance got along extremely well.

When Nick dropped Katie off at her apartment, he pointed out, "Seems you and Scott's co-worker get along well."

She shrugged it off. "It was for their wedding."

"He seems like a nice guy. Have you considered going out with him?"

"Well, he asked Stacey for my number. I haven't decided if I'm going to give her permission to give it to him yet."

"Why not?" he asked, leaning on her doorway with his arms crossed. "You two seemed to hit it off really well."

"I don't know."

Entering her apartment, she headed for the kitchen while he came in and closed the door. "Why don't you know? What's holding you back? Are you afraid of making another mistake, like you did with Seb?"

"That's a good question. Water?" she asked, pulling a bottle of water out from the refrigerator. When he nodded, she grabbed one for him as well. "He almost seems too good to be true."

"Too good to be true, or not what you're looking for?" Nick challenged.

"What does that mean?" she asked, standing on the other side of the counter from Nick.

"What are you looking for in a man?"

Katie choked on the sip of water she'd just taken. When she cleared her throat, she asked, "Why?"

"Well, I know how I feel about you. How do you feel about me?"

"I'm sorry?"

"Look, let's be realistic here. I don't think I'm being conceded, nor do I think I'm being arrogant when I say that I think we'd make a perfect couple. Seth says it all the time."

"If we do that, we can't be on the same unit."

"Who says?" he demanded.

"The FBI."

"What if we give you an alternate position within the FBI and not as an actual agent?"

"Meaning?"

"Have you ever considered a position as receptionist of our unit? We're still flippin' 'em left an' right."

"I don't know. I wanted to be an agent."

"Why?"

"Because it's been a desire."

"Why?" he pressed.

"To tell you the truth, I don't know."

"Just consider it. In the meantime, know that I respect whatever your decision is, but also know that I love you."

Katie looked at him, wide-eyed, as he left her apartment. "Seriously?" she asked, stunned, as the door closed behind him.

*   *   *

Katie flew through the police academy with honors, and headed into the police force with Andy as her training officer. She and Nick continued to battle over whether or not to have a relationship, but Katie kept resisting. She didn't want to make the same mistake she made with Seb. Fear held her back from going forward.

As 'The Hunter' came after Katie, she continued to dodge his attempts at her life, until the night where the group was having dinner at the restaurant.

"I had a horrible day." Katie dropped her head in her hands. "I really need my friends tonight."

"What happened?" Nick asked.

"A guy killed himself right in front of me."

Claire came in, and when she saw Katie, she groaned. *Why was Katie always around? Why wouldn't she just leave her friends alone?* "What are *you* doing here?" Claire demanded.

"She's eating dinner with us. What's *your* problem with her?" Nick shot back.

"Guys, seriously, I just want peace and laughter," Katie pleaded.

Claire crossed her arms in a huff. "Then you may want to look elsewhere."

Katie threw her napkin on the table, and left the restaurant, hearing the argument she left at the table between Nick and Claire. Feeling weary of fighting for everything in life, she sat down in her car for a moment to collect her thoughts. "Seriously, God, why is everything a battle? Why do things always seem so challenging?"

Hearing nothing in response, she put the key in the ignition, and turned. A ball of fire engulfed her as her car exploded around her.

* * *

Katie gasped as she sat upright in her bed. "Why did both of those end in my death?" Katie asked the Lord aloud, as her heart raced.

"Maybe He wanted to show you that you are where you are for a reason," Pete offered, as he was sitting in a chair, reading a book.

"What are you doing in here?"

"Yer screamin' was scarin' Nana, so she had me sit in here. Nick's been takin' his anxiety out on workin' around the station. So, care t' tell me about your dreams?"

"What's in that stuff?"

"Tell ya what, why don't you head t' the bathroom before –
"

He was cut off by the mad dash made by Katie for the bathroom, where she promptly threw up for several minutes. Not sure what she was throwing up, the heaving made her head pound more fiercely than it already was. She had to make sure her aim was good, as it flowed without ceasing.

Finally, when she didn't think she could take any more, it stopped. Pulling herself up to the counter, she brushed her teeth and used mouthwash afterward for good measure.

When she returned to her room, Pete was still there. "Why are you still here?" she groaned.

"Because you were sent on a journey. Do you want to talk about it?"

Narrowing her eyes, she asked, "Did you do that on purpose?"

"No." He chuckled. "It's just a blessed side effect. You see, the tea takes your fever away, but it also allows one to go through journeys, where it lets one deal with something they have struggled with, but don't know how to resolve it. Or, it allows them to see where a different choice may have had a different effect on their life, and those around them. We've all had those split second decision moments. This allows you to take a journey to see what would have happened if you made the other choice."

"So, you're telling me that I had to sort out the 'what ifs' in my life, and this is one way to do it?"

"Exactly. Did it work?"

"Oh yeah!"

"Good. Then it did what it was supposed to do."

She sighed. "I didn't realize that I actually had those questions in my mind, but now that I've seen the 'what ifs' I'm thankful for where I've landed."

"Meaning?"

"With Nick."

"I see."

"If God didn't take me down the path He did, I might not be with him right now. And, I can honestly say that I would walk it again if the result is that I still have him."

"You love him that much?"

"I love him more than I love myself. There isn't anything I wouldn't do for him."

"Good, then let's go find him," he said, putting his arm out for her to loop hers through.

As they walked out into the station, the bright sunshine almost blinded her. While her eyes adjusted, she clung to Pete's arm. "Don't worry. He's only over in the stables. It's a short walk," Pete encouraged. "Hey, Nick!" Pete yelled when they walked through the doorway, "Yer ol' lady's awake an' lookin' for you."

"Katie?" Nick poked his head out of the stall. Hugging her for only a moment, he rested his hands on her face. "No fever. Good. How's yer head?"

"Good," she responded, absentmindedly, as she stood there in flannel pants and a t-shirt. "Um, can we talk?"

"Of course. Do you want to walk around?"

"No. The porch or a bench will work."

"I got the barn. You take care a' yer lady," Pete dismissed him.

As they slowly made their way over to the porch, Katie explained, "I had some very real dreams while I was asleep."

"Oh really? What about?"

"I don't know if I can explain it in a way that you won't be upset."

"That sounds kind of scary."

Katie eased into her seat, while Nick took his seat next to her. "Pete said the dreams one experiences, answers questions that the person has no other way to figure out how to process."

"Meaning?"

"Well, it answers questions in one's mind."

"Such as?"

"Such as those 'did I make the right choice' moments."

"Okay. Do you want to give me details, or do you just want me t' know that yer questions are answered?"

"Do you really want to know?"

"Are you satisfied that yer questions were answered?"

"Yep."

"Then, I'm good."

"I knew I had a smart one in you," she said, relieved, as she hugged him.

Chapter 5

Summer Lovin'

Over the next week, Nana pulled Katie into the kitchen to show her how to cook lunch and dinner, which Katie didn't mind. Learning a few things allowed her to feel more comfortable in the kitchen and cooking from scratch.

The first morning she had her in the kitchen for breakfast was a treat for Nana. "All right, we need t' crack all a' these into this bowl."

"That's a lot of eggs!" Katie remarked as she struggled to see straight. Still refusing the coffee, she craved caffeine more than anything.

"We have a lot a' mouths t' feed. C'mon now, you've done a great job so far on lunch an' dinner, don't let me down now," Nana encouraged.

"Fine," Katie sighed. Picking up the first egg, she cracked it on the corner of the cabinet and lazily opened the egg, emptying it into the bowl.

"Oh, for cryin' out loud! Them boys wanna eat this mornin'!" Nana snapped. Grabbing two eggs in each hand, she cracked them on the sides of the counter, and dumped them into the bowl before picking up another four.

"Cool! Can you teach me how to do that?"

"Let's start with one in each hand first," she said, helping her to crack the eggs.

After fishing out several eggshells, Katie finally got the hang of doing two at a time, so Nana left her to those while she went for the sausage and bread. Breakfast, to Katie, was actually good, and she enjoyed helping Nana in the kitchen. She half-wondered if Nana was prepping her to take over whenever Nick decided to take the station, especially since Paige mentioned that Nana doesn't let *anyone* in her kitchen.

*   *   *

With only three weeks left in their trip, Nick and Katie took a walk before dinner, out into the station. As they walked hand-in-hand, Nick sighed. "Ahhh, I love this land!"

"I can tell. It definitely works for you."

"Do *you* like it?"

"I enjoy it. I really like that I've been able to breathe these last couple of weeks. Not worrying about anything allows me to enjoy the beauty around me."

"Glad you feel that way," he said, draping his arm over her shoulder as they sat down on a bench that overlooked the entire station. "It's a beauty, huh?"

"Oh yeah! And that sunset is absolutely stunning!" she said, memorizing the scene before her of gold, red, and orange that were painted across the sky to draw later. When she looked back to Nick, he was on his knee in front of her. "What are you doing?"

"Katie Marie MacKenna, I love you with all my heart. Would you do me the honor of being my wife, whether it's here or in the states?"

"I…of course!" Katie agreed. As he stood, he placed a stunning ring on her finger. "It's gorgeous!" she gushed.

"As are you," he whispered before pulling her up off the bench, kissing her. The kiss started slowly, and then escalated into a passionate one. "Just wait until I don't have to hold back," he whispered, pulling slightly away.

He steadied her as she wavered. "That was amazing," she mumbled.

"Trust me when I say that it is nothing compared to the way I feel about you. Once we're married, there will be no mistaking how much I love you."

"And I you," she said, looking deeply into his eyes. "You are an amazing man, who I am blessed to have in my life. I never want to lose you."

"You never could. If something were t' happen here on earth, we'll be with each other for all eternity in heaven."

"When do you want to get married?"

"Whenever you want."

"We'll talk about it when we get back. Let's just enjoy and celebrate for a bit."

"I think that's a great idea. In the meantime, we'll tell my family at dinner."

Sitting on the bench, hand-in-hand, Katie felt a sense of relief to have had those dreams while she was sick. In doing so, it answered any 'what ifs' that were deep in the recesses of her mind. Grateful to God to have been given the opportunity, she didn't want to waste another moment enjoying her time and her love with Nick.

As they were sitting on the bench, waiting for Nana to ring the dinner bell, Nick mentioned, "I don't think we should tell them."

"What do you mean? You want to keep our engagement a secret?" Katie asked, upset.

"Not a secret, but wouldn't it be more fun t' let them see for themselves?"

A smile crossed Katie's face. "You're being a brat, aren't you?"

"Yep. Nana and Pop have been pushing so hard lately for me t' take over the station, a little lightheartedness, I reckon, is due."

"Sounds good."

"Don't purposely hide it, mind you, just wait an' see who sees it first."

"Sounds like a plan," Katie said, as Nana rang the dinner bell.

Walking hand-in-hand back to the main house, Katie couldn't help the giggle that escaped her. "You need to quit, or they'll see it right away," Nick mentioned.

"Walk any slower an' ya may get there by breakkie," Flynn commented, walking up next to Nick.

"Shut it," Nick snapped. "We're on vacation. We'll go as slow as we want."

"Not if Nana catches ya."

"Oh, she'll let me do whatever I want."

"Why do you get the special privileges?"

Nick smirked. "Because Nana loves me more."

As soon as he said it, Flynn playfully shoved him, so Nick let Katie's hand go as they played around the rest of the way to the main house. Shoving her hands in her pockets, Katie couldn't help but feel blissfully happy, and prayed it would never go away.

As they settled around the table, Katie kept her hand covered with her napkin on her lap. As soon as the first plate was passed to her, she could feel Nana looking at her. Glancing to her left toward Nana, Katie smacked Nick's leg.

"Is there something you wanna tell us, Nick?" Nana asked.

"Nope," Nick said, passing the plate to Flynn on his right.

Nana picked up a spoon full of mashed potatoes and flung it in Nick's direction. As it splatted on the wall near his head, he spun toward her and commented, "Your aim is getting better. Did ya get a new pair of glasses?"

Snickers were heard around the table as Nana lowered her glasses to look at Nick over them. "Gettin' brazen over there, aren't ya?"

"You know you love me."

"I do. Wanna tell us about that shiny thing on Katie's finger that I can see from all the way over here?"

"*What?*" Paige spun toward Katie, wide-eyed, as she sat to Katie's left.

"Maybe *you* need t' get a pair a' glasses, there, Paige," Nana quipped. "She's sittin' right beside ya. She even took the plate with that hand."

"Oh my gosh!" Paige gushed, first grabbing Katie's hand before she grabbed Katie. "You have made me a happy woman!" Then Paige reached behind Katie to Nick and pulled him toward her with a kiss on his cheek. "Sneaky little buggar!"

Nick smirked. "They pay me t' be sneaky in the FBI, Mum."

"Cheeky too," Nana added.

"I learned that from you," he shot back at her.

"So, when are ya gonna give me some grandkids?" As soon as Nana asked that, Katie just about choked on the lemonade she was drinking.

"Why don't we get t' the wedding first, huh, ol' lady?" Nick sassed, while Katie cleared her throat.

"Are ya gettin' married here?"

"No. We're going t' set a date when we get back."

"So, dat means you part a' the family now, huh?" Barwon asked, crossing his arms as he sat across from Katie.

Katie nodded. "I believe it will be. Yep. Can ya handle a seppo as a family member?"

"I'm okay with it," Flynn said. "That way when we *do* end up in a fight, where she has to *prove* those fighting skills you've been talkin' about, Nana won't shoot me."

"Want me to prove it now?" Katie challenged.

"You know we can't."

"Sure ya can," Nana said, feeling Katie may as well prove herself now, so she won't have to later.

Flynn's face went pale. "Are you bloody serious?"

"Sure. *After* dinner," she clarified.

"I have an idea," Nick said, with a grin on his face.

"Do I *want* to know?" Katie asked, nervously tucking a portion of her hair behind her ear.

"Well, to finally put an end t' the discussion of who top-dog is on this station, how about an ol' fashioned mud wrestlin' contest? Anyone who wants t' challenge either me or Katie can join in."

"Have you lost your mind?" Katie asked, stunned.

"Bloody hell! You *are* serious!" Flynn said, wide-eyed.

"Is that possible?" Aaron Slater, another ranch hand asked. "I mean, I know we're not allowed t' fight on the station, but technically that's not fightin'."

"Is he sayin' what I think he's sayin'?" Adoni, another aboriginal ranch hand asked, excitement dancing in his eyes. (Adoni means the sunset, which was when he was born.)

"He sayin' we can wrestle in da mud!" Kalti, another aboriginal ranch hand grinned. (Kalti means 'a spear.')

"Can we?" Owen Miller, another ranch hand, asked.

"After dinner, I don't see a problem with it…as long as it doesn't get outta hand," Nana agreed.

"You dink you can beat me?" Barwon challenged Nick.

"I think it'll be close," Nick said.

"I make bet with you?"

Nick furrowed his brow. "For what?"

"I beat you, when you run the station, you make me foreman?"

"Hmm, I think that position should be earned through hard work, though, don't you?"

"How about honorary, until I earn it?"

"I think that could be arranged."

"An, you call me 'his nibs'?"

"How about I have the blokes under you call you that?"

"How about *you* call me dat?"

"How about if you win, I call you that when I shake your hand? Otherwise ya have t' earn that title."

"I agree," he said, shaking Nick's hand.

"This should be fun," Flynn grinned, knowing he would target Katie first to shut her up.

*   *   *

After dinner, Nick, Pete, and Flynn went outside to set up the hoses in order to create a mud pit. There were four hoses aiming toward the center, first set at full blast until a well-formed mud hole was created, then they turned them down in order to keep the mud wet until they were finished.

"Ready," Nick announced, when they came back in with muddy boots.

"Yer gettin' mud everywhere!" Paige exclaimed, upset. "What a mess!"

Nana scoffed. "Paige, this is a runnin' station. There's usually mud everywhere. It'll clean. Let the boys have some fun."

Paige put her hands up in surrender. "Okay. I give."

There was a loud ruckus as they all headed out to the porch. "Are you sure this is okay?" Katie quietly asked Nick.

"Yeah. Just do your best an' hold on as long as you can."

"Okay."

"Take Flynn out as soon as you can. Pretty sure after those comments from when we first got here, he'll be gunnin' for you."

"I figured as much."

"If it gets too rough, pull yourself, but wait as long as ya can. I don't want anyone else giving you a hard time. This is a match t' see who the big dogs are. This is, in essence, the pecking order. The further you can get up this chain, the better off you'll be."

"Got it."

"Now, go make me proud," he said, and tapped her behind before grabbing her hand and heading out to the middle of the mud pit.

"Y'all comin' or what?" Katie asked.

"I don't wanna fight a girl," Kendall Adams, another ranch hand, protested. "I was taught better."

"Afraid you'll get hurt?" Katie challenged.

Murmurs were heard through the guys as they stayed on the porch.

"She's serious," Nana said, and shoved Flynn out into the mud, where he landed face down. When he turned and glared at her, she said, "Get out there an' prove yer words. If the rest a' ya aren't a bunch a chooks, you'll get out there too."

"What about you, Barwon?" Nick crossed his arms. "Weren't *you* wanting t' prove somethin' earlier?"

"Not with her."

"Barwon, you and I both know you won't hurt me," Katie encouraged. "*You're* not the one I'm targeting anyway."

"I would never!" Barwon's eyes opened in surprise, to the point that Katie saw the whites of his eyes, even from where she stood ten yards away.

"I know. C'mon out here. I thought you were fixin' to teach Nick a lesson on who is boss?"

Barwon huffed, deep in thought. Then he puffed his chest before strutting out into the mud pit. On his way by Flynn, he picked him up by his collar and dragged him out to the middle of the pit with him.

"Anyone else?" Nick asked.

"Maybe," Aaron said. "Kinda want t' see what the four a' you do."

Nana went behind him and shoved him off the railing he was sitting on. "Might as well, yer muddy anyway."

"I'll go," Kalti said, and walked out to the middle.

"Me too!" Adoni followed him.

Kendall shrugged before he headed out as well, closely followed by several others. When they were in the middle of the pit, Barwon and Nick stood toe to toe.

"You ready for this?" Nick asked, as the others were circled around them.

"*You* ready?" Barwon asked.

"Give it yer best shot, mate," Nick said, and shoved Barwon back. When he only stumbled back a step, Barwon went to lung at Nick, but Nick sidestepped him, and Barwon hit the mud, face-first, and it was on!

Katie barely looked up in time, as a mud-covered Flynn lunged for her, knocking her back into about three inches of mud. While the others broke off into groups of two, Katie did her best to take Flynn out. He was slippery with all the mud, so it took her a bit to get a grip on him enough to flip him off her. When she did, she scrambled onto his back and got him into a headlock.

"Let me go!" Flynn shouted, grabbing her arm.

"Do you give up?"

"No!"

"Then I'll put you to sleep," Katie warned.

"You can't!"

"Watch me," she said, and tightened her grip around his neck, cutting off his air supply. He struggled only momentarily before he slapped her arm, giving up.

"Over here," Nana called him out of the center. "First one out, eh?" she teased, as he struggled to get through the mud, slipping and falling every few feet.

No sooner was he gone then Aaron sideswiped Katie, only for her to get hit on the other side, sandwiched between Aaron and Maka, another aboriginal ranch hand. (Maka means 'small fire'.)

Shaking her head to clear it, she quickly ducked as Maka went to grab her neck, and he grabbed Aaron instead, which ticked him off, so Aaron hauled off and hit Maka in the stomach. Maka and Aaron were known to bicker a lot on the station. When they did, Katie crawled out from between them, only to get hit by Steve Keller, another ranch hand. This one she saw coming, so she pushed up on him. Using the momentum from him lunging at her, she tossed him several feet, and he slid on his back. Scowling, he scrambled to get up, but promptly fell back into the mud again, this time face first. When he looked back up at her, it was too late, she was coming down on him, elbow first into his back, shoving him back down into the mud. Then, she grabbed his wrist and flipped it behind his back.

"Give up yet?" she asked.

"No!"

Pulling up on his wrist, she put immense pressure on his shoulder, as she had her knee in his back. "Now?"

"No! I won't let a sheila beat me…even if she looks as good as you do. Wish we were in a different position at this time, though," he sneered.

Angered at his rudeness and blunt pass at her, she pulled up on his arm so hard she dislocated his shoulder. He let out a howl that rang through the yard.

"Yer done," Nana called to him. "Get over here an' I'll reset that."

"Fine!" he grumbled. He let Katie help him up, but promptly shoved her back to the ground once he was upright. Nana was about to object, when Katie kicked his ankle out from under him, and he fell again, hard!

"Get outta there before she kills ya!" Nana shouted. While she looked angry, she was very impressed with Katie and how she held her own with the guys.

While Steve stumbled over to Nana, Katie noticed that several men had left the center of the pit, leaving only a handful. Seeing Aaron and Maka still going at it, she decided to split them up by diving in between them.

"What the –?" Aaron got out before Katie placed her foot within inches of his neck and he froze.

Maka looked at them wide-eyed before he put his hands in the air. "I give. You done, mate?" he asked, putting his hand down to help Aaron up.

As they stumbled off to the side, Katie turned to another pair who looked to be going at it pretty rough. She sighed. *Did she dare break up Ed Thomas and Jarrah?* They were another pair who were often at each other's throats, but these two had some massive size on Katie. (Jarrah was Aboriginal for a type of Eucalyptus tree).

Looking toward Nana for direction, Nana shrugged. *What was the worst thing that could happen? If she got them out, that would only leave Nick and Barwon, and she was not touching that fight. They were going at it hard!*

Standing by the pair with her arms crossed, she asked, "Do y'all need me to break this up, or are ya givin' up? I've already dislocated someone's shoulder. Want me to do yours too?"

The pair froze and looked at her. The trio covered in mud stood motionless for only a moment before Jarrah pulled on Katie's ankle, dropping her to the mud with a splat on her behind. She kicked forward, shoving him off Ed. When Ed was clear, he went to jump on Katie, but Katie used his momentum, and she shoved upward with her feet, sending him into the air.

When he landed with a splat and a groan, Katie looked up to see Jarrah flying toward her, sending her back almost to where Ed landed. "Give up yet?" he asked.

She giggled, when all she could see that was white on him was his eyes. Even his teeth were covered in mud. "Depends."

"On what?" he asked, surprised by her response.

"On whether or not Ed's goin' t' take you out for me," she said, and curled up into a ball when Ed leapt over her, landing squarely on top of Jarrah. Deciding to stay out of that one, she maneuvered her way through the mud out toward Nana.

"Good job, love." Nana patted her on the back. "You'll fit in here quite well."

"Is Steve okay?"

"Oh, he will be. His pride is hurt worse than his shoulder."

"He deserved it. What he said was rude."

"Actually, they've been kind since you came. Nicky an' I both threatened them within an inch a' their lives if they hit on you or said somethin' crude t' you. If he did, then he must a' been ticked."

"Oh, he was," she agreed.

"Then I'll let it slide. Have a seat, this looks good," she said, gesturing toward Nick and Barwon's fight. Jarrah and Ed's fight was finished, with Jarrah getting the upper hand. They were sitting on the side, watching the mud-coated pair still in the middle.

Going for what seemed like forever, Nick finally had enough and took Barwon out. He didn't want to have to deal with him later.

"I give!" Barwon shouted, spitting mud out of his mouth, as Nick had him face down on the ground with his knee in his back, and both of his arms pulled behind him.

"*Who* is his nibs?" Nick challenged.

"You are!"

"Good! Now we have an understanding," he said, and released him. When he helped Barwon off the ground, he shook his hand, as he said, "There will be a day where you *will* earn that title if ya fight for it as hard as ya fought for this."

Barwon grinned, showing his white teeth. "I will."

While he and Nick made their way out of the mud, Nick put his arm over Barwon's shoulder and said, "How about I call you 'boss' until you earn that title?"

He grinned again. "Really?"

"As long as you know who the *real* boss is, I'm okay with that. It'll give you motivation t' earn that title, yeah?"

"Yeah!"

"Good job, boss," Nick said, shaking his hand when they reached the porch.

"You two finally gettin' along?" Nana asked.

"Yeah."

Barwon shrugged. "He okay…for his nibs."

*　　*　　*

The rest of the trip could not have gone better for Katie. She and his family got along famously after those first couple of rough days. His twin, Nate, was still in jail by the time they left, so they didn't have to deal with him. As far as Katie and Nick were concerned, the less they had to see him, the better. The only thing they didn't get to was going to church. She hoped next time they came that they would be able to attend.

Before they left, Nana and Pop gave one more ultimate push for Nick to take over the station. He insisted on holding off, because there were still several issues they needed to clear up at home, and Nick wasn't ready to leave Cleveland yet either…at least that's what he told Katie.

*　　*　　*

Collecting her mail the day they got home, Katie dreaded wading through it all. Nick had to go into the office the following day, while Katie prepared ahead of time and gave herself a couple days to acclimate to the time change. Knowing she would have the entire day to wade through it, she tossed the mail onto the counter and made a beeline for the shower before going to bed.

*　　*　　*

After watching the news while she ate her breakfast the next morning, she knew she needed to tackle the ominous mountain of mail that loomed in front of her, so she gave up fighting it any longer. "Obviously I was missed," she sighed, separating the bills from the junk mail, grateful to have all of her bills set up for automatic deduction so she wouldn't have to deal with them. "What's this?" she asked, picking up a 5x7 envelope from the stack.

When she opened the envelope, Jax's class ring dropped onto the counter. She gasped as she picked it up, knowing the ring was supposed to be tucked away in the jewelry box on her dresser. Looking in the envelope, she found the rest of the jewelry that was supposed to be in the box.

Running into the room, she flipped open her jewelry box. The only thing inside was a piece of paper folded in half. When she opened it, the lettering was done in magazine cutout letters, which said:

Katie,

Life for you seems to have fallen into place. I have tried to destroy you in many ways but those attempts have failed, so the only thing left to take from you is your heart. You have two choices:

1) Stay with Nick, and I kill you both.

2) Break up with Nick, and you both live.

Now, if you tell anyone about this at all, I will assume option 1, and I will kill Nick in front of you and make you watch. I will also kill whomever you tell in front of you as well. Then I will let you live for an undetermined amount of time before I kill you, allowing you to soak in the understanding that you have yet again cost others their lives.

Choice is yours,

The Hunter

Her body trembling, Katie dropped her head into her hands, doing her best to stop the world from spinning around her. *Was he serious? Of course he was, he had already tried to kill her! Giving up Nick would break her heart and potentially kill her. Could she do it? If she didn't, The Hunter would kill them both, and this wasn't Nick's fault.*

Looking toward heaven, Katie pleaded with God, "Lord, please help me. This will be the most difficult thing I have ever had to do in my life."

Chapter 6

Summer is Slippin' Away

By the time Nick returned from work that evening, Katie was a disaster. Crying for the entire day as she paced the living room over and over again, praying against the choice, she knew what she had to do.

"Evenin', love!" Nick said, coming into her apartment after work. "Do you want to go – what's wrong?" he asked, suddenly noticing her puffy red eyes and tear-streaked face. "Aww, love, what happened?"

When he went to hug her, she pushed him away. Breaking out in tears once again, she pleaded with him, "I can't. Please don't make me do this."

"Do what?" he asked, confused.

"I have to break up with you. I can't marry you." Taking off the ring he'd given her, her body shook once again as she begged, "Please take this and just go."

"What? I – *what*?" Nick asked, stunned, as he felt his heart sink down into his stomach. Forcing the vomit down that threatened to come up, he stared helplessly at the ring she placed in his hand. "I don't understand," he choked out.

"I can't tell you. Just know that I love you, but I can't marry you."

"Katie," he shook his head, "this doesn't make sense."

"Please go. Just go," she said, opening her apartment door. "I'm sorry, but we can't see each other anymore."

"What did I do?" he asked, pale and shaken.

"It's not you. It's me."

"This doesn't make sense, Katie. Please help me understand?"

"Just leave," Katie insisted.

"Please reconsider this? I love you so much. This is going to kill me."

"It's killing me too. Trust me."

"Then why are you doin' it?" he demanded, his frustration bordering on anger, while the hurt and anguish churned within him.

"Please. Just go," she said again.

Looking defeated, he left her apartment, but didn't go home. Instead, he went to Seth's house, distraught.

"What happened? You were in a great mood earlier," Seth said, opening his door. "Did something happen to Katie?"

"No, well, yes, well, I –" he tried to explain, but the tears choked the words he wanted to say. Instead, he opened his hand, showing the ring to Seth.

"What happened?" Seth asked, taken aback.

"I don't know. She said it was her. I don't know what happened. I went t' work an' everything was great. I came home an' she was a mess. She gave me this an' told me we couldn't see each other anymore. I don't understand, Seth," he said, sitting on the chair at the end of the couch, his head dropped into his hand with the ring still in it. "Why would she do this t' us?"

"Let's get to the bottom of this. We're FBI agents. If we can figure out counterterrorism and organized crime families, I'm pretty sure we can figure out why Katie doesn't want to see you."

Nick looked at him, torn up inside. "I don't want t' disrespect her request. I just wanna know why."

"And you should know why. What did she do today?"

"I don't know. I didn't have the chance t' find out anything except that she had been cryin' all day. I don't know what t' do here, Seth. I've never experienced this much hurt. What do I do?"

"Get yourself together. You're strong. You can figure this out."

"I can't! I don't know where t' start. I literally feel sick t' my stomach."

Placing his hand on Nick's shoulder, Seth promised, "We *will* figure this out. She's not that complicated. Let's work on this as a side project."

"I *don't* know where t' start."

"We'll take it one step at a time, starting with calling the guys. Two heads are better than one, but six make a formidable group."

"Six?"

"You're forgetting Chad and Eugene?"

"I don't want t' deal with that blue flamer t'day. Please, have mercy on me."

"Blue flamer?" Seth asked.

"Eugene Kennedy is in this just t' get the glory. I don't want t' deal with his pity or pious attitude t'night. It may not end well."

"Over the last few weeks, Chad's gotten him under control. It was a little hairy there for a bit, until they came to an understanding. Their code word, from what I can figure out, is if Chad mentions a rodeo, Eugene shuts up."

"What do ya mean?"

"He may have threatened to tie him up and leave him in a pig farm once or twice."

"Oh!" Nick said, wide-eyed. "I guess Chad's got more guts than even I gave him credit for."

"Eugene's been a good boy lately. His investigative skills are quite unique and productive. I'll be willing to bet that he may prove more valuable than you know."

"Fine. Call in the cavalry."

*   *   *

Katie curled up on her bed for the rest of the night, in tears. Her heart was shattered in a million pieces, unable to think. Food was the farthest thing from her mind. As a matter of fact, the thought made her ill. *Why would God bring Nick into her*

160

life to have this happen? She had to trust in Him, but could she? She felt so alone.

"The LORD is close to the brokenhearted and saves those who are crushed in spirit," she heard Psalm 34:18 go through her mind.

"I know You're close to me, but I don't know what to do," Katie prayed. "I don't want to see Nick hurt in this. I had to make a choice. Please forgive me for breaking his heart. I just don't know what else to do."

I Corinthians 13:6-8a slowly crawled through her thoughts, *"Love does not delight in evil, but rejoices with the truth. It always protects, always trusts, always hopes, always perseveres. Love never fails."*

"I'll hold onto these verses until You show him the truth. I'll protect him by keeping him at a distance until You deem the time to be right. Your timing in this is what I'll hold on to. I'll have faith that You'll work this out. I pray for his heart. I pray You will protect him and his heart. I pray that if it is Your will for us to be together, that You will show him the truth. 'Love does not delight in evil, but rejoices in the truth'. I pray for the truth to rise to the surface, but not through me. 'It always protects, always trusts, always hopes, always perseveres. Love never fails.' I am holding on to that promise, Lord. In Jesus' most precious name I pray, Amen."

*   *   *

"What do we know?" Seth asked, pacing in front of his couch and sofa. The chair still contained the distraught Nick, while the couch had Dakota, Todd, and Eugene, and Chad leaned against the wall with his arms crossed, deep in thought.

Katie's ring sat in the middle of the coffee table in front of the group.

"We know she loves you with every fiber of her being," Dakota pointed out.

"If that is accurate, then what would propel her to destroy his faith, trust, and love for her?" Eugene asked.

"That's the question," Chad agreed.

"What are you gettin' at?" Nick asked.

Chad came off the wall, and stood in the middle of the guys with his arms crossed. "Knowin' where she's from, and her background, there aren't many women like her, even in the south."

Seth shook his head, confused. "I still don't understand."

"The question is not whether or not she loves him. We *know* she does. The question is what would force her to push him away?"

Todd suddenly sat up in his seat as a thought hit him. "Protection. She's protecting him. But from what?"

"Or who?" Dakota countered.

"It's *whom*," Eugene corrected.

"Shut up," Dakota snapped.

"Y'all are right," Chad said, crouching down in front of the coffee table. Picking up the ring, he toyed with it as he explained, "She loves him just as much as he loves her. The *only* thing that would force her to shove him away is to protect him from some*thing* or some*one*. Now," he looked each man in the eyes as he said, "there is only one thing going on, that I can think of, that would make her do that."

"Rossi or Gombeda," Nick finished.

"We've already figured out that it's Rossi junior," Chad explained. "While you were gone, we found out that Gombeda passed about eight months ago. After that, Rossi junior has been on his own."

"Let's just call him 'Junior' for short," Seth suggested.

"Right." Chad placed the ring back on the table before he stood. "Now, we know Junior is 'The Hunter' by this point, so what does he wanna do?"

"He wanted to kill Katie, because she took away his family," Nick explained.

"Is that all?" Chad challenged. "Think about it. Not only did she fix it so his dad went to jail, but got his brother to be the one to turn state's evidence."

"Technically, that was me," Nick pointed out.

"Then, what's the best way to hurt those who have hurt his family?"

"He knows as long as the two of you have each other, he can do his best, but he won't win," Todd continued.

"United, you stand," Seth started.

"Divided you fall," Dakota finished.

*   *   *

"I was expecting you to come back all happy and healthy, but you look like crap," Andy said when Katie walked into the precinct.

"Thanks. You look like you've seen better days yourself," she countered.

"I'll get this off in another couple of weeks, and be back to my old self," he said, gesturing toward the cast on his leg.

"Was kind of hoping you'd come back *better* than your old self," one of the officers teased.

"Shut it!" he snapped. Then he turned back to Katie as she sat down at her desk. "You need to go see Carlton," he said, referring to the psychiatrist. "You really look horrible. What happened?"

"Well," she started, hoping to hold herself together, "Nick and I got engaged while we were on vacation."

"Saw that on your profile. That's why I thought you'd come in a heck of a lot better spirits than that."

Dropping her head in her hands, she admitted, "I broke it off yesterday."

"What? Why?" he asked, stunned. "Seriously Katie, please tell me that's some sick joke."

"No," she groaned.

"MacKenna!" Chief called from his office. "Get in here!"

"Yes, sir," she said, pulling herself up from the desk. Dragging her feet, she headed into his office.

"Shut the door and have a seat," Chief ordered.

Reluctantly, Katie closed the door and took the seat across from Chief.

"I got a disturbing call this morning from Director Shaw."

"I'm sure you did."

"That's not quite the answer I was expecting."

"This hasn't been the summer I was expecting either."

"I thought you were engaged?"

"So did I."

"What happened?"

Katie sighed in response as she dropped her head into her hands.

"MacKenna? What's going on? It seems that there's some conflicting information being sent around. What does Joey Rossi have to do with this?"

Looking at him in wide-eyed shock, she couldn't formulate the words that wanted to spill out of her as The Hunter's words ran through her mind, *'if you tell anyone about this at all, I will assume option 1, and I will kill Nick in front of you and make you watch. I will also kill whomever you tell in front of you as well. Then I will let you live for an undetermined amount of time before I kill you, allowing you to soak in the understanding that you have yet again cost others their lives.'* Not wanting to put another person in danger, she sat up with a determined look on her face. "I'm sorry, sir. I can't tell you."

Giving her a cross look, he demanded, "Why not?"

"Sir, you will have to trust that I know what I'm doing. Now, I give you my word that my calling off the engagement will not affect my job performance. Who is my partner until Andy is back on duty?"

"You need to get clearance from Carlton again."

"What?" Shock rang through her body. "I already got clearance before I left for vacation."

"Go see Carlton. That's an order," he said, irritated. "Ya know, you can be a stubborn little thing."

She stood, resigned more than ever to keep her secret. "Yes, sir. I've been accused of worse."

"Get out of my office and go see Carlton," he growled.

Katie left his office, her heart beating out of control. What she just did could have been construed as insubordination. However, since it wasn't job related, she knew she could get away with it. Saying a prayer for clarity of mind once again to challenge the system in order to get back to work, Katie knocked on Carlton's door.

"Come on in, Officer MacKenna," she called. When Katie walked in, Dr. Carlton held her finger up as she was on the phone. "Yes, sir. I understand….Please calm down. I understand your frustration, but –" she was cut off by the other person on the phone. "Yes, sir," she said, and hung up. "Wow. Not sure what you did, but you really ticked Chief off. What's going on?"

Katie shrugged, as she sat down in the chair opposite the doctor. "I broke up with Nick."

"Why?"

"That's personal."

"Really?" she asked, stunned by her response. "Katie, we've talked about plenty of personal issues. Why is there a sudden block?"

"Please just trust me. I know what I'm doing."

Dr. Carlton studied her for a moment before she asked, "How are you feeling after your vacation?"

"Rested," Katie answered cautiously, knowing how the doctor operated by this point.

"Do you feel that you're ready to return to work, even though your partner isn't ready yet?"

"I feel ready to do my job," she said confidently.

The doctor paused, as she watched Katie sit there looking strangely calm. "When did you and Nick break off your wedding plans?"

"Yesterday."

"Who broke it off with whom?"

"I broke it off with Nick."

"Why?"

Expecting the doctor to make an abrupt turn in her questioning, Katie simply responded, "It's personal."

"Hmm," she said, doing her best to put the pieces of the puzzle together by what she knew of Katie. "Do you love him?"

"Yes."

"Then, why did you break up with him?"

"Because I love him."

Not expecting that answer, the doctor was thrown for a moment before she asked, "Katie, I need you to be straight with me. Did someone threaten you?"

"No ma'am," she lied, not knowing if she could trust her. Katie knew the Rossi family had people in the police force, but she didn't know who they were.

"Then, how can you say you love him if you broke up with him?"

"I just do. Can I return to work yet?"

"It's against my better judgment, but I guess so," she said, pulling out a form. "I still want to see you each week, though. If you feel the need to talk otherwise, my door is always open."

Katie stood and accepted the paper. "I know. I'll make an appointment for next week on the way out."

"Sounds good." As Katie went to leave, Dr. Carlton stopped her. "Katie?"

"Yes."

"I understand that your secrets are your own, but those secrets can be dangerous if you don't regulate them well."

"Secrets *are* dangerous, but I have faith in God's promise that love never fails."

*   *   *

A couple of weeks after her return, Andy got his cast off and was cleared to return to light duty. Since Chief was still concerned with Katie, he kept them both on light duty until Andy was ready. In the meantime, he had them going through old files, pulling what they could find in regards to the Rossi family.

"I don't understand why we're doing this," Andy said one afternoon in frustration. "The Rossi family was shut down years ago by the FBI."

"Because we were told to," Katie responded, dryly.

After several more minutes of silence in the conference room they were working in, Andy had it, and demanded, "Why did you and Locke break up?"

"What business is it of yours?"

Taken aback by her answer, Andy continued to push, "Have you two talked since you broke up with him?"

"Nope. He's been keeping his distance. Since I know his general schedule, I work out at a different time than he does."

"Help me understand why you did it?" he asked. "Why would you break it off with a guy you love so much, and who loves you with all his heart? You two seemed to be the perfect pair."

"Please don't ask me that question. I can't answer it."

"Can't…or won't?"

Katie sighed, shaking her head.

"Can't…or won't?" Andy asked again, a little more sternly.

"Andy, please don't push me on this?"

"Why not?"

"Please?" Katie begged.

Taking a few more minutes to process through the files, Andy gave it one more shot, "I feel I know you well enough to understand you."

"Oh really?"

"Yep. And, using my brilliant skills of deduction, I'll bet you still love him."

"Wow. Do they pay you for that type of analysis?"

"I love your sarcasm." He chuckled. "But, seriously. I've got a few more observations. Want to hear them?"

"Not really, but I have a feeling I don't have a choice."

"You got it. You're stuck in this room with me for another five hours."

She rolled her eyes. "Great."

"Ya see, I'm thinking you have a secret that has to do with Nick. Since Chief's making us go through the Rossi files, I'm also thinking that Nick and company think it has to do with Joey Rossi. Am I close?"

"You're a mess."

"But, am I right?" he pressed.

"Just leave it be."

"Katie, this is killing you. Anyone with a pair of eyes can see that. Why would you intentionally break both of your hearts?"

"Can we just concentrate on what we're supposed to be doing?"

"What *are* we doing?"

"Going through the old files, pulling anything that has to do with Rossi. Thankfully we'll be hitting the portion that's on the computer here shortly. This is irritating at best."

"Nice side-track. It's going to work for now, but know that I'll figure it out."

Katie looked him square in the eyes, as she said, "I want you to leave it. If you care about me at all, you *will* leave this alone."

He sighed, shaking his head. "The kind of love that you two have is a once in a lifetime kind of love. The two of you are soul mates."

"Then, I'm trusting if God wants us together, He'll work it out. Love never fails."

"I pray you're right, because the two of you were meant for each other. I don't know what's going on, but I'm going to trust if God wants the two of you together, that nothing will stand in the way."

"Thank you."

*   *   *

For the rest of the summer, Katie avoided Nick. As each day passed, Katie felt like she was slowing dying, slipping away into a void.

One afternoon, Katie pulled out her sketchpad. Avoiding it for the entire summer, she feared if she didn't draw, she would return to the Ice Queen. When she sat down to draw, her hands froze in place. Her mind was blank.

"Father, I need to draw. You know that drawing allows me to center myself. Right now I feel so off-center, it's not even funny. I love You and trust that You know what's best for me, but I'm tired. I feel so alone, so desperately alone."

As she sat, Joshua 1:9 came to mind, *"Have I not commanded you? Be strong and courageous. Do not be frightened, and do not be dismayed, for the Lord your God is with you wherever you go."*

"I know You're with me. I know Andy's there for me, along with the other officers. I just don't know who to trust. I can't tell anyone or it could get them killed." Tears formed in her eyes as she continued, "I don't want anything to happen to anyone that I love…especially Nick. Father, I know I broke his heart. I pray for You to strengthen him. Please allow Him to see the truth without me telling him. Please allow people to figure this out without my help."

"The name of the Lord is a strong tower; the righteous run to it and are safe, " she heard Proverbs 18:10 in her heart.

"I know. I just ask You to keep Nick safe. At this point, I don't care what happens to me. I only care what happens to Nick."

"Trust in the Lord with all your heart and lean not on your own understanding; in all your ways acknowledge Him, and He will make your paths straight. "

"Proverbs 3:5 and 6," Katie said, nodding in understanding. With those verses in mind, she drew a picture of a lighthouse placed on the side of a cliff. Its light blazed brightly from the tiny bulb at the top, as the storm raged all around. The black clouds churned above in the skies, while the lightening crackled across the sky. When she finished, she wrote 'Proverbs 18:10' on the bottom, along with the date. "I will trust in You. I trust You will protect me…that You will protect us both."

Chapter 7

Ain't No Cure for the Summertime Blues

The summer was torture for Katie. Unsure of what was going on with Nick, she would rush home in order to hear him enter his apartment in the evening. She promised herself that as long as she heard his door, she knew he was okay, and this would be worth it.

"Katie, you've been depressed for weeks," Andy said, while they were driving around. They were officially both cleared to return to full-duty that morning, so Chief sent them out for patrol.

"I'm sorry," she sighed, looking out the window.

"You've lost your spunk. I've purposely set you up for some slams, only to have you apologize or say something sensitive. I'm worried about you."

"Thanks, but I'll be fine."

"I don't know about that."

"Please, can't we talk about something other than Nick?"

"Okay. Your two-year stint ends in January. Are you going to Quantico?"

"Of course."

"When you graduate Quantico, what unit are you going to go on?"

Katie spun her head toward Andy, wide-eyed.

"Ahhh, got ya. You didn't think about *that* one, did you?"

"No," she admitted. "What am I going to do? Do I go to another unit? Should I request another unit?"

"That's a question only you can answer. Good news is if you go in January, you have until the end of May to figure it out. Training for Quantico is what? Twenty weeks?"

"Yes."

"Well, you've got several months to figure it out. Personally, I think you should at least *talk* to Nick and see if you can work together."

"I can't."

"Why not?" he asked, taken aback by her response.

"Why not, what?"

"Why can't you talk to him?"

"I just can't."

Pulling into Cook's Café for lunch, Andy continued to push. "Why not? Just because you broke up with the guy doesn't mean you can't talk to him."

"Andy, please trust me when I say I can't. I would love to tell you why, but I can't."

"Fine," he said, getting out, slamming his door. "Let's go eat."

Katie played with her lunch, eating only the little she knew she had to in order to function. All in all, she calculated that she had dropped a good fifteen pounds through the summer.

"You're not looking healthy. Maybe you should consider another job if it's putting this much stress on you," Seb pointed out as he delivered their meal.

"I'll be fine. It's not the job anyway."

"It's her and Nick," Andy added. "They broke up."

"Really? I was wondering why you've been so silent," he said, pulling a chair over to the end of their table, sitting down. "What have you been doing with yourself when you're not at work?"

"Good question. What *have* you been doing?" Andy asked.

Katie shrugged. "You know…drawing, church, things like that."

"Do you not see him in church?" Seb probed.

"No. He goes to the first service, so I go to the second."

"Interesting. Are you avoiding him?"

"Yes."

"Why?"

"Because it hurts. Why are you sitting here? Don't you have a job to do?" she scowled.

"I do, but that's one of the perks about owning half the business. I have other people to do the work when I need to step out for a few. And, since it's been a while since I've seen you, I took a break."

"Wonderful," she said, tongue-in-cheek. "Look, Andy and I need to talk and you really can't be hearing it."

"I get it." He stood. "Know that I'm there for you if you need me, okay?"

"Thank you," she said, and he left, much to her relief.

"Afraid he's going to try the 'sympathetic friend' routine and try to slide into Nick's spot?" Andy asked.

"Yeah. I really don't want to date him. He scares me. He can be a bit overbearing."

"Is that all?" Andy asked, sensing there was more.

"He pulled some mind games and got a little physical when we went out. He scares me. I don't mind him being a friend, but I know he wants more."

"Hmm, then I would keep my distance."

"That's the plan."

"I don't envy you, but you need to get some friends so you're not dwelling on Nick. You look like you've aged several years."

She sighed. "I feel like it."

*   *   *

When Katie got home that night, she had a letter for her in the mail that contained some photos of Nick. Included was a typed note that said:

Katie,

I have been keeping a close eye on you and Nick. I am happy to see that you have finally learned your lesson. Continue to keep your mouth shut, and Nick will stay safe.

The Hunter

Feeling like she was going to throw up, Katie went to bed early, knowing she wouldn't have to go to work the next day. As she lay in her bed, she flipped through the photos. Noticing in each photo that Claire was looking at Nick, a thought struck her. *Was that done on purpose? Could there be someone else who was now involved as 'The Hunter'? Claire would be privy to all information as an agent in regards to the case.*

Tucking everything away in a shoebox at the top of her closet, her mind was working overtime. *While Joey was a calculating individual, could Claire be involved as well? Could she have been the one to send the initial letter? How would Katie know?*

Unable to sleep, she threw on a pair of shorts and t-shirt, and headed downstairs to the track. She needed to clear her mind and exhaust her body. Pushing it to the limits, while minimally eating, she felt her body had been put through too much. *How long could she keep this up?*

"Haven't seen you in forever," Nick said as she passed the weight room.

She jumped, startled by his voice. She could see Todd, Dakota, and Chad in the weight room as well. "Sorry. Been busy. I need to keep running," she said, focusing on the track as the tears formed in her eyes, feeling as if she had gotten punched in the stomach.

He left her alone for the lap, but on her second lap, Chad ran up beside her. "Now, I know ya don't want to talk to Nick, but what about a fellow southerner?"

"Fine. You can run with me, but don't report back to him," she warned.

"There's a bench over there, wanna talk?"

Reluctantly, Katie agreed.

While she sat on the table portion with her feet on the seat, Chad leaned back on the table, as he sat on the bench with his legs sprawled in front of him. "Wanna tell me why you look like somethin' the cat dragged in?" Chad asked.

Glancing to the weight room, where Nick went back in with Todd and Dakota, she sighed. "It's been a rough several weeks."

Chad turned so he was facing Katie, with his hands intertwined in front of him. "Southerner to southerner, we need to talk. Ya see, sometimes those guys just don't get the southern mindset."

"I agree," Katie said, cautiously, the words from the threat still playing through her mind.

"Ya see, down south, we look out for our own. Family is family. There are times where we wear our hearts on our sleeve. When we love someone, there isn't anything we wouldn't do for that person, even to go so far as to put ourselves in danger to protect them," he said, studying her.

Fidgeting in place, Katie nervously nibbled on her nails.

Knowing he hit the target, he pushed forward. He was on a fishing expedition and the next few questions would be crucial. He had to ask them, though, so as not to scare her off. "Since we haven't had much contact with you, we haven't been able to check in with you to see how you're doin' at work."

"It's good."

'So, it's not a work issue,' Chad thought. "You only have until January, and then are you still plannin' on headin' to Quantico?"

"That's the goal."

'So, it's not fear of the FBI.' He continued his assessment. "And, you're still comfortable with that goal?"

"Yep."

"Have you been eating right lately?"

"No," she admitted.

'Neither has Nick,' he thought. "Have you been taking care of yourself otherwise?"

"Sure."

"What about your drawin'? Are you still doin' that?"

"Yes."

"I was wonderin' if I could see them? I've heard a lot about your work and wanted to see them for myself."

"Maybe, some day."

"What about today? Those guys are workin' out. What if we go upstairs and check 'em out?"

She shook her head, slightly alarmed. "No. Not today."

"Okay. Can you tell me about what you've been drawing?"

She shrugged. "Depends on what I'm feeling at the time."

"I'm tryin' to reach out to ya here. Can ya give me somethin'?"

"To what end?"

"Really? You don't trust me?"

"I don't know you."

"This is true," he agreed. "Have you been goin' out with your friends lately?"

"Nope."

'Not a friend issue either.' He continued to probe, "Have you…have you heard from The Hunter lately?" he asked, and watched her immediately cringe. *'Bingo.'*

Getting up from the table, she said, "I need to go. I have some things I need to do. Take care," she said, and disappeared out the door before he could get another word out.

Shoving his hands in his pockets, he slowly made his way back to the weight room. He felt he knew the true reason for the break up due to Katie's answers.

"Well?" Nick asked, anxiously, when Chad walked into the weight room.

"It's The Hunter," he said, getting on the treadmill.

"So, what's Junior done to her?" Nick asked.

Dakota sat up on the bench after placing the bar on the rack. "That's what we need to find out. What if we break into her apartment and see what we can find?"

"We can't do a B and E," Todd looked at him, stunned, "even if it *is* only Katie's apartment."

Dakota shrugged. "Legally we can't, but this isn't a legal issue. It's a concerned friend issue."

"We can't break the law just because she won't talk to us," Todd argued.

Nick hung his head and sighed. "Is there anything we *can* do?"

"Watch her," Chad said. "She's not going out with her friends. She's keeping *everyone* at a distance."

"How long can she keep going on like this?" Dakota stood, and then paced with his arms crossed in front of him. "She's starting to look anorexic."

"She said she's not eating well," Chad agreed. "What if Claire or Emma went to see her?"

"Claire hates her and she knows it. She's *definitely not* a good option." Nick shook his head. "Emma's almost too old to help her. Stacey's too busy, and she's not really talked to any of the people she hung out with in college. I'll bet if we tagged her in a photo, Ty or Ryan will see it and give her some major grief, though."

"Great idea!" Todd perked up. "I'll get a picture of her tomorrow and post it."

"I can do a follow up with them in private message," Nick suggested, a spark of hope finally filling his spirit. "She listens to them."

"Here's hoping." Dakota pointed out, "If not, she won't make it to Quantico. She'll collapse first."

*   *   *

The guys followed through with their plan. Todd tagged Katie in a photo that he got when he and Dakota ran into her at Cook's around lunchtime.

Once Nick got Ty and Ryan on instant message together and explained the shape she was in and why, their concern was confirmed. Nick paid for their plane tickets, and they set to fly out that weekend.

*   *   *

Seeing Katie in the picture Todd tagged her in, his heart sank. The sparkle was lost from her eyes. The rosiness was replaced with sunken cheeks. The bright spirit Dominic saw in the photos from earlier in the summer was extinguished. What really scared him, was the amount of weight it looked like she lost. He printed the photo and placed it beside the others he printed out from the summer. If things didn't change soon, he would have to come out of hiding and do something about it before it got too late.

*   *   *

Seeing the photo, Joey Rossi printed the picture with delight. His plan was finally working! He did his best to have her killed, but it never occurred to him to split Nick and Katie up, until it was suggested. Things could not be going any better as far as he was concerned.

*   *   *

The next weekend, Katie shuffled out to the kitchen around ten that morning to make her peanut butter toast and pour her orange juice when she got a knock on her door. "What now," she groaned, going over to the door. When she looked through the peephole, her spirit did a backflip in excitement. Flinging open the door, she squealed, "What are you doing here?"

When she jumped into Ryan's arms, he swung her around. Setting her down, he furrowed his brow in concern. "Where did you go? You've lost *a lot*. What's going on with you?"

"How did you get here?" Katie asked, hugging Ty.

"We about lost it when we saw that picture on your profile. What's going on?" Ty asked, scared. "And now to actually see you, it's worse than we thought."

"How did you guys get in here?" she asked.

"We called Nick. We wanted to make sure you were here."

"Come on in," she said, grinning ear to ear. "However you got here, I'm happy to have you guys."

As they went in, Ryan noted all of the stacks of papers on the counter. "Are you caught up on your bills?"

"Yes. I have automatic deposit for my paycheck, and the bills are automatically deducted. How long are you guys here for?"

"I have a week before I have to be back to school," Ty explained.

"If I need to be here longer, I can," Ryan offered.

"Not necessary." She shook her head. "I'll be happy to have y'all for the week."

"Katie," Ty said, seriously, "have you started drinking alcohol?"

"Nope."

"Are you eating?" Ryan asked.

"Wow. Twenty questions. Why can't we just relax and enjoy each other?"

"What happened? Why do you look this way?" Ty pressed.

"If you're going to be this snappy, y'all can get back on the plane," Katie huffed, crossing her arms.

"We're only concerned for you. If you saw one of us looking like this, wouldn't you be?" Ryan asked, showing her the photo.

When she looked at it, it shocked her just how much she changed over the last several weeks. "I'll be fine."

"The bags under your eyes have bags," Ty pointed out.

"I guess."

"Have you been drawing?" he probed.

"Yes."

"Can I see?"

"Sure," she said, and went into her room for her sketchpad. When she handed it to Ty, she said, "I wish I knew y'all were coming. I can't take off work."

Ryan shrugged. "Don't worry about it. We can explore while you're at work."

As Ty flipped through her drawings, he became increasingly concerned. "There are a lot of dark and stormy type scenes in here. The last sunlight picture looks like the sunset picture you posted from Australia."

"It is. That was the night Nick proposed," she explained.

"Then, it heads into dark pictures. Katie, your spirit is reflected in your art," he pointed out. "There's not a single lighthearted picture after the sunset. Quite honestly, this concerns me. They're not only dark, but they're stormy, as if you have darkness churning through you."

"That's enough," Katie said, snatching the sketchpad from him.

"You're breakin' my heart, Katie," Ty pleaded. "Talk to us."

"I can't," she explained.

"I'll tell you what," Ryan stepped in, not wanting to fight with her, "why don't you go get a shower and get dressed and we'll go out afterward. You can show us some of the sights."

"Sounds like a plan," Katie agreed.

As soon as she disappeared into the bathroom, Ty and Ryan went into her room. It took Ryan a few minutes to find the shoebox. "Pay dirt!" Ryan said, bringing the box down so Ty could look in it.

They took pictures of the notes, along with the photos before Ryan replaced it exactly as he found it. While Katie was finishing in the bathroom, Ryan texted the pictures to Nick, in hopes of Nick being able to find out where The Hunter was and how to stop him.

*   *   *

"Keep this between us," Nick said, showing the guys the photos he printed from Ryan's texts at Seth's house. "I don't want Emma or Claire to get a hold of these…especially Claire."

"Why not?" Eugene asked.

"Look at the way Claire is looking at me in each of the photos," Nick pointed out. "It's as if she knows something. I'm wondering if *maybe* she does. We know Rossi has gotten people in the FBI to work with him before. What if the reason Katie won't tell anyone is because she doesn't know who to trust?"

"Look at what this says in the end," Chad showed him the picture of the first note. "She doesn't want to tell anyone, because she doesn't want anyone else killed because of her. We know she feels responsible for the attacks, and for Jillian and

Aaron's deaths. What if she's afraid to tell someone, because she doesn't want anyone else hurt?"

"Okay, now that we have this part figured out. How do we get her out of this mess?" Dakota asked.

"Both of us out of this mess," Nick added.

"All of us out of this mess," Chad pointed out. "This is affecting all of us."

"First off, we need to find Junior," Todd said.

"Oh, like we've had such wonderful luck in accomplishing that." Dakota sighed. "We don't know where he's at, and he's been able to avoid all cameras for several weeks."

"He's sending his men to do whatever he needs done," Nick explained. "Claire's not had any luck in her attempts."

"And we can't track him either," Todd added. "It's like he's moving in a camera dead zone."

"Claire can't track him?" Chad asked, astounded.

"That's what I said," Nick grumbled.

"*Claire* can't track him?" Chad asked again, a little more forcefully.

"Yeah." Nick shook his head, confused. "Did ya not hear me the first time?"

"*Claire can't track him,*" Chad said, making his words clear.

"Right. Claire can't find him. Ya know, yer really irritatin' me," Nick said, his Australian accent flaring, as well as his temper.

"Claire can't track him," he said again.

"What the bloody hell are you gettin' at?" Nick demanded.

"Watch your mouth," Seth snapped. Then he turned to Chad and asked, "What are you trying to say?"

"Claire can find *anything, anywhere*. If there is even a remote trace of them, she *can, has, and will* find them," Chad pointed out. "Unless she doesn't want to." He gestured toward the photos of Claire.

"No. There's no way she would do this to him." Todd crossed his arms, adamant. "There's no way she would do this."

"She hates Katie with a passion," Dakota reminded them.

"No, she's changed." Nick couldn't believe his ears. "She even apologized to her."

"What's the true definition of insanity? Doing the same thing over and over again, and expecting a different result. Claire knows this. If it were me, and something was having an opposite effect of what I wanted, I would do the opposite in order to get the desired effect," Chad said, gesturing to the photos again. "Gentlemen, we may have a spy amongst us. If she catches wind of this, we could all be in danger, according to this letter."

"We need to act as if we don't know anything," Nick said, sternly. "No one is to know what we know. At this point, he thinks Katie's cooperating with him. The only possible way to get a message to her is through Ryan and Ty. In the meantime, I've scrubbed my phone and had them do the same. If Claire is watching Katie's phone, then Junior will know."

"How do we get a message to Ty and Ryan?" Todd asked.

Nick looked at him with a renewed vigor and hope. "Carefully."

* * *

While Katie was at work the next day, Nick met up with Ryan and Ty at the Rock and Roll Hall of Fame. "How's she doin'?" Nick asked, looking at an exhibit, while Ryan and Ty stood less than five feet from him. Neither guy looked at the other.

Ryan pointed to something in the exhibit and pretended to say something to Ty, when in reality, he said, "She looks like crap. She's depressed and her pictures are dark and stormy."

Nick shook his head. "Sorry t' hear that. That breaks my heart."

"Hers is broken as well," Ty pointed out, "scary broken."

Nick covered his mouth as he said, "We've figured it out. I need the two a' you to scrub yer phones and also give Katie a message."

"Already cleaned the phones as soon as I sent the texts," Ryan explained.

"What's the message?" Ty asked.

"Tell her we know who the two Hunters are and to not trust anyone but you two, me, Seth, Dakota, Chad, Todd, and

Eugene. That's it. No one else is to be trusted at this point until we locate The Hunter."

"Got it," Ty agreed. "Consider it done."

"Where are we meeting next?" Ryan asked.

"The penguin exhibit at the zoo on Thursday at two."

"Sounds good," Ryan agreed. "See you then."

With that, the two groups went separate ways. Nick continued to stop and stare at several exhibits before leaving the museum in case he was being watched. When he left, he headed for Lake Erie, sitting on a bench along the shoreline. That gave him time to think and process all that was going on while he watched the waves roll in and go back out. The water gave him a sense of peace and calmness.

Could Claire really be working with Joey Rossi? Why would she if she was? She was part of the team. She knew just how much Katie meant to him. He would have to trust those in his circle, otherwise no one else was to know what was going on until he could get to Katie safely.

Katie. His love for her for at times was more than he could stand. This summer was torture for him. Now that he had Katie in his life, he couldn't imagine his life without her. This summer showed him just how deep his love for her truly was.

* * *

"I don't understand," Katie said, upset, as she stood in her kitchen with her arms crossed.

"Just leave your phone here," Ryan pleaded. "Look, we'll leave ours as well." He set his phone down on the counter.

Ty set his on the counter beside Ryan's, as he said, "We want you to enjoy your evening. We just want to relax and have fun without distraction. If we all leave our phones and go somewhere that you've never been, we can experience it together. C'mon! It'll be fun."

"This is fixin' to be a long week if I keep getting these kind of surprises," she grumbled, placing her phone on the counter next to theirs before they left.

Once they arrived at the restaurant and were seated, Ryan leaned over to Katie and whispered in her ear. At first she pulled away before he said, "I need to tell you something and want privacy. Ty is already aware of it."

"Fine," she sighed and let him whisper in her ear.

"We have to admit something to you."

"What?"

"We snooped and found some things out. Don't stress. Nick, Seth, Dakota, Todd, Chad, and Eugene are working on things. They suspect Claire may be involved. He said to tell you to continue doing what you're doing, knowing they're working on it. They know about the notes."

She gave him a hug, and when she was near his ear, she whispered, "If you two weren't my closest friends, I would have to hurt you. Thank you for snooping."

"Don't trust anyone but those already mentioned…minus Claire. She's suspect at best."

"Understood. And, thank you."

"We're meeting him on Thursday. Do you want us to send him a message?"

"Please tell him I love him with all my heart," she said, her body shaking with excitement and fear at the same time. "I don't know who to trust."

"No one but us, Nick, Seth, Todd, Dakota, Chad, and Eugene. No officers, nothing."

"I understand."

He placed his hands on each side of her face so he could see her eyes. "We love you and are scared for you."

"I know."

"Stay focused on what you know to be true."

"I will."

With that, they ate most of their meal in silence. Katie toyed with her food until Ty and Ryan refused to leave until she ate her entire meal. She wasn't allowed to use the restroom until they got home either. They weren't taking any chances with a possible eating disorder, or abduction from the restaurant, on top of the problems she already had. Truth be told, they had her leave her phone in case someone had accessed it, and could be listening or tracking her movements. Paranoia seemed to be the order of the day.

*　　*　　*

Through the week, Ty and Ryan often took frequent trips with Katie when she got home from work. While she enjoyed her time with them, it exhausted her.

On Thursday, Nick walked into the penguin exhibit. It took him several moments to find Ty and Ryan. "Did you get a chance to talk to her?" Nick asked, covering his mouth so it wouldn't reflect on the glass of the penguin exhibit.

"Yes. She's actually eating now and looking a bit healthier," Ryan explained. "She said to tell you that she loves you with all her heart."

"Wonderful to hear," Nick said, doing his best to hide his delight.

"Any message in return?" Ty asked.

"Tell her just to have faith. Love never fails."

"Got it. Same for you. Do what you can do to get this fixed. Find who's doing this," Ryan said, irritated. "You both look like crap."

Nick chuckled. "Point taken. I owe you guys for what you did."

"Nope. The plane tickets were plenty. Just take care of her...or you're dealing with us."

"I will. Have a safe trip. I cannot thank you enough," Nick acknowledged before he wandered off to another exhibit.

"Think they'll figure it out?" Ryan asked.

"You have to have faith," Ty said. "We all have to trust that God has this under control."

Chapter 8

Dog Days of Summer

The days seemed to drag as far as Katie was concerned. Not knowing what was going on in the investigation was bothering her, but she couldn't let it show. Instead of letting it sidetrack her, she focused on her job each day. She had to, her partner was counting on her, and she was counting on the Lord to fix this.

"Enough is enough, Katie!" Andy snapped as they drove around. "Are you seriously going to tell me that you haven't talked to him yet?"

"No, I haven't."

"Why not? Why aren't you even going to give him a chance?"

"Because I can't."

"Why not?" he demanded. "It's obvious you two love each other. What's the problem?"

"I can't tell you."

He growled. "What's your problem?"

"I can't tell anyone."

"Why not?"

Katie's heart raced as the anger pulsed through her.

"Why not?" he questioned.

"I just can't."

"Ohhhh, this is going to be a long day if you don't start talking. You've been sulking all summer long."

"I have not!" she snapped. "I have done my job well."

"Yes, you have. Can you imagine how much better you will be at your job if you give it your full concentration?"

"Who says I'm not?"

"It's obvious."

"Why do you say that?"

"Seriously?"

"What are you trying to say?"

He pulled into a parking lot and threw the car into park. "I'm trying to say you are a phenomenal officer, but your mind is only half here. Could you imagine how much better you would be if you were able to concentrate on everything around you? I'm afraid for you. I'm terrified that one of these days we're going to get called somewhere, and you won't see the person who shoots you! Then, I'll have to take the worst possible message to Chief. Together, with our hearts broken into pieces, we're then going to have to go to Nick and explain it to him as well."

"Nick and I are no longer together."

"Oh! You are *so* full of it!"

"Wow," she said, shaking her head. "At this point *you* are the one full of it."

"You can be extremely infuriating!"

"I've been called worse."

Andy took a deep breath and slowly let it out, taking a few moments to calm himself before he responded. "Katie, I've seen you in the field. I've spent countless hours with you on shift. I've seen you with Nick when the two of you came over for dinner with me and my girlfriend. She likes you. I like you. What I don't like, is what I've seen these last few months. You have gone downhill so fast, it's not even funny. You've lost your spark. You've lost your heart. You've lost your hope."

"I've lost my love," she finished.

"I know. What I *don't* know is why? Why aren't you even talking to him?"

"I can't."

"Why not?"

"Please just trust me," she begged.

"Oh, I trust you. I just don't want to see you killed because your mind is elsewhere."

The radio in the vehicle crackled alive and a call came over for shots fired at an apartment complex within a couple blocks of their location. "Time to get your head in the game," Andy said, as Katie radioed that they were responding. They pulled out of the parking lot, lights and sirens running.

*   *   *

"Pay attention," Andy ordered, as they, along with several other units exited their vehicles for the apartment building. He grabbed her shoulders and made her look at him. "I mean it. *Pay attention!*"

"Yes, sir," she acknowledged, pulling her gun out of the holster.

As they entered the building, the body of a young man dropped from over the balcony, landing right in front of Andy and Katie. Andy knelt down to check for a pulse, but only shook his head, while keeping an eye in every direction possible.

"Fields and Harmon went around back with Michaels and Wilkins," Katie mentioned, while she, Andy, Terry Baldwin, and his partner, Ed Norton, split up in teams of two. Each of the units took the staircase opposite each other, meeting in the middle of the hallway each time.

As they entered the third floor, the hair on the back of Katie's neck stood on end and she struggled to control her breathing. *What was she doing? If she were to get killed there today, Nick would never know how much she truly loved him.* She decided at that moment that enough *was* enough. When she got home that day, she would take the chance and make contact with Nick…one way or another.

"MacKenna! Look out!" Terry Baldwin shouted as he jumped on top of Katie, shoving her to the ground. A split second later, a gun went off twice from down the hallway, creating an echo in her ears as they landed on the floor with a thud.

"Terry?" Katie looked at him, wide-eyed, pushing him up. Fear and terror filled her eyes as she rolled him off her and placed her hand on the side of his face. "Terry, you're too stubborn and obnoxious to let them take you this way."

"I can't…ohhh, make it stop," he groaned.

Looking down at his leg, panic began to overtake Katie when she realized the artery in his upper right leg had been hit. Blood was pouring from his leg at a high rate of speed, as it also sprayed from his upper right arm. A bullet had hit the brachial artery in his right arm, while the other hit the femoral artery in his right leg. The shooter couldn't have hit more fatal targets if he tried. Her stomach lurched when it registered in her mind what his fate would be. "Look at me!" she shouted.

"From the left!" Terry's partner, Ed, yelled to Andy as another few shots went off.

One of the shots landed in the wall above Katie's head. When she turned to look, another bullet bit into her right shoulder, closely followed by searing heat, as it threw her into the wall, and exited out the back.

"Katie!" Andy exclaimed in shock at what was going on around him, but was doing his best to keep his cool. "Are you okay?"

Groaning, Katie growled, "Get us out of here!"

From either of the staircase entrances, police officers flooded in, going after the gang members who were using the hallway as a battleground. Andy rushed to Katie's side, "Katie?"

"I'm…I'll be fine," she said, grabbing her shoulder. "Terry isn't, though." Struggling to sit up, she rested her right hand on the side of his face again. "Look at me, Terry."

"Ahhh," he sighed. "I've known you've liked me since the academy. Admit it." He jumped and groaned in pain.

"Terry, look at my eyes," Katie coaxed, putting pressure on her shoulder. The gunfire slowed that was whizzing around them, while the gang members fought the police officers.

He shook his head and sighed. "Such beautiful eyes."

"Tell me about your favorite place. C'mon, please tell me about your favorite hiding place. We all have them."

He slowly exhaled. "It's okay, Katie. I know what you're trying to do, but it doesn't hurt as much anymore."

"Terry, don't you dare go anywhere!" Katie growled and jumped as her shoulder seared in pain. "Tell me!" she demanded. "Where do you go to hide?"

"There's a little state park down south by about an hour or so," he started. "There are trails to hike and hills to climb."

"Go to the top of one of those hills for me. Is there an open area?"

He nodded. "There is."

Noticing how pale he was, she pushed forward, "Go to the middle of that field in your mind and lie down. Look toward the sky. Can you see it?" she asked, a tear slowly crawling down her cheek.

With his eyes closed, he imagined the area she described. "Yeah. There are puffy white clouds."

"Perfect," she said, feeling Andy's hand on her other shoulder, letting her know he was sitting there with her. "What do you see in the clouds?"

"All sorts of things."

"The sun. Can you feel the warmth on your face?" she continued.

"Yes. It feels wonderful," he said, taking a deep breath.

"Look at me, Terry."

"It's beautiful. I wish you could see this."

"I will, when the time is right. I want you to stay there for me right now."

Opening his eyes, he reached up toward her face. "I'll save you a place," he said, and let out a last breath of air as his hand dropped to the floor.

"Oh, dear Lord," Katie breathed out as tears streamed down her face. Shaking her head, she explained, "He was a thorn in my flesh, but I wouldn't wish this on anyone."

Andy pulled her toward him as she sat there, her spirit broken. "We need to get you to the hospital, Katie. You're bleeding. It's through and through, but we have to get you to the hospital."

"Ambulance is downstairs. How are they doing?" Ed asked while other officers were busy clearing the floor and securing the scene.

"Terry's gone," Andy said, somberly.

"Gone? As in dead?" When Andy nodded, Ed placed his hands on his hips and swore. "And Katie?"

"She'll be okay, but we gotta get her to the hospital."

"Let's get her downstairs," he said, helping Andy get her off the floor. As they assisted her down the stairs to the waiting ambulance, a couple other officers cordoned off the scene with tape, while two other officers stood over their fallen brother. As much as they wanted to cover him, they knew they couldn't until they got permission. In the meantime, they would guard him with their lives.

*   *   *

Resting in the emergency room bed, with the medicine finally taking effect, Katie lay there with her arm in a sling. She did her best to figure out how she was going to get home, when Andy walked into the room with Chad and Eugene from Nick's unit.

"Ohhhh," Katie groaned, "What are you doing here?"

"You two got this?" Andy asked. "I have a ton of things to take care of at the station. The paperwork on this one is going to be horrific."

Chad shook his hand. "Yeah, we got it, man. Really sorry for the loss of your fallen brother."

"You and your precinct have our condolences," Eugene added. "And, thank you for contacting us."

"Just take care of her, or you're dealing with me and Chief. And, trust me, that won't go well," Andy warned.

"We will," Chad assured him.

"Pretty sure you would not have called us if that was in question," Eugene pointed out.

"Chief said to take it easy for a few days before you come in," Andy explained. "Please do so. I want my partner back."

"I will," she promised, and he left the three of them in the room. "So, um, what are y'all doin' here?"

"Well, it was either us or Seb." Chad shrugged. "Pretty sure we were the better choice."

"We have acquired your paperwork and prescriptions, and we will pick them up before depositing you to your apartment," Eugene said, holding up the paperwork.

"They stitched me up and gave me an anti-biotic," Katie explained.

Chad offered her his arm. "We know. C'mon, let's get you home."

As the tears crawled down her cheeks, she explained, "Terry didn't make it."

"We know. C'mon, let's go," Chad coaxed.

Katie sniffed. "He was arrogant and cocky, but he was a good officer."

"I will retrieve the nurse for a possible sedative prescription as well," Eugene said, and disappeared out of the room.

Chad pulled the stool over to her bedside and took her hand. "Katie, our brothers and sisters in the law enforcement community are fully aware of what dangers lurk around every corner, but those brave individuals put that uniform back on each day and go back out there. Just like them, you'll have to do the same."

"I don't know if I can."

"Oh, you can and you will. It'll take several days before you'll be able to see sunlight around you, but trust me, it's there."

Shaking her head, she looked toward the ceiling, praying for the tears to stop. "This may be the last straw."

"Andy told us what happened in the hallway. He told us of the colorful past you and Terry shared. When Terry saw you in the line of fire, though, he didn't hesitate to jump in front of you to stop you from getting hit. He took the bullets for you, and you gave him the peace he needed to see and feel before he passed. Andy said you refused to let the fact that you were shot deter you from making him focus on beauty, even though there was ugly all around him at that minute."

Sitting up, Katie wiped the tears from her eyes.

"You gave that man a present of peace. No matter what the past was between you two, you restored grace and mercy within him. Not everyone can do that. You looked past yourself for another."

"Here," a nurse walked into the room with Eugene behind her. "Take this with a cup of water," she said, handing Katie a pill, along with a plastic cup of water from the pitcher. After Katie took it, the nurse explained, "It will take only a few minutes to kick in. Doctor Simmons said to make sure she takes this for at least ten days." She handed Eugene Katie's prescription.

"We will acquire this for her as well, and will ensure she takes them as directed," Eugene agreed.

"Do you need a wheelchair?"

"No, ma'am, we got it," Chad assured her.

"Okay. Doctor Simmons' information is on the paperwork, and she'll have to come back here tomorrow for a wound check to make sure there's no infection. Also, please make sure to change the dressing every eight hours."

"Yes, ma'am," Chad agreed.

"Tomorrow we'll check her out and let you know when she needs to go see the doctor again."

"Yes, ma'am."

"Um, we need to get out of here," Katie said, her head spinning. Struggling to keep her eyes open, she wavered a bit.

"I will retrieve the car and meet you at the entrance," Eugene said before he disappeared.

Chad took Katie's left arm and put it around his shoulder, guiding her slowly toward the doors where he knew Eugene would be waiting. "Just focus and breathe. We're almost there."

Katie nodded in response while she took slow, deep breaths. "My head is spinning."

"I know. Focus for me. Trust us," he coaxed.

Nodding in response, she was relieved to see Eugene pull up to the entrance.

"A little further," Chad encouraged. When they reached his car, Chad opened the back door for her and she slid into the seat.

As Chad closed the door, Katie gasped and jumped when she saw a person in the back seat floor wearing a black hooded sweatshirt. "Ummm…" she squeaked out, while tapping on Chad's shoulder as he got in the passenger's side front seat, unable to form words.

"Shhh," Eugene whispered as they drove off. When he was sure they weren't being followed, Eugene explained, "We are going to drive around for a bit. You had better make it quick, though, she is on sedatives."

Nick came up off the floor and uncovered his head.

"Nick!" Katie breathed out, her heart pounding ferociously in fear mixed with excitement. "I can't! He'll kill us both! Please!"

Feeling her body trembling, Nick hugged her like he never wanted to let her go. "We have to go somewhere safe. I can't do this anymore."

"We need to know if Claire's involved before you disappear on us," Chad pointed out.

Katie gulped. "Disappear? To where?"

"We'll disappear to South America."

"Will they not find us?"

"No. They'll think we're dead."

"How? How will that be possible?"

"Do you trust me?"

Katie sniffed, wiping the tears of joy off her face at seeing Nick. "If you…if you can't trust the FBI, who can you trust?"

"Ohhh," he chuckled, pulling her into himself. "I missed you beyond words! I love you."

"The sooner we clear up a few things, the sooner you can be together," Chad reminded them.

"Can we?" Katie asked. "Is it possible?"

"The main one we need to find out about is Claire," Nick explained. "Other than that, the other issues can fall by the wayside for all I care. As long as I have you, I'll be a happy man."

"That would make me the happiest woman on this planet," she said, and kissed him with passion that was beyond what it should have been. "I don't…" she looked at him, "I don't want to ever let you go again. This is killing me."

"I know. It's killing me too, but it's only for a little while longer. I *will* figure this out. I promise you."

*   *   *

Over the next few days, Eugene and Chad continued to stop by Katie's apartment to make sure she was doing what she was supposed to be doing in regards to eating and taking her medicines. They even went with her to Terry's funeral. As much as she didn't want to go, she knew she had to. Terry was a fellow brother in blue, and for that, she was proud. With Chad and Eugene at her side, and Andy and her fellow officers standing around her, she focused on his family. She prayed with every bone in her body for the Lord to work everything out to His will…whatever that entailed.

Chapter 9

Summer Rays of Hope

"You want me to do *what*?" Katie asked, stunned, as she sat in the Chief's office eight weeks after Terry's death.

"Look, you've only got another two months before I have to lose you to Quantico. I would like you to shadow one of our detectives until then, and see if maybe we can change your mind."

"I'm supposed to stay with Andy!"

"Katie, Andy told me how you took care of Terry. How you helped him focus on the good of the world and find peace before he left. I've also watched and have seen for myself just how strong you really are. I feel your talent is being wasted as an officer. I want you to move to shadowing a detective. And," he held up his hand to stop her objections, "the detective I want you to shadow is working on a specific case in conjunction with another agency."

Katie furrowed her brow. "I don't understand."

"Nancy!" Chief called his secretary.

Poking her head in the door, she asked, "Yes, sir?"

"Please have Detective Petrovich come in here?"

"Yes, sir," she said, and disappeared.

Less than five minutes later, a thirty-year-old lady with a thin build, walked into the office. With her hair in a pixie cut, it allowed her blue eyes to stand out on her etched face. "Sir, Nancy said you wanted to see me?"

"Yes. Remember when I told you about the young officer I wanted to shadow you?"

"Yes, sir," she said, coming in and sitting in the chair opposite Katie.

"This is Officer Katie MacKenna. Officer MacKenna, this is Detective Dana Petrovich," he introduced them. As they shook hands, Chief continued, "I want her to shadow you, mainly because she is to head to Quantico in January. I want her to experience what it will be like to work with the FBI."

"But, you're a police detective, right?" Katie asked.

"Yes, but I'm working in conjunction with an FBI unit on a case right now. Pretty sure that's what you're hinting at?" Dana asked Chief.

"Yep." Turning toward Katie, he clarified, "I feel this will be an experience for you that will help you in making a decision on whether to go on to Quantico, or stay with us and take the test for detective."

"But, sir!" Dana objected. "People wait years to take that! You can't seriously offer that to her! She's only a rookie! She's barely in year two!"

"She's almost done with year two, and her background dictates a quicker transition," Chief explained.

"*She* is still in the office," Katie snapped. "And, I do believe it will be my decision regarding which direction I take?"

"Yes, it is. But the selfish part of me still hopes to keep you," Chief encouraged.

"I appreciate that." Katie then turned to Dana, and explained, "And, if you're willing, I would like to learn from you."

"Sir, may I have a word with you? In private?" Dana asked.

"No, ma'am. I know your feelings in the matter, but I am overruling you on this."

"But the guys will simply not like this…at all!" she objected.

"I'm aware. And, if anyone gives you any sort of guff about it, I will deal with them immediately. I will not tolerate my decisions being second-guessed in my station."

Dana sighed, crossing her arms. "Yes, sir."

"That includes from you," he said sternly.

"I've worked so hard –"

"I'm aware of that. That's why I want her to learn from you. You are a phenomenal detective, or you wouldn't be representing the precinct in this joint venture. You are brilliant and I wanted to put her with our best. Can I count on you?"

Dana mulled things around in her mind for a moment before she finally nodded.

"And be nice to her. She was the one who talked Terry through his passing."

"That was you?" Dana asked Katie. "From what I was told, it was an experienced officer."

"She has a ton of life experience," Chief pointed out.

"And, yes, that was me. It wasn't easy, but I wanted him to have peace before he passed. He was in immense pain. He also gave himself for me," Katie pointed out, her body shaking in remembrance of the incident. "While I would give myself for anyone here, he did. I only hope to be as good an officer, with as much courage as he had, each day I put on the uniform."

Looking at her in shock, she then understood why Chief was giving Katie this opportunity. "All right. I'll do it, with one condition," Dana stipulated.

"What's that?" Katie asked, nervous.

"You listen to what I tell you. If I tell you to stay in the car, you do so. If I tell you to duck, you do it and ask later. When we're working with the other unit, you are to listen to me. If I am to be responsible for you, I don't want you screwing anything up for me. I also don't want to have to clean up any messes you may create. Do we have an understanding?"

"Yes, ma'am," Katie agreed.

"It's Dana," she said, putting her hand out. When Katie shook her hand, she said, "I'll stand up for you, but you have to listen to me…and, take good notes."

"Yes, ma'am."

"And quit calling me ma'am. I keep looking for my mother."

"Yes, ma' – I mean, Dana. Sorry, it's a respect thing. It's engrained within me."

"I get that, but I'm Dana."

"Got it."

"Good. Now head on out. Please send Andy in when you go through the bullpen," Chief said, writing in a folder on his desk.

As they left the office, Andy looked questioningly at Katie before Dana told him to go talk to the Chief. "He's not gonna like that one," Dana said, glancing over her shoulder toward where Andy went into Chief's office. "As a matter of fact, there may be quite a bit of backlash on this one. Let's bail and head to lunch before we go to the FBI office to connect with them. That way we can get to know each other a bit."

"Sounds good. Where are we going?"

"Wherever you want?"

"Your choice," Katie offered.

"All right," Dana agreed. "This may not be so bad after all."

*   *   *

During lunch, Dana shared a little about herself, and then Katie returned the gesture. Continuing their conversation on the way over to the FBI office, Katie only explained what happened up to when she graduated college, when Dana said, "Wow. You've not lived an easy life…that's for sure. Do you have any doubts on what you want to do or where you want to go in life?"

"No. Not really."

215

"You know, I think with our conversation here, I now know why Chief is having you come with me on this assignment."

"Why is that?" Katie asked, as they absentmindedly walked down the hall toward a conference room.

"Because of who we're looking for," she said, and opened the door to the conference room.

Katie gasped as she saw Seth's unit around the table.

"Oh! No way!" Claire groaned. "Seriously? Out of every single officer on the force, *this* is your informant?"

"You know each other?" Dana asked, looking from Claire, to Katie, and back again.

"Unfortunately," Claire grumbled.

"I dunno if this is a good idea," Nick calmly protested, but looked as if he was about to yell.

While deep inside, Katie knew it was for show for Claire, it still gutted her on the inside.

"Like it or not, she's our inside person when it comes to the Rossi family," Seth stepped in. "We *need* her in order to find Junior."

"Are you bloody serious?" Nick snapped. "This is the best you can do?"

"Honestly!" Claire complained. "I didn't like it the first time around. How is she going to help us this time?"

"She knows Joey Rossi," Seth pointed out. "She can also be used for bait, if she is willing?" He looked at her for her answer.

"Wait. Bait? What?" Dana objected. "Does Chief know? She's supposed to be an observer. He said absolutely nothing about using her as bait *or* an informant."

"At this point, it doesn't matter. You can use me however you need to," Katie spoke up. Looking toward Nick, she continued, "I've been a target multiple times thanks to Joey. I'm also going to Quantico in January, so I'll be yours after that anyway. If it will get you to find Joey, use me however you deem necessary."

"There," Seth said, satisfied. "She's volunteering."

"No. Not until I talk to Chief," Dana said firmly. "I'm responsible for her. Until I talk –"

"I'm here," Chief said, pushing his way past them into the conference room with Director Shaw right behind him. "They called me just after the two of you left. Knowing the both of you the way I do, I figured I would have to be here."

"Sir? You don't have any objections to this? They are using her as an informant and as *bait*, not just for observation."

"Trust me. I know."

"I struggled with the idea as well," Director Shaw pointed out. "However, we're running out of options here. We've gone months without a sighting from him. Not sure what rock he's hiding under, but we need to find him…and she's our best bet on doing that."

"How?"

"Come in and close the door, please?" Director Shaw asked. After Dana pushed Katie in a couple of steps, she closed the door. Feeling the temperature of the room hovering around freezing at best, Director Shaw explained, "Look, our investigation has led us to none other than Joey Rossi. Junior, as you guys call him, has disappeared off radar for quite some time. He's been lurking in the shadows. I feel an option would be for Katie to visit Lucca in prison and see what comes out of it."

As the color drained from Katie's face, Dana shouted, "No! No way! You will paint a target on her back she will *never* be able to run from. That's like kicking a hornet's nest! I can't believe you agreed to this!" she yelled, exasperated. "Teasing him by sending in the *one* person who put him away and took one of his sons away from him? No. This is crazy! I can't *believe* any of you, who are supposedly her friends, are even entertaining this idea. You should all be ashamed of yourselves! What? Just because she broke it off with Locke, you all are going to desert her and feed her to the wolves. I cannot believe I'm the only one passionate about not putting her on the front line in this room," she finished, looking from face to face. As she did, they each hung their heads. Walking up to the Chief, she stated, "I *will not* be responsible for this. If you approve this, then *you* will be the one responsible if he kills her! Has she not been through more than enough? Hasn't the precinct been through enough? We've lost three officers this year, and you're purposely putting another one in the line of fire. No," she crossed her arms, "I *will not* be a part of this!"

Getting within a couple inches of Dana's face, Chief sternly ordered her, "You *are* and you *will*. You will protect her with everything that is in you, while you teach her how you work."

"No."

"She needs you."

"She needs *you*, but all you're doing is throwing her to the wolves! You're no better than her father!"

As soon as she said that, other than a couple of gasps heard around the room, complete silence filled the air. Feeling the heaviness in her chest, Katie took a deep breath. Saying a prayer in her heart for courage and faith, she whispered aloud, "Love never fails."

Dana spun toward Katie. "What did you say?"

Standing tall, Katie reiterated, "Love never fails. The Lord has never failed to show me that He loves me. If He's not done with me, there is nothing that will be able to take me out."

"There's a dangerous difference between having faith and having a death wish," Dana pointed out. "*This* situation is a death wish. It's *so* beyond dangerous, it's not even funny!" Turning back to the Chief, she demanded, "If it were me, would you send me in there to see Lucca Rossi?"

"No," he said quickly, a little too quickly.

"Then why would you place her in this position?"

"I know you don't understand this —"

"Understand this? How can *anyone* understand this?" Walking over to Nick, Dana questioned, "You supposedly loved her. Even if there is a remote part of you that still loves her, how can you put her in this position? Do you really hate her *that* much?"

Unsure how to answer, Nick looked toward Director Shaw for help.

"She's like a daughter to me," Director Shaw started, but Dana cut into him.

"If she is, then why are you putting her in the line of fire?"

"Because right now she's fighting blind. If we can do it in a controlled environment, we may be able to flush him out."

"Controlled environment? Seriously? You are kicking a hornet's nest in a supposedly controlled environment. Someone *will* get stung!"

"I understand your concern –"

"Obviously not!"

"Petrovich!" Chief snapped. "I've let you go on long enough."

"I vehemently object!"

Chief rolled his eyes. "Obviously."

"How can you be so callous about her life?"

"We're not. We are trying to flush someone out who's trying to *take* her life."

"I want no part of this."

"If you choose to walk out that door, you are giving up any say in this matter. Once you do, you are not to speak to a single soul about this…not even to her partner, Officer D'Antonio. If you do, there *will* be consequences. Have I made myself clear?" Chief threatened.

Walking over to Katie, in a low voice, Dana asked, "Do you want to do this?"

"I'm tired of hiding. This has been going on over a year now. I just want to do something to make this stop," Katie responded, weary.

"Do you want me to stay?"

"I want your help. Out of anyone in this room, I know you have my best interest at heart."

Dana nodded before she turned to the others in the room. "This is the deal –"

"Deal? What deal?" Seth snapped. "There's no *deal* in this."

"Yes, there is. You want her to help? You want her for bait? Here's the deal –"

"Wait a minute! Who says we have to make a deal?" Seth demanded.

"If you want me, you have to listen to Dana," Katie spoke up, standing slightly behind Dana.

"Fine," he growled. "What are we talking about?"

"If you want her, then you have to go through me. I have to approve all moves in regards to her. I seem to be the only one concerned for her safety here. I am also not going to leave her side. That means I will even be sleeping in her apartment. Deal?"

"Do *you* agree to this?" Seth asked Katie. "She's invading *your* home."

Katie nodded. "Yes."

"Director?" Seth asked.

"Do what you need to do. I want Junior found yesterday," he said, and he and Chief left the conference room.

"Fine. We are in charge of *what* she does, but you will have control over *how* it's done," Seth reluctantly agreed.

"Okay then. First off, clear the room except you, me, and her. We need to set some ground rules."

After everyone left, the trio sat down at the table. With Seth on one side, and Dana and Katie on the other, Dana started, "Look, there was absolutely no disrespect intended. I only feel that you guys are putting her life in danger. Does her life not matter to you?"

"Oh, more than you know," Seth countered, "but we have exhausted all resources up to this point. Frankly, I don't like that she's being hunted. I don't like that we've had to come to her apartment after break-ins by him. I don't like that she was shot at, and even had someone kill themselves in front of her after he tried to kill her, only to have her car blown up later that night. I *really* don't like that we had to unbury her from a blown up warehouse that killed two of *your* officers. Now, while she and Nick have a past, I promise you that we are only looking out for her. We even sent Agents Chad Johnson and Eugene Kennedy to pick her up from the hospital when she was shot. They also made sure she ate and got her medicine through the next week. Now, if I'm not mistaken, Agent Johnson even helped her work through the loss of the young officer who died in her arms during that time. Does that sound like someone who doesn't have her best interest at heart?"

"Then why are you sending her into her worst nightmare, which will undoubtedly result in a phone call from him to his son to put a contract out on her?"

"I'm betting on it."

Puzzled, Dana pressed forward. "How is *that* looking out for her?"

"Because, unless I miss my guess, you're tired of being watched and hunted down, correct?" Seth asked Katie, who only nodded in response. "Then if that's the case, we need to push him. I want to do it in a controlled environment, though. With you continuously by her side, this will work out better than even I could have planned. With a second pair of eyes looking out for her, she will be in that much less danger. When we kick the hornet's nest, as you called it, we can track who he calls, where it goes, and hopefully will see if we can locate Junior in the process. Once we locate Junior, I promise you we will take him down. At that point, both Junior and Senior will be behind bars, leaving Katie the chance to finally breathe after almost two years."

"Katie?" Dana asked.

"That would be nice," she said, mulling it over in her mind. "What do I need to do?"

Relieved, Seth explained, "We need you to go to the prison and meet with Lucca Rossi."

"Why?"

"What you don't know is ever since he was arrested, he has wanted to meet with you."

"What? Why?" Katie asked, stunned.

"Look, the only ones who knew about the request were me, Director Shaw, and both the head of the prosecuting and defense attorney teams," he said, sensing her real question was if Nick knew about it. "He's requested this, because he wants to have a controlled conversation with you. If Dana goes with you, would that be less intimidating?"

"It would give you a witness, that's for sure," Dana pointed out. "Where you go, I go, until this is over."

Taking a deep breath before she slowly let it out, Katie agreed, "I'll do it."

"You'll have to face Lucca Rossi himself," Seth warned.

"I know."

"And, Dana is correct, this *will* trigger a contract on your life."

"I already have one on my life," she pointed out.

"You have a controlled torment on your life at the moment. He's holding you hostage. Once a contract is put out, you will have to continually look over your shoulder. They can be anywhere at any time."

"Will this get Junior and Senior out of my life for good?"

"That's the goal."

"Then that's the hope I will hold on to."

"Then, you'll do it?"

"At this point, I feel like I'm being continuously watched, never knowing when he'll pull the trigger. If I have another pair of eyes looking out for me, I feel more comfortable in doing this."

"You won't go anywhere without me," Dana promised.

"Then, yes. I'll do it," Katie agreed.

Seth stood, relieved. "I'll get it set up as soon as possible."

"In the meantime, I'll need to meet with your unit so you can catch me up," Dana said.

"Can I just stay in here?" Katie asked. "With as stressful as this is, the last place I want to be is in a room with Nick."

Dana patted her hand. "I understand."

"Thank you. I pray this will be over soon."

"Me too, Katie. Me too," Seth said before he left the room.

Chapter 10

Summer Storms

The night before Katie was to meet with Lucca Rossi, she tossed and turned all night long. Stumbling to the shower in the morning, she wasn't sure what she would face when she sat down in front of Lucca, so she prayed the entire time, even up until they were sitting in the room waiting to see him.

"I'm scared," Katie admitted to Dana, who stood leaning against the wall next to Katie, because she wanted a good position in case Lucca pulled something.

Dana sighed. "Unfortunately, that's painfully obvious. You look like you haven't slept in days."

"I haven't."

"You're going to need to be sent to a private island when this is finished just so you can relax, knowing you're alone."

"Tell me about it." She sighed. "Once this portion is over, I'll be able to breathe."

"Noooo, actually, this will probably trigger the biggest storm you've ever faced in your life."

"So, hold my breath until this is over?"

"Yes. And in the meantime, I won't leave your side."

"I appreciate that."

When they heard voices, Katie's heart skipped a beat. Panic began to take over and she stood. "I can't do this."

Placing her hands on Katie's shoulders, Dana calmly said, "Yes, you can. You are a strong young lady. Just remember the man whose home you went to for dinner. Remember the man who you sat at the table with."

"It's being overwritten by the man who was in that massive file," Katie said, trembling. "I can't do this!"

"Breathe. He's here." Dana turned her toward the door, where Katie and Lucca made eye contact as the guard unlocked the room door. "I'm not leaving you. Sit down and let him say his peace."

Katie gulped, only nodding in response. While she lowered herself to her seat, Lucca took the seat across from her and the guard handcuffed him to the table.

"Hello, young lady," he said, and she jumped. "Please, relax. I have requested to speak with you many times and was delighted when the request was finally granted."

"I, um, am surprised that you would want to talk to me at all," Katie said, voice trembling while she tucked a piece of hair behind her ear.

When Dana reached over and placed her hand on Katie's to calm her, she asked Lucca, "Why did you want to see her?"

"Who are you to her?" Lucca questioned. "I don't ever remember seeing you prior to now."

"I am a police detective. I'm here to ensure there are no problems."

"I see." Lucca nodded in understanding. "I have no inclination to hurt young Katie, only to speak with her. May I have a moment alone with her?"

Katie's eyes popped wide-open as she squeaked in response.

"I'm afraid that's not an option," Dana explained. "The fact that you get to speak with her at all should be more than plenty."

"Fair enough," he conceded.

Katie nervously cleared her throat. Wiping the sweat off her forehead, she asked, "What, um…why do you want to see me?"

"May I continue to call you Katie?"

"Yes, sir."

"Ohhh, I love that you have proper respect. That was one of the things I admired about you. What I don't understand is why you would set out to destroy my family," Lucca said, throwing her off.

"I assure you, sir, that was *never* my intention."

"What *was* your intention?"

'*Mayday! Mayday!*' Katie thought. '*He's trying to set you up! Get a grip woman!*'

"*What* was your intention?" Lucca insisted.

Katie took a deep breath. As she slowly let it out, she said a prayer for purity of heart and clarity of mind. "My intention was to be the best possible friend I could be to Giovanni."

"Is that how you justify taking his family away from him?" Lucca fired. "How is *that* being a good friend?"

"You were forcing him to do something that was not in him. You were forcing him to be someone that would destroy the tender heart that is in him."

"What did he want to do?"

"Sir," she started, knowing he was fishing for information. How she answered these questions would be crucial to Giovanni's safety. "If you don't know where his true heart is, then you didn't know your son at all."

"How *dare* you!" Lucca shouted. "You have some nerve! I cannot believe you have the audacity to claim to know my own son better than me."

"Did you ever ask him what he wanted to do?"

"He was to take over the family."

"Per your orders, yes. And your other son would be confined to working security in the organization as well."

"You are a brazen young lady. You come waltzing into our lives and dictate who is to do what? And they called me overbearing and tyrannical. You have the makings of being a perfect boss in a criminal organization."

"No, I don't."

"What makes you say that?"

"Because I have a heart. I've seen what you do to people who don't agree with you or your strong-armed tactics. You are a heartless individual."

"I find it amazing that you feel you know more about my family than I do. You have no idea what it feels like to have your love killed right in front of you."

"Oh yes I do!" Katie spat, anger taking over any feeling of fear or terror about meeting with Lucca. "I had to watch my love of four years die in a car accident while I sat right next to him. I've had multiple people taken from me throughout my life."

"Imagine me being responsible for taking the life of your fiancé," Lucca said, coldly.

"I don't have a fiancé," Katie quipped. "Your son has taken care of that one."

"Are you threatening the life of a federal agent?" Dana questioned.

"I would *never dream* of doing such a thing," Lucca responded in an icy tone. "I have the utmost respect for our law enforcement individuals."

"That's a load of crap and you know it!" Katie snapped.

"Now you question my loyalty?" Lucca asked, appalled.

"I question everything that comes out of your mouth."

"It amazes me how much liberty you take with your tongue. You should really consider using it more wisely before it gets you killed."

"Now you're threatening a police officer?" Dana questioned.

"I would never. I am only warning her that it may cause her harm. I am offering her helpful advice. I would never hurt young Katie. I have more respect for her than that."

Katie rolled her eyes. "Incredible. I have never met anyone who can twist words the way you do. You seem to somehow spin things to your advantage whenever you can, just like you tried to spin your will onto your sons."

"You leave my sons out of this!"

"I can't. Giovanni is the reason, I assume, that I'm here."

"Do *not* speak his name in my presence ever again," Lucca spat, then realized what he did and adjusted his position.

Katie couldn't help the laughter that escaped her mouth.

"Are you laughing at me now?" Lucca asked, appalled.

Resting her chin on her hand as she propped her elbow on the table, Katie watched Lucca in amusement.

"You *are* laughing at me!"

"I was waiting for you to slip, and you actually did. I'm surprised. Living in these close quarters must have dulled your senses."

"Now you choose to antagonize me as well?"

"Lucca, you're a smart man, but you use intimidation to keep people in line. Now that you're stuck in here, you've lost the strength of utilizing that tactic. And, I would imagine that you have an immense amount of time to think about your son, *Giovanni*," she said, emphasizing his name, and he cringed, "and just how he not only betrayed the family, but you as well." Katie sat up with arms crossed in front of her. "That brave young man with a strong heart, took down every last little bit of what took you an entire lifetime to build. What you built on fear, he took down using his heart. Whatever your game is, you will never win."

"Whatever my game is, you may not figure out before it's too late."

"There ya go, threatening her again," Dana pointed out. "Keep in mind that this conversation is on tape." She gestured toward the camera. "If anything happens to either Katie *or* Agent Locke, you will be the first one they look at."

"How am I supposed to hurt them from here?" Lucca asked, innocently

"Your sadistically barbaric ways will catch up to you one day," Katie pointed out. "Oh wait! They have. I believe the judge said life *without* the possibility of parole. So, you will have an *extremely* long time to dwell on where your son, *Giovanni*, may be living his life free of you, while you sit here rotting in jail. And," Katie stood, leaning on the table, "I'll be out there as well, enjoying everything that life has to offer."

Lucca seethed. "For a limited time."

"Strike three. We're out of here," Dana said, ushering Katie out of the room. "He's all yours," she said to the guard as they left.

*   *   *

"I really need you to breathe," Dana mentioned when they were clear of the prison.

"What just happened?"

"What do you mean?"

"I don't remember much of the conversation. If someone ordered me to tell them about it, I don't know that I could recall it all."

"Really? You did an amazing job."

"I really don't know what I said. I think I blocked it out."

Concerned, Dana glanced at Katie before she turned back to the road. "You do realize we need to go tell Seth what happened. You're going to have to think about it and prepare yourself to tell the team."

"I don't want to."

"Not an option. This is part of your job. You're going to have to be around Nick," Dana pointed out. Seeing Katie cringe at hearing Nick's name, she explained, "I know it hurts. Imagine how I feel every time I see Andy."

"You and Andy were together?" Katie asked, stunned.

"Yep. The job is what tore us apart. While he has recovered, it wasn't as easy on my part. I was given a lot of guff when I became a detective and he didn't. They said I emasculated him. Both of us stood our ground, but eventually it broke my heart too much, and I confided in a coworker. I felt as if I did something wrong, even though he said I didn't."

"He's a good guy."

"Unfortunately, I did something stupid after all of that."

"Which was?"

"I turned to another detective who understood my position, and, well, one thing led to another. We went from talking, and me confiding in him, to…yeah," she said, regret all over her face.

"You cheated on him?" Katie asked, stunned.

"Yeah."

"Why? He's a great guy!"

"I know. Trust me. I know! It was my fault. I know he's better off with the girl he's with now. I just hope they stay together. They're good for each other, and she makes him happy."

"Wow. I…I'm sorry. I just don't understand."

"There are days I don't either. Along those same lines, Locke seems to be a great guy, and I don't understand why you broke it off with him. Is there someone else?"

"Oh! No way! I don't cheat. No offense, but I just don't. I would rather break up with a guy than rip his heart out by cheating. And, to put it bluntly, if I'm looking at someone else, then the guy I'm with isn't who I'm supposed to be with anyway."

"No offense taken. It was the one and only time I ever cheated. Trust me. I feel dirty on the inside and sick to my stomach when I think about what I did to his heart. It would kill me if some guy cheated on me as well. To be completely honest, I don't even know why I did it. It didn't start off that way. That's for sure."

"It never does."

"Ready to head up?" Dana asked, pulling into a parking spot.

"If I have to."

She chuckled. "You do."

"Then let's get this over with."

*   *   *

When she walked into the FBI office, she could feel the room divided. That's when she turned to see their secretary, who started while Nick was gone on vacation. Remembering that, Katie decided to keep an eye on her as a possible suspect. She was having a hard time, as much as she didn't like Claire, imagining that Claire would hurt Nick this badly.

After Dana and Katie explained what happened in the meeting, Claire gave an update. "It didn't take him long to make two phone calls. One was to his lawyer, while the other was to a burn phone."

"Did you get a location?" Seth asked.

"The lawyer is in his office."

Seth rolled his eyes.

Claire smirked. "I know what you meant. I was trying to lighten the mood in here."

"Considering most of it is coming from you, I would think *you're* the one who needs to lighten up," Dakota pointed out.

"Fine," she huffed. "He contacted a burn phone located here," she said, putting it up on the screen for all to see.

"And the conversation?" Seth questioned.

"I'm waiting for the prison to send the recordings."

"Get them as soon as possible."

"You know they'll be in code."

"Then get them to the code breakers a-sap," he said sternly.

"Yes, sir," she snapped. "Grumpy today?"

"The Rossi's make me grumpy," he said, crossing his arms. "I'll be happier when these people are all behind bars."

"Do we know for sure that Joey Rossi is The Hunter?" Claire asked. "I mean, honestly. Why are we even doing this? Have you even *heard* from him since you guys got back from vacation?" she asked, looking at Katie.

Not sure how to answer, she looked to Dana for help. "Just because we can't find him right now, does not discount what all he did over the previous year," Dana pointed out. "He took lives. He is responsible for people either dying or getting hurt."

"Even though we haven't heard from him in months?" Claire challenged.

"There is no statute of limitation on murder," Katie pointed out, recovering from the initial question. "While he hasn't taken any agent lives, he has taken the life of two officers, as well as an innocent man in the warehouse explosion. Just because he's lying low, doesn't make him any less responsible."

"I wasn't talking to you," Claire snapped.

"Yes, you did. You directed the first question to me. You want to do this here and now?"

"Do what?"

"You've carried animosity against me from day one. I have done nothing to you, but you feel it is your right to tear me apart every chance you get and take shots at my reputation. I'm getting sick and tired of dealing with your juvenile attitude!"

Claire stood, leaning on her desk with her hands, while no one else in the room said a word or moved a muscle. "You have cut Nick's heart out with a spoon and then stomped it before kicking it into the dirt."

Walking over to Claire's desk, opposite her, Katie leaned in, and pointed out, "Nice try. You've had a problem with me before Nick and I even started dating. What? Were you upset that you couldn't have his heart, so you felt it necessary to ensure that no one else got it?"

"I broke up with him," Claire shot.

"Only because he no longer wanted to be around you, since he saw into your dark inner core. The mask that you hide behind will never cover the darkness that swirls around in your soul."

When Claire slapped Katie, all of the men in the room jumped up to help, as Katie scrambled over Claire's desk, shoving her to the ground.

"Nick, get Katie!" Seth ordered, pulling Claire off the ground. "You're the only one who can hold her back!"

When Nick wrapped his arms around Katie, Katie melted. Feeling his body so close to her, with his arms around her, anger and resentment churned deep inside her, and without thinking, she shouted, "You will not get away with what you're doing! Others may not know, but I do!"

"Oh really?" Claire snidely retorted, as she struggled in Seth and Dakota's arms. "What *exactly* are you talking about?"

"You are part of this! You're keeping me from Nick!" As soon as she said it, the room fell deathly silent.

Narrowing her eyes, Claire demanded, "What do you mean by that?"

"You can find anyone, anywhere…if you want to. You aren't finding Joey, because you're working with him. I've seen the photos. I know your heart is dark as a moonless night."

"You know absolutely *nothing*!"

"I know you –"

"As much as I hate you, I am *not* doing what you accused me of doing!" Struggling to get free, she shouted, "Ever since you broke up with him, he hasn't been the same. Why would I hurt him just to get to you? I love him!"

Nick stood there stunned. He wanted to release Katie, but he held onto her, knowing Katie could potentially rip her apart. And, with as angry as Katie was, he was sure Claire would at least end up in the hospital if Katie got hold of her.

Coldly, Katie responded, "You don't know what real love means. All you do is try to control him. Control is not love. Love is being willing to give him up, just to ensure that he lives!"

"What are you saying?" Claire asked, taken aback as Seth released her. "Has someone threatened Nick?"

Noting that Claire looked genuinely stunned, Katie asked, "Are you working with Joey Rossi?"

Appalled, Claire quickly responded to the accusation, "Definitely not!"

"Then who is?"

"What do you mean?"

"Someone in this office is working with Joey Rossi."

"You can't be serious!"

"I'm very serious. The maps that show dark areas of the city, where there aren't any cameras, are on that machine at your fingertips. Besides, how can you seriously tell me that you haven't seen Joey Rossi in months? You can find anything you want to on that thing."

"I didn't!"

"Prove it!"

Claire went over to her computer and tapped away at the keys as quickly as her fingers would move. After a moment, she looked over to the receptionist. "Where is she?"

"Who?" Seth asked.

"Amber, the receptionist. It says she logged onto my computer several months ago. Looks like it was when we were out on a raid. Look for yourself," she said, showing him the screen, which had a date and time stamp of when she logged in. "Why would I do this? *How* could I do this if I wasn't even here?"

Nick ran over to his phone and got on with security, who immediately locked down the building. After he hung up, he glared at Seth, "This is an inexcusable security breach!"

"I agree," Seth said, furious. "Dakota, go find Brenda Birch and get her up here five minutes ago. In the meantime, Chad and Eugene get with security and locate Amber Stevens immediately!"

"Yes, sir," the three men responded before disappearing from the office.

"Katie, you and I have not had a great past," Claire started, as soon as the men left the room, "but I promise you that I would never hurt you *or* Nick like this. I would never betray this unit or any part of it. They are my family. They have looked out for me, even when I was at my worst. I haven't had much family, and there is nothing I wouldn't do for them. Whether I like you or not, you are a part of that family. Just like sisters who don't get along, you and I can go at each other, but *no one* messes with you or me, or they're dealing with the other one."

"You're serious?" Katie asked, speechless.

"What would you do if someone came after me?"

"I would hunt –" Katie stopped short. "I got it. So, you're saying you had nothing to do with the notes?"

"Why would she take photos of herself that would potentially paint a target on her?" Nick asked. "She couldn't take those pictures if she was in them."

"So, you don't think it was her anymore?" Katie asked.

"No." Nick shook his head. "She didn't do it."

"Thank you," Claire said, tears in her eyes. "I would never hurt you guys like this. Have you guys been thinking this entire time that it was me?"

"The evidence told another story," Todd pointed out.

"I understand, but if we begin to not trust those around us, then he wins."

"I agree. So, what do we do?" Todd looked to Seth.

"I think we hire a new receptionist, if she'll have the job," Seth said, looking right at Katie.

Katie looked at him, startled. "What?"

Walking over to Katie, he put his hands on her shoulders. "You are an amazing individual. We need someone at that desk who we trust."

"But, I'm supposed to be an agent."

"With your heart, do you really feel that you could do this job and not lose it? You helped Giovanni for the very same reason."

"I did."

"Your heart is already jaded. It will only get worse. You will only experience more loss and be placed in dangerous positions even worse than you already are. Please let us protect you this time, and occupy that desk?"

"I need to think about this."

"Think about it and let us know."

"Um, in the meantime, we need to hide her," Claire said, reading the transcript on the screen in front of her. "A contract has been put out on her."

"Have you located where the call went to?"

"I have the area," Claire confirmed. "Unfortunately, I can only narrow it down to the warehouse district."

Nick grabbed his phone and dialed Damian's phone number.

"Hey, Nick," Damian answered. "What's up? Usually I'm the one making the call."

"Hey, mate, has there been any recent activity in any of the warehouses down near you? Any new occupants since, say, the beginning of summer?"

"Yeah. There's been a couple. Why?"

"Give 'em to me," Nick said, grabbing a piece of paper and a pen while Damian gave him the information. "Thanks, mate," he said before he hung up the phone. "There are a couple new occupants."

"Get with Claire and get search warrants. I want these places searched top to bottom," Seth ordered. When no one moved, Seth shouted, "NOW!"

As everyone scrambled, Dana pulled Katie aside. "Normally I wouldn't even bother with mentioning this, but if I don't, I would feel as if I didn't follow through with my promise to look out for you."

Crossing her arms, Katie groaned, "What?"

"You know, it's not a bad idea if you come in as a secretary. You've been through so much in your life. Would it really be a bad idea for you to work as a receptionist? You'll still be helping the FBI, but you'll do it in a safe capacity. In the meantime, you'll also be providing a safe zone for those on this unit. Knowing they can trust the person behind that desk will let them do their job without looking over their shoulder to make sure they're not getting taken out from within. You don't think this has affected Locke's performance?" Dana challenged.

Katie glanced over to Nick, who was watching the conversation with interest. "It has," he agreed. "Without you in my life, I'm not operating as well as I should."

"Which places his life in danger," Dana finished. "In breaking up with him, it not only ripped your heart out, but his as well. In doing so, Junior handicapped and gutted both you *and* this unit. You said he was a calculating individual. You said that Giovanni told you Joey was ruthless and cunning, especially when it had to do with anyone who harmed his family. Your life is in danger. If that contract gets fulfilled, what do you think that will do to Locke?"

"Kill him," Katie said in understanding. "So, if I work here, they can hide me while they look for Joey, and keep me safe when I'm not working."

"They can keep you safe in here," Dana agreed.

"What's going on in here?" Brenda Birch demanded, as she and Dakota came into the office.

"Amber was a mole. She passed confidential information to Joey Rossi, as well as threatened the life of a federal agent and a police officer. She was an accomplice to at least those crimes, maybe more," Seth explained.

"*What*?" Brenda asked, horrified, as her face went pale. "I checked her out myself!"

"We have another option for the position. You won't even have to do a background check on her, because it's already done."

"Who?"

"Katie."

Chapter 11

Explosive Summer Night

When the units raided the warehouse district, they found everyone but Joey. When they finally found Amber in the building, there was a text message on her phone to another burn phone, warning Joey that they would be searching the warehouse district for him. So, armed with a map where there were no cameras, he took off, hiding deeper than he already was.

Dana went with Katie to the police station to talk with Chief and to empty out her locker. With an escort, that allowed Katie to relax. She felt paranoid, not sure who could potentially be working with Joey Rossi. Continuously watching every direction around her, her skin crawled with fear. Every muscle in her body was on edge.

"We need to get out of here," Katie whispered to Dana.

"Do you have everything you need from here?"

"As much as I need."

"We need to see Chief before I drop you off at the FBI."

Katie sighed. "Fine. Let's get this done and over with."

By the time they got upstairs to Chief's office, Katie was a nervous wreck. "Come in!" Chief yelled from behind his closed door. When the pair walked in, Chief gestured toward the chairs across from him. "Have a seat."

It took a little over an hour for Dana to catch the Chief up on the events of the last two days. "So, as you can see, this is the best possible position for her," Dana finished.

"While I understand that, I'm sorry to see you go," Chief said, disheartened.

"I agree, but I need to look out for myself for once," Katie explained.

"I understand. You do. You've been through a lot over the years. I hope, for your sake, that you may finally find peace."

"Me too, sir."

"Just know you have a position here if you want it. Now, you may have to go through the academy if too much time passes, but I have faith in you."

"Thank you, sir," she said, shaking his hand before the two women left the office. When they were outside in the fresh fall air, Katie admitted, "I think this will be a good move."

"I know it will," Dana said confidently. "You'll be protected, yet still be able to help from the safety of a federal building. And," Dana said, opening her car door. As soon as she did, shots rang out around them. When Dana's car window exploded as a bullet crashed through, she dove for the ground. "GET DOWN!" she shouted as loudly as she could.

Within seconds, police officers flooded the parking lot to find the shooter. Dana crawled on the ground around her car to Katie. When she got around to the other side, Katie was gone. "Oh no! Not again!"

With bullets still whizzing through the air, Dana dialed Nick's office phone. "Locke," he answered.

"Nick, gunfire erupted around us at the precinct, and now Katie's disappeared."

"She's *what*?"

"Are you hit?" An officer ran up to Dana.

"No. Find that shooter!" she ordered.

"There's multiple. The shots are coming from several directions. We've taken out two of them, but there are at least three more."

"Have you seen Officer MacKenna?"

"No. Why?"

"She was here right before the gunfire started," she said before she got on the radio. "Anyone have eyes on MacKenna?"

"Dana!" Nick snapped into the phone. "Where's Katie?"

"We don't know," she admitted. "We were getting into the car when shots rang out around us. We can't even look until…" she stopped short at the abrupt silence.

"Find her!" Nick growled and hung up.

Shoving her phone in her pocket, she stood, brushing herself off. "I plan to."

*   *   *

Ducking behind the vehicles, Katie maneuvered her way through the maze to the park across the street. She flattened herself against a tree, breathing heavily. *I can't place anyone else in danger. If they hide me, others will be in danger. The question is where to go.* Looking toward heaven, Katie whispered a prayer, "Lord, please direct my thoughts and steps. Help me to find somewhere safe. Amen."

She heard Proverbs 1:33 in response, *"But he who listens to me shall live securely, and will be at ease from the dread of evil."*

"Okay. Where am I going?" Katie whispered.

Suddenly, an arm wrapped around her body, as a hand covered her mouth. "Shhh, I'm an A.N.G.E.L., like Danny Hawk and Ethan Carson in Australia. Do you remember them?" a man asked.

With Katie's heart racing, she only nodded in response, remembering the men she met in Australia who helped her.

"My name is Mark English. I'm an American A.N.G.E.L., which stands for available to nurture God's eternal love. That's our code, so people know we are telling the truth. Are those the words they told you?"

Katie nodded again.

"I was sent to help you get to Nick Locke, and to help the two of you get away. If I let you go, are you going to run away?"

Shaking her head, she felt a sense of relief flow through her body. When he let her go, Katie whispered, "I need to know what's going to happen."

"No. You only need to know what you are told. Now, I know where he is being sent. Do you want to go to him?" a rather bulking man, who had short blond hair and blue eyes stood before her, asked.

"You know where he is?"

"No. I know where he'll be."

"How?"

"We know what we need to know. Now, I don't have a lot of time. Do you want to come with me or not? I can keep you safe from Joey Rossi, but we have to move now."

"Okay," she said, pulling her cell from her pocket. As he tucked his coat over her shoulders to cover her uniform until they could get to the safety of the woods, Katie popped the battery out before she threw it away. Then she tucked her hair into the baseball cap that he gave her as they nonchalantly made their way through the park as not to draw attention to themselves. Knowing it would take a while to get there, Katie paced herself, while keeping an eye in every direction for evidence of someone following them, while she prayed she made the right decision in leaving with Mark.

*   *   *

"Where do we start?" Seth asked, as their unit, along with several officers and Dana stood in the middle of the precinct parking lot.

"The campus?" Dakota suggested. "She knows that place like the back of her hand."

"What about Cook's?" Todd asked. "She knows Seb will hide her."

"Where would she feel safer?" Dana asked Nick. "You know her better than anyone here."

"She doesn't have any place like that. Wherever she can draw is where she feels safe."

"What if she went to run, but someone took her?" Chad proposed.

"Ugh!" Nick growled. "This will be like finding a needle in a haystack!"

"We'll spread out," Seth decided. Sending them out in groups of two, Seth and Nick were left standing there. "If she wasn't taken, where would she go?"

"She really doesn't have a safe place that I know of," Nick said, unsure.

"What about you? Wouldn't she go somewhere that you know, knowing that you would be the only one to find her? Have you ever shown her a safe place for you?"

He nodded, cautiously. "I have."

"Where?"

"C'mon, I'm driving," Nick said, running for his car with Seth on his heels.

"Where are we going?" Seth asked, getting in Nick's Explorer.

"To my safe place. You're right. If she runs, she'll run where she knows I will be the one to find her."

*   *   *

Nick and Seth pulled up to a bench that rested next to Lake Erie. "I come here to think, and she knows it because I've brought her here."

"It's quiet," Seth commented, as they walked over to the bench.

"Yep. In this extremely loud and chaotic city, there are quiet places outside. Sitting here, I listen to the waves coming in and out, and imagine that I'm at my parent's house on the ocean."

"Nice," he said, crossing his arms. "So, you can hear pretty much everything around you here."

"That's the other reason I come here."

"I see. Um," Seth looked around him when he heard a stick crack in the distance, "I think we may have company."

Both men stood and scanned the area as closely as they could, but the sun had gone down about an hour before, so light was at a minimum.

*   *   *

"Okay," Mark said, as they walked through a wooded area, "we're close. When I tell you to run, I want you to run and not look back. Got it?"

"What do you mean?" Katie whispered, left in her uniform pants, a t-shirt, and Mark's jacket. She threw her uniform top away about a mile back, and her hair was slowly seeping from the baseball cap.

"We're not alone. I'll need to see who I can take out before you make a run for it."

"You can see them?"

"Not all of them, but I see some."

"Do they have guns on Nick?" Katie asked, horrified.

"Look, you've trusted me this far, don't lose that trust now. My job is to get you here safely. I'll need to take care of a couple guys that I *can* see, and hopefully the Spirit will reveal the ones I can't."

"Your lips to God's ears," Katie breathed out.

"Amen." Taking another good look around, as they stood just inside the tree line, Mark said, "Okay, change of plan."

"Change? What? Now?" Katie panicked.

"Relax and breathe. I want you to count to twenty and then run. Do it slowly, as if you're counting the time difference between lightning and thunder in a storm. Do you understand?"

"Like, one, one thousand; two, one thousand sort of thing?"

"Right. Count to twenty. I'm going to go, um, disarm a couple of these fine young upstanding gentlemen who are positioned through here," he said, sarcasm dripping from his voice.

Katie stifled her giggle as she nodded.

"Now, know that God has an amazing plan for you. You only have to listen for His voice and follow the steps before you. Also, if someone tells you they are an A.N.G.E.L., make sure they explain to you what that means. The devil has some minions of his own that are wandering around here too.”

“Here? As in, in these woods?”

“Yes, ma’am,” he said, feeling the hair on his neck standing on end. “Now, are you ready?"

Taking a deep breath before she slowly let it out, Katie nodded. Grabbing his arm before he went to run, she said, “Thank you.”

“Your service to the Kingdom is thanks enough for me,” Mark said, and then disappeared into the shadows.

“Okay,” Katie whispered, “One, one thousand…” she continued the count until she reached, “Twenty. Ready or not, here I come.”

Seeing Nick and Seth beside the bench, Katie’s heart leaped. “He’s here!” she said, and ran as fast as her feet would go. The baseball cap flew off after a few steps, sending her hair cascading down her back. “NICK!” she shouted at the top of her lungs.

“There she is!” Nick’s face lit up when he saw her running toward them.

As she ran across to them, shots were suddenly fired from various directions in the wooded area. “Get to Katie, and get her out of here!” Seth shouted, shoving Nick toward Katie.

Grabbing her, Nick threw Katie into the back seat. When a bullet shattered his window, he felt the breeze of the bullet as it passed his face and he jumped. “Get in, Seth! We gotta get out of here!”

"Get her out of here!" Seth shouted from behind the bench, while he was firing toward the direction he saw the gunfire from.

"Get in!"

When another bullet shattered the side window of the Explorer, Katie screamed as she ducked further into the seat.

"Get her out of here! I'll cover. Go!" Seth growled.

"But –"

"GO!" Seth roared before he fired off a couple more rounds. Changing the magazine, he shouted, "Don't make me tell you again! GO!"

Tires spinning, Nick floored the vehicle to get it out of the line of fire. Seth emptied his magazine toward the wooded area as he watched his friends spin out of sight. Then, as suddenly as it started, the gunfire abruptly halted. Confused, Seth strained to see what he could, when Mark walked out of the wooded area with his hands in the air.

His empty gun trained on Mark, Seth watched him cross the area between them, his heart racing out of control. "Who are you?"

"I'm the one who got Katie here. My name is Mark. Look, I just took out several men in the wooded area. You're going to have your hands full finding them all, but they are all put down."

"As in?"

"Sleeper hold, dude! I had to be quiet about it, but you're going to have to act fast to get them all in custody before they wake up. In the meantime, I wanted to let you know that they are currently asleep. I gotta get back to work."

"I can't let you leave."

"Oh yes you can."

"I have to take you in for questioning."

"Are you going to make me put you down too?"

"You wouldn't," Seth challenged. "I'm a federal officer."

"And I'm special operations trained. I could do it in my sleep. Look, the only reason I came to you, was to tell you about the sleepers and to deliver a message."

"Which is?"

"That they are in God's hands now."

"Who?"

"Nick and Katie."

"But –"

"You'd better hurry to the sleepers. The first one I took down is over there," Mark pointed toward the left of the wooded area.

When Seth looked back to talk to Mark, he was gone. Seth looked in every direction possible, as he anxiously searched for Mark, but he seemed to have completely disappeared. Getting on his phone, he barked orders to get personnel to the scene to arrest the individuals in the woods. He would have to trust that Nick could get Katie to safety on their own.

258

Chapter 12

Summer Scramble

"I don't understand?" Ryan said, as he spoke with a panicked Seb on the other end of the phone.

"It's all over the news up here, man!" Seb explained, pacing the kitchen of Cook's Café. "They said there were two officers in the parking lot at the time of the shooting. Then Katie's face is plastered all over the screen with a number if she's found. Joey Rossi's is up there too in connection with the shooting and her disappearance. I have *no idea* what's going on. Do you?"

"We'll be up there as soon as we can get a ticket," Ryan said, and hung up. He turned to Ty, and explained, "We need to get a hold of Nick. Do you have his number handy?"

"Yeah. Why?"

"Because it looks like The Hunter's found Katie, and now she's missing."

* * *

"What do you *mean* both are missing?" Ryan demanded on the phone with Seth as they waited for their plane to board.

"I *mean* that no one can find Nick, Katie, *or* Joey Rossi."

Ryan swore before he snapped, "You're the FBI. How do *you* lose people? Nick is one of yours. Katie was going to be one of yours. And Joey Rossi? You've had *months* to find him! Are you telling me that you're that incompetent?"

"I'm telling you that we are searching frantically for them."

Claire nervously cleared her throat as she stood in front of Seth's desk in the office. "Sir?"

"What?" Seth snapped.

"Is that Ryan?"

"Yes. Why?"

"I, uh, you may want to mute that."

"What? No!" Ryan growled. "We're fixin' to get on this plane in less than ten minutes. *Do not* put us in the dark that long!"

"Here." Seth put the phone on speaker. When he did, the entire room went silent. "Whatever you have to say, if it pertains to Nick and Katie, they need to hear this."

"You may want to change your mind," Claire warned.

"Does it pertain to Nick and Katie?"

"Afraid so."

"What is it already?" Ryan snapped over the phone. Hearing his flight being called, he added, "C'mon, we're boarding. What is it?"

"Nick's SUV was found, um, at the Whiskey Island Marina," Claire started.

"A little quicker, Claire," Seth hinted. "Their plane is boarding."

"Sir, there were two charred bodies in the fried vehicle," she said. A few gasps were heard in the room, otherwise it was silent. "They haven't confirmed it yet, sir, but the size of the bodies state that they may be Nick and Katie."

"Are you sure?" Seth asked, looking pale and shaken. As his heart sunk into his stomach, he had to force the vomit to stay down.

Wiping a couple of tears from her eyes, Claire continued, "They said that the vehicle was lit on fire. It was pretty well scorched before fire was even alerted. I'm, um, sorry, Seth. Really, I am. Ryan, Ty, I'm really sorry."

"I, uh, we'll be there in about five hours," Ryan squeaked out before he hung up his phone.

As soon as the line went dead, shouts erupted from every corner of the office, demanding answers from Todd, Dakota, Chad, Eugene, and Emma toward Seth.

Seth hung his head in his hands, and shook it. "I don't know what to say."

"Are you telling me that's real?" Dakota demanded as everyone surrounded Seth's desk. "Are you telling me that Nick and Katie are really dead?"

"Did Joey Rossi really take them both out?" Todd shouted.

"Is this a ruse?" Eugene asked.

"*What*?" Seth asked, stunned.

"I'm fixin' to take someone out if this is some kind of game for you!" Chad yelled. "I don't find anything about this even remotely funny!"

"Neither do I!" Seth defended himself.

Emma slammed her hands on the desk to get Seth's attention. When he looked up at her, she very sternly, but calmly explained, "I have worked in this office for years. I *know* not everything is as it seems. If you tell me, beyond a shadow of a doubt that Nick and Katie were in that vehicle, then I will believe you. If you tell me you're not sure, you'd better get an answer as soon as possible."

"They're taking the bodies to the morgue downtown," Claire interrupted. "Dr. Sandy Simmons is heading there now to help with the autopsy in order to confirm or rule that fact out."

Turning back to Seth, Emma pressed, "I want to hear it from you."

"I don't want to answer that until we get a decisive answer from Sandy," Seth explained. "I swear to you that the last time I saw Nick and Katie, they were speeding down the road to get away from that gun fight I was in by the lake. I have no more of an idea of what's going on than you do."

"Did you have anything to do with this?" Emma clarified her question.

"With burning Nick and Katie?" he asked, horrified. "Are you kidding?"

"No. I'm not."

"Does it *look* like I know what's going on? I can't believe you're asking me that."

"I can't believe you're dodging her question," Dakota pointed out. "They weren't in that vehicle, were they?"

"I don't know."

"Stop it!" Todd shouted, his tone sharp. When Seth looked at him, stunned, he explained, "I cannot believe you're dodging Emma's questions. Did you, or did you not set this up?"

"You seriously think I set up burning Katie and Nick in a vehicle? Nick's my best friend!" Seth said in his defense, as he stood, resting his hands on the desk. "Do you honestly *think* I would make it so I could never see him or Katie ever again? You *do* realize that's what would happen if I set them up like this? That desk will sit empty, and I will never see or hear from him. I was the one who ordered Nick to go and get Katie out of the line of fire! If I even had an inkling that it would be the last time I would ever see him, don't you think my last words to him would be a lot more kind and not angry. It kills me to think I won't see my brother again! Wouldn't it be easier to just set them in a safe house and hunt Junior down?"

"It would," Emma said, relaxing her stance. Letting out a slow breath of air to clear her mind, she started again, "If you had nothing to do with this, then Junior is the one more than likely responsible. If that's the case, what do you want us to do?"

Anger flashed through his eyes before Seth growled, "Pursue him with extreme prejudice!"

*   *   *

"Find him!" Chief growled before leaving the room full of officers and detectives, floored by the news about Katie and Nick, and the update on the joint search for Joey Rossi.

263

"Where do we start?" one officer asked.

"Check with every person you know on the street," Andy suggested. "Get his photo circulating. Cameras or not, our snitches are the best resource we have out there."

"The FBI raided a couple warehouses where they thought he was, but he escaped by the time they got there," Dana explained.

"Then, let's get out there, folks. We're not going to find the little miscreant in here," Andy pointed out. As people dispersed, Andy grabbed Dana's arm. "Can we talk?"

"Yeah."

"Let's go search together. Both of us know Katie, and you know Nick from working with him. We're going to need all the information we can get to find them."

"I agree."

"Then, where do we start?"

"Nick has an informant in the warehouse district."

"Who?"

"He's a runaway, named Damian."

*   *   *

"C'mon, it's dinner for information," Andy coaxed.

"I don't know who you are," Damian argued.

"I'm Officer D'Antonio and this is Detective Petrovich," Andy explained. "There's a diner right over there," he pointed it out. "We can go right over there and sit at an outside table. Look, kid, I'm not going to take you in or anything. We're only trying to find Katie, Nick, and Joey Rossi."

"Mainly Joey," Dana clarified. "If we find him, pretty sure we're going to find Nick and Katie."

"Joey Rossi took Nick and Katie?" Damian asked, his face draining of color. "Nick and Katie are with *him*?"

Hunger and shock taking over, Damian passed out. As Andy caught him, he ordered Dana, "Go get him some food."

"Right. Back in a few," she said, jogging toward the diner.

"C'mon, Damian, we need you," Andy said, tapping his cheek.

"What? Where?" Damian shook his head to clear it. "What happened?"

"You passed out on us. We need you to focus, though. Dana's going to get you some food, but I need you to focus and tell me what you can remember about Joey Rossi."

Sitting up, Damian rested against the wall. With a look of fear, he asked, "Are you telling me that Joey Rossi has Nick and Katie?"

"No. I'm telling you that they're missing, and that Joey Rossi has something to do with it."

Slamming his fist onto the ground beside him, Damian swore. "If he's gone, then I'm really in trouble."

"No, you're not. If he's gone, then I will take care of you until you can get on your feet. Katie's told me about you. I know your intentions to be self-sustaining are true. Let me help you."

"Really? You would do that?"

"Yes, but right now, I need you to help *me*."

"Right," he said, clearing his mind. "Joey Rossi."

As Damian explained the warehouse situations over the last several months, Dana brought everyone dinner. When he finished, Damian explained, "After that call from Nick, the FBI swarmed the area, but from what I could see, Rossi was gone."

"So, you've *seen* him down here, then?" Dana asked.

"Oh yeah. If I would have known you guys were still looking for him, I would have told Nick, but I thought that was over with. I haven't heard anything since the explosion, until Dakota showed me his picture at the raid."

"Do you know where he went?"

"No, but I can tell you that he doesn't quite look like the picture did. He had a thick beard, and his hair was raggedy. When I saw him, he also had on sunglasses and a black baseball cap."

"Does he still resemble the picture?"

"Yeah, but you have to really look at him to see it."

"So, you're saying he could walk right by us and we might not see him?"

"Exactly."

Tucking her legs beneath her, Dana thought for a few moments. "Can you tell me where else you've seen him besides the warehouses?"

"Yeah. He would go to lunch over at the diner."

"Really? Anywhere else that you saw?"

"Not really."

"Okay, here's my card," Andy said, handing him a card with his cell phone number on it. "If you have anything that comes to mind, let me know. Also, if there is anything you need, or anything you may think I want to know, give me a call. Of course, I'll be happy to take you out to eat at times as well."

"Here's the number of the cell Nick gave me." Damian wrote the number down. "It's a pay-by-use, so I have to use it sparingly."

"Don't worry about that. Next time we meet, I'll give you another card."

"Thanks, man."

"Thank you. Again, let me know of *anything*, no matter how insignificant it may be."

"Got it."

*   *   *

As Dana walked into the FBI office, she immediately felt the heaviness of the room. "What's going on? Have you guys found him yet?"

"Nope," Seth said, not taking his eyes off the computer.

"We can't find him either. What's going on in here? Have you guys found Nick and Katie yet?" When he looked up at her, Dana saw the pain in Seth's eyes. "Did something happen to them?"

"We're, um, determining that as we speak."

He jumped when she slammed her hands on his desk. "*Look at me!*" she demanded.

"I am trying to hold it together here!" Seth snapped.

"So am I. She was lost under *my* care. I take that beyond seriously. You are holding something back. *What happened?*"

"They found a vehicle burned all the way to the shell, with two bodies inside," Claire spoke up.

"Claire!" Seth growled. "You need to keep your tongue in check."

"She has clearance," Claire pointed out. "And, she's right. You had a deal with her. You *are* holding back. She has a right to know."

Seth sighed, knowing she was right.

Dana gulped. "Was it them?"

"We're waiting for the call to confirm or deny that."

"Cut with the formalities!" Dana hissed. "What does your gut tell you?"

Dropping his head in his hands, Seth felt like he was going to throw up. "I don't want to go there right now."

"What does your gut tell you?" she insisted.

He reluctantly looked up her. "I'm afraid to find out. Every time that phone rings, I feel like I'm going to get horrible news."

Crouching next to him, she rested her hand on his arm. She quietly asked, "Do you feel that they were in that vehicle?"

Glancing around the room, he let out a slow breath of air. "I really don't know what to hope for. If it was them, then they were together when they died. If it's not, then there's a strong possibility that Junior has them. If that's the case, then they are in even greater danger than before. He can torture them for days. To be honest, I'm terrified of both scenarios."

"I understand."

"I don't think you do. Nick is my best friend. Katie is close to my heart. Yes, they were broken up at the time, but I would still do anything for her, and you know it."

"I do."

"Then, know that I am doing everything possible to find them…and Junior."

When Seth's phone rang, everyone jumped. "Are you going to answer it?" Dana asked when the phone rang a second time.

"I'm afraid to."

"Answer it or I will," Emma threatened.

"Simmons," Seth said, answering the phone on speaker.

"Seth, it's Sandy," his sister's voice came over the phone.

"Have you finished the autopsies?"

"Yes."

"And?"

"Until we get the dental records, we can't be one hundred percent sure, but Seth, um, we found Katie's necklace on one of the bodies, and Nick's watch that you gave him on the other body. I'm afraid that after everything we've examined, it's both of our determinations that the bodies are of Nick Locke and Katie MacKenna."

As soon as she said it, everyone in the room looked as if they were punched in the stomach. Claire threw her hand over her mouth as she ran from the room for the bathroom.

"You're sure?" Seth said, a single tear flowing down his cheek as his hands shook.

"I'm afraid so. We're waiting for the dental confirmation, but yes. I'm really sorry, Seth. He was like a brother to me, and I loved Katie too."

"Thanks, Sandy. I'll, uh, talk to you later."

"Okay. Again, I'm really sorry. Please pass my condolences to your team."

"I will."

"I love you, Seth, and wish I had different news."

"I love you too. Talk to you soon," he said, and hung up the phone. "Does, uh," Seth dropped his head into his hands, "does that answer your question, Dana?"

"Yes. I'll, um, pass this along to the Chief. We'll continue our citywide search for Joey Rossi," she said, standing. Before she left the office, she said to the room, "I am really sorry to have heard that news. Please know our entire precinct is hurting as much as you are. We will use that anger to find the person responsible for this," she said, and left the room.

When she was gone, Emma stood. "I'll, uh, go after Claire," she said, and left the room.

"We're going to go look for Junior," Chad sniffed, while he grabbed his coat, hiding that he was crying.

"We shall contact you as soon as we acquire some information," Eugene added before they left the office, leaving only Todd, Dakota, and Seth in the office.

Todd and Dakota walked over to Seth's desk. While Todd hopped onto the counter behind his desk, Dakota leaned on the corner of Seth's desk with his arms crossed, both looking down at Seth. "What?" Seth growled. "I'm not in the mood for games."

"Neither are we," Todd said sternly.

"What is your problem? We just lost Nick and Katie!"

"Did we?" Dakota probed. "Ya see, I have learned over the years to trust my instincts. You, me, and Todd are the only ones in this room. I swear on my own life, and that of my family, that if you tell me they're still alive, I will not tell a soul."

"Same here," Todd agreed. "You have my word. I also swear on my life, and that of my family, that I will not tell a soul."

"They're dead! Did you not hear Sandy on the phone?" Seth shouted. "I loved that man like a brother. Knowing I will never see him again tears me up inside. What would *you* do if Todd were taken out?"

Looking toward Todd, Dakota nodded in understanding. "I'm sorry. You're right. It may be more of a wishful thinking."

"Trust me. I wish with all my heart that it wasn't the truth, but they're…." He dropped his head in his hands, unable to finish.

"I'm sorry that I accused you of falsifying this," Dakota apologized. "I can't imagine losing Todd. He's my brother from another mother. We're as close as you and Nick are. The idea of not hearing Nick's Australian Strine every day, just…I can't imagine that this is what took him out, man. I mean, I know we will all have our time, but…" he sighed, shaking his head.

"I feel the same," Todd said, his eyes red. While the tears threatened to overflow, he refused to let them fall. "This seems so surreal."

"This is going to rock the entire building," Dakota added. "He was well liked and admired."

"We need to, um," Seth wiped his face off, "We have to find Junior. He's the one ultimately responsible for taking both of them."

"Can we?" Dakota questioned. "If he doesn't want to be found, *can* he be found?"

"Even our wonder brain behind the computer screen, Claire, hasn't been able to find him in months," Todd reminded them.

"Give me twenty-four hours and I will find that boy!" Claire growled, coming into the office with Emma, her eyes puffy and stained with tears.

"You haven't been able to find him for months," Todd said again.

Claire narrowed her eyes. "I *will* find him."

"Do your best. That's all I ask," Seth said, hoping to calm the emotions that were flying around the room.

"That's not good enough anymore." Claire sat down at her computer. "He's messed with my family. He *will* be found."

*   *   *

"Look, I understand why you came straight up here," Seth said to Ty and Ryan, as they sat in a conference room in the federal building. They went to the FBI office directly from the airport. "My sister, Sandy, is a doctor, and she helped with the autopsies. Knowing how well she knew both Nick and – "

"Whoa! *Knew*, as in past tense?" Ty questioned.

"Sandy called about an hour ago, confirming that the bodies found in the torched vehicle were Katie and Nick's."

"You're sure?" Ryan asked. "You're one hundred percent sure?"

"We're ninety-nine point nine percent sure," Seth explained. "We're waiting on the dental records to be one hundred percent sure."

Ryan ran his fingers through his hair before he slammed into the back of the chair with his elbows and crossed his arms. "You guys promised to keep her safe."

"We did what we could. She was fired upon in a police station parking lot. We can't be everywhere at once."

"What was she doing with Nick?" Ty asked, sorting through all the information he heard since their arrival.

"What do you mean?"

"She and Nick were broken up, as far as anyone else knew. What was she doing with Nick?"

"You and I both know they may have been technically broken up, but if she were in danger, he would move heaven and earth to get to her and get her safe," Seth pointed out.

"Is there something you're not telling us?" Ty asked.

"Yes," Seth admitted.

"What?"

"I talked with Sandy privately. She explained that they were shot prior to the vehicle being set on fire," he admitted.

"So, you're telling me that she somehow got to Nick. Then they ran for a marina, only to get shot there, and their vehicle set ablaze?" Ty verbally sorted through the information.

"Yes."

"And, y'all are still looking for Joey Rossi?"

"Yes."

"Then, we'll contact her father and get permission to take her back to Oklahoma with us."

"You don't want her buried near Nick?"

"They're not really in there, and you know it. They're in Heaven, with God. She would want her body buried near her mother," Ty explained.

"I understand."

"If you really do understand, then you would have protected her better!" Ryan snarled.

"How *dare* you!" Seth roared. Both guys looked at him in wide-eyed shock, as he stood and slammed his fists on the table. "Nick Locke was like a brother to me. We went through hell and back out in the field, literally dodging death at every turn. I find it highly offensive that you even *remotely* think I would not look after him or Katie as much as I would look after my twin sister or any of my blood brothers."

"Obviously you didn't," Ryan shot.

"We're finished here," Seth said coldly, as he walked to the door where there was a security officer standing by. "Take them to the entrance and *do not* let them back in."

"But –"

"No!" Seth cut Ryan off. "I *will not* stand by while you insult me or my brothers and sisters in this building who lay our lives on the line each day. Katie knew the risks, and she agreed to the circumstances prior to meeting with Lucca Rossi. We have done everything in our power to protect them both, but it wasn't enough. Our hearts are broken, and so are yours. Please contact Mr. MacKenna, and see to your friend's body, while I contact my brother's family to do the same."

"Know that you and your co-workers are in our prayers," Ty compassionately said before leaving the room, closely followed by a still brooding Ryan.

"Thank you."

"And, thank you for serving our country," Ty expressed, and then he and Ryan followed the security officer without another word.

Chapter 13

Summer Tears

"The first to say a few words, is her childhood friend Ryan Darcy," Pastor Eric Davis said, and then took his spot next to his wife, Serenity, as everyone stood around Katie's grave.

"I've struggled over the last several days to find an answer to why Katie was taken from us. I even went so far as to try to forget her. I tried not to remember her smile, her laughter, her drawings that showed her heart and soul. I tried not to remember holding her hand at her mother's graveside. I tried not to remember all the times we spent together through our younger years. I tried not to remember walking her to school, and going out with her on Friday nights to the movies before high school started. I did my best to forget the time I turned my back on her, and yet, she turned around and forgave me." Tears slowly crawled down Ryan's cheeks, as he admitted, "In the still of the night, I still wake up thinking she's still here, until I see the evidence in front of me. The world has lost a strong leader today. Through her circumstances, where normal people would crumble and fall, she always came through stronger than ever. So," he sniffed and wiped the tears that continuously streamed down his face, "I refuse to forget her. I refuse to let her memory be erased. I will do everything in my power to ensure this town never forgets this brave young lady," he said, and took his seat beside Katie's dad.

Eric stood. "Next is Tyler Bennett," he said, and sat back down next to Serenity.

Ty wheeled himself to the end of Katie's casket, and rested his hand on it. "We know she's not in there. She's where there's no more pain...no more anger...no more hurt. She was a fighter. She fought to start over after a tumultuous childhood. She fought to show the world that she would not be silent, nor would she stand by and let someone else be run over. She fought to continue her dream of helping people in any way she could. At one point, she even gave up her love to save his life. To me, that speaks volumes to her character. While it tore her up inside, she refused to put him in any further danger. Their love was strong, though, and no one could separate them. In the end, she died sitting next to him. I only hope and pray to find a young lady with as much strength and passion as she even remotely had. I pray that while we bury her body today, that her spirit will live on in the drawings and memories she left behind. I take solace in knowing that she and Nick will be together in Heaven today, and I'm sure she's introduced him to Jax and Anna." While he chuckled at first, sobbing quickly took over, to the point that he couldn't stop. "I'm sorry I couldn't be there for you. I'm sorry you had to fight alone."

"C'mon, Ty," Eden gently tugged him, until he went back with him.

"And finally, her father, Brent MacKenna," Eric said before taking his place beside Serenity again.

Brent placed a single red rose on her casket, covered by an American flag, before he kissed it. Standing near the end of her casket, he struggled with the words that wanted to pour from his soul. "I buried my Meg many long years ago, and stood right there," he pointed toward Meg's grave, "doing my best to explain to those in attendance who Meg was and what she meant to me, while my little Katie bug stood right there, holding Ryan's hand. I remember it like it was yesterday, but alas, it wasn't." He sighed, looking at her picture that was beside the casket. "Look, I know Katie has touched each one of those here in attendance. I am grateful for those officers and agents were able to make it today as well," he said to Dana, Andy, Chief, Director Shaw and his wife, Seth, Dakota, Todd, Emma, Chad, Eugene, and Officer Herman Williams. "It blesses my heart to know that she has touched so many lives. I only wish she were around to see it." Doing his best to control his crying, he continued, "I didn't do right by her in the beginning after I lost Meg, but she still found it in her heart to give me grace and forgave me. She helped restore our relationship, and for that, I can never thank the good Lord enough." Crossing his arms, he pushed forward, "I'm with Ryan in saying that I have done my best to forget her, but ya just can't. Her laughter still rings in my ears. Her smile still lights my heart. Her last email will forever remain in my inbox. Her drawings will remain on my walls. And, her spirit will remain in my heart. I have now lost both of the most beautiful ladies in the world. They were entrusted to me for a short time, and for that, I will never be able to express my gratitude enough to the good Lord." Looking toward the sky, Brent pleaded, "Father, please help me! I don't know…" his voice trailed off, as his sobs took over.

Serenity got Brent and took him back to his seat, as Eric went back up. "We are at a loss today. This brilliant, strong young lady had her secrets. She did her best to protect those she loved, even with her own life. I do take solace in the fact that she and Nick were together in the end. I cherish the knowledge that she is currently with our Lord and Savior at this very minute. It's moments like this, that I remember the words in Ecclesiastes 3, which tells us, 'There is a time for everything, and a season for every activity under the heavens. A time to be born and a time to die, a time to plant and a time to uproot, a time to kill and a time to heal, a time to tear down and a time to build, a time to weep and a time to laugh, a time to mourn and a time to dance.' Today, we mourn Katie's life. We weep, yet we hear her laughter in our minds, and know that her heart is dancing right now in the presence of the Lord. There'll be days where we will struggle to make it through. No one can take the place you each have in your heart for Katie, but God can help heal the wound, leaving only the scar that bears the knowledge of what the world lost today. Try to remember her laughter and passion for life. Don't let the world lose her heart or her drawings that showed the beauty she held onto in the world, even through her darkest times. Let us pray," he said, and everyone bowed their heads. "Lord, You give each but one life to live for You. This young life was taken too early as far as we're concerned, but You are the One who holds the ultimate plan. As we each struggle to answer the question of why she was taken so soon, we must focus on the fact that You have a plan and a purpose. We know that whatever is done in Your name will never die. And it's that promise that we hold You to. Please do not let her memory fade, or her life will have been in vain. Thank You for the blessing and gift You have given us in having her in our lives for the time that she was here. We ask your forgiveness for the anger and frustration we are dealing with in losing her so soon. Thank You, Father, for the knowledge that we can come to You when we need to. I pray for a blanket of peace and comfort to be placed around each one here. I ask for You to allow us to band together as we help each other through this difficult time. Thank You for providing each other to help when we don't think we can face the day. In Jesus' most precious name I pray, Amen."

When he finished, Chief Anderson got in front of everyone and did 'last call' with her badge number, closely followed by the ring of the bell. As everyone left, they placed a rose on Katie's casket.

Gathering at Brent's home afterward, they shared stories about Katie. Some brought tears to their eyes, while others allowed them to laugh or share her drawings that were strategically placed throughout the room.

When the last person left, Ty stayed and sat with Brent in the living room. "You know why I'm still here, right?" Ty asked.

"I do. And I appreciate it. It's days like this that I feel crushed beyond belief. It brings back memories of the loss of my Meg. You don't know how badly I want to grab that bottle and drink these feelings away."

"I do. Trust me."

Looking up, with tears streaming down his cheeks, he begged, "Please! Please tell me this is some sort a' nightmare, and that I'll wake up to find my Katie Bug is still alive?"

"I wish I could. With every bone in my body, I wish I could. And I'm with you. I want a drink so bad, I can taste it, but God had left us with each other to help carry the other one through. He did not restore you with His grace to have you crumble when things suddenly go south."

"Go south? Katie is gone! She's *never* comin' back!"

"I know!"

"Why?" He sobbed. "Why did He take her? What did she do to deserve bein' burned to death?"

"I honestly wish I had an answer. I wish I could tell you, but I don't understand it myself. All I know, is that the world lost a beautiful heart today."

"Death. Why does it sting? Why do evil people continue to live, while good people die? I want so badly for her to come back to me. I know I did her wrong, but for the last few years we have been doing well. She forgave me."

"That's right. She did. Now you need to live for her."

"My family line will die with me."

"But your family's heart will live on through whatever you choose to do. Today, from this moment on, the choices you make can make a difference in another person's life. Just like Eric made a difference in your life, your legacy can live on in the lives you touch. Make a choice to make a difference. You didn't deal well with Meg's death. You're a new man today. You have to make smart choices to face things differently than you have in the past. Choose to make a difference."

"Is that possible?"

"There are tons of things you can do. Go to the soup kitchens. Do a work in the church. Go find a charity and volunteer your time. There are so many things you can do that can make a difference in someone else's life."

"How do I start?"

"We start in the morning. Your new life starts in the morning. Just like the world is fresh and new, so will you be. In the meantime, I'm not leaving you until I know you're in stable spirits. It's in the quiet that we make poor decisions."

"You don't need to."

"Oh yes I do! I need to do this for you, as much as for me." Resting his hand on Brent's knee, he explained, "I'm hurting at the core level just as much as you are. I loved Katie. I loved her probably more than I should have. I need to be here to keep you accountable, as much as you need to keep me accountable." Pulling his challenge coin from his pocket, he set it on the table. "Both of our futures depend on us relying on each other, and in turn relying on God. Are you up for the challenge? I know God is."

"I am, brother. Let's do this."

*   *   *

"Are you sure you don't want us to come with you?" Claire asked Seth as he waited to go into the terminal.

Taking a deep breath to control the emotions that continuously wanted to overflow since he heard the confirmation from Sandy, Seth explained, "No. This is something I need to do myself. Nick and I were close. While I appreciate you guys coming down here to send us off, Katie's funeral and the memorial service for Nick were hard enough. I really need to take him home by myself."

"When are you going to be back?" Emma asked, wiping her tears for what seemed like the umpteenth time that day.

"I really don't know. I'll stay in contact with Director Shaw. I need to be there for his parents and grandparents. I don't want to put a timetable for this. I feel like we're going to need to help each other through this. Without them, I don't think I'll be able to heal. I can't look at that empty desk for another day right now. I just can't."

"Look, man, we do know how you feel. We're all close in that office," Dakota reminded him. "But, as you pointed out to me, if anything happened to Todd, only then will I truly know how it feels."

"I miss his colorful vernacular," Eugene admitted.

"Is that…is that an attempt at emotion?" Claire asked, stunned.

"He grew on me," Eugene admitted.

"I'll miss the big lug," Chad expressed. "It added for some fun sayings around the group with my Texan, Eugene's pompous vocabulary, and Nick's colorful Aussie lingo. I am really sorry he's gone. Things will not be the same without him."

"I agree," Emma added. "Things won't be the same."

Shoving his hands in his pockets, Seth looked around. "They won't. Look, I need to go…preferably before I lose it in the middle of an airport," he said, wiping his eyes.

After everyone gave him a hug, Seth made his way through security. His heart broke at the thought of never seeing Nick again. *Could he really go through another funeral? The memorial service when they placed his star on the wall was bad enough. Would this help, or hurt him worse than he already was hurting?*

Looking toward heaven as he made his way to the gate, he said a prayer for the first time in his life, "Look, if You're really there like Nick told me You were, I need You. I know You don't know me, but I hope to one day know You. If you could possibly send me someone to help me find You, I would appreciate it. Until then, I feel extremely lost. Thanks," he said, sitting down to wait for his plane.

"You're looking a little rough, friend," an older gentleman said in the seat next to him.

"I just lost my best friend, and now I have to take him back home," he admitted.

"The name's Colonel Ethan O'Donnell," the Colonel put his hand out. "And you are?"

"Colonel? As in the military?"

"Yes, sir."

"Thank you for your service," Seth said, shaking his hand. "I'm Seth Simmons."

"Pleasure to meet you Seth. Are ya headed all the way to Australia?"

"Yep."

"First class?"

"Yeah."

The Colonel showed him his ticket. "Looks like we're travelling the same route."

"Looks like we're actually sitting next to each other," Seth pointed out. "What are the odds?"

"Yeah. What are the odds?" The Colonel smirked. "God has a funny way of making things work out for the good of those around if they only pay attention."

"What does that mean?"

"Did you not just pray for guidance from the Lord?"

Seth narrowed his eyes. "How do you know that?"

"Because I was put in this place to answer your questions about Him, by Him."

"Are you serious?"

"Yep. You've already met a friend of mine," he pointed out.

"Really? Who?"

"Mark English."

As soon as the Colonel said his name, Seth looked at him in shock. "Mark was real?"

"Yep. Real as you and me. He's already filled me in on what happened."

Sitting back in his seat, Seth crossed his arms in front of him. "What do you mean he filled you in? I find this very unsettling."

"I'm sure you do, but why does it surprise you when the Lord actually answers your prayers?"

"Why does He care about me at all?"

"He cares about everyone. If He didn't, He wouldn't have sent His Son for you."

"What do you mean? Who is His Son?"

"Jesus."

"I've heard Nick talk about this Jesus, but I don't really know much about Him."

"Well, then, I guess it's a good thing that we have at least twenty-two hours for me to tell you about Him."

Seth couldn't help the chuckle that escaped him. "Okay. I give. Obviously, I was meant to run into you. At this point, I don't know what else to do but to go with the flow. I've lost one of the people closest to me. He was like a brother."

"Nick?"

"Yes."

"Ya know, people are put in our life for a reason. We don't always know why, but I promise you that if his death brings you to the Lord, Nick would be totally okay with what happened."

"What do you mean?"

"If you come to a saving knowledge of Jesus Christ through his death, Nick would be thrilled. It's each of our goals, as one of His, to bring others to Jesus' message of love, grace, and mercy."

"What's the message?"

"Jesus Christ came down from Heaven. He lived here among us, leaving us an example to follow. He made strong friendships, developed disciples, and performed many miracles and blessings while here. Then came the time He knew was coming. While He prayed in the garden after having supper with His apostles, Judas, one of His inner circle, betrayed Him for thirty pieces of silver. Judas sold Jesus out for money. As a matter of fact, when the soldiers arrived in the garden, Judas betrayed Him with a kiss on the cheek."

"Seriously?"

"Oh, that's not the worst of it. They took Him into custody, and beat Him within an inch of His life with a cat of nine tails. Do you know what that is?"

"Yes," Seth said, feeling horrified at the direction of the story.

"While He was getting beaten, His best friend was in the courtyard denying that he ever knew Him. As a matter of fact, Peter denied that he knew Jesus three times, just as Jesus told him he would. Would you ever deny knowing Nick?"

"Never!"

"Peter told Jesus the same thing. They were as close as you and Nick were."

"Why would he do that?"

"Because he was afraid for his life."

Seth shook his head.

"Anyway, back to the story. So, while Peter was in the courtyard, the soldiers beat Jesus with the cat of nine tails so badly that His flesh was torn from the bone." The Colonel knew Seth was hanging on his every word, so he pressed forward, "Before the blood dried, they placed a purple cloak on His back, signifying royalty. Because Jesus professed to be King of the Jews, they mocked Him by placing the purple cloak on His back, and shoved a crown with three-inch thorns on His head.

Now, when the blood dried, they tore the cloak off His skin, ripping it all over again. They shredded the cloak and made a lottery game out of it. And, if that wasn't enough humiliation and agony, they made Him carry the cross they were about to kill Him on through the streets of Jerusalem on the day of His death, amongst people who were mocking Him and spitting on Him. He was so battered and beaten, though, the soldiers had to pull someone from the crowd to carry it the rest of the way. When they arrived, they nailed His hands and feet to the cross with three inch spikes before placing the cross in an upright position."

"They killed Him?"

"Yes."

"I thought He was supposed to be alive?"

"Just a minute. I'll get there. Allow me a moment to share His heart first?"

"Go ahead."

"Ya see, He wasn't up there alone. There were two criminals hanging on either side of Him. While one continued to mock Jesus, the other told that guy to shut up. Right there, in His last minutes, one of the men asked Jesus to forgive him of his sins. And, do you know what Jesus did?"

"Probably forgave him."

"Not only did He do that, but He also promised the man that on that very day he would be in paradise in Heaven with Him. While He was dying, He cared enough for that man to forgive him. Know what else He did?"

Seth shook his head.

"He made sure His mother was taken care of. He gave His mother to His best friend, John."

"Really?"

"Yep. Even in His dying minutes, He wanted to make sure His people were cared for. He even made sure *you* were cared for."

"How?"

"He took *your* sin on His body. He paid the penalty for any sin you would ever commit on this earth. As a matter of fact, He did this for the entire world. There was so much sin on Him, that His own Father, the Almighty God, turned His back on His own Son."

"Why did He do it then?"

"Because Jesus loves you. He loves me. He took our sins on His body so we could enjoy the paradise of Heaven when we pass from this world, just as your friend is right now."

"But, if Nick was one of Jesus', why would He take him so soon? He was a great agent, and an even better man. There aren't many like him."

"I understand that, more than you know. I have lost a lot of good men through the years, but I know I will see them again."

"That's what Nick said."

"And if you're one of His, you will see him, too."

"Do you really think this Jesus will forgive me for all I've done? As an agent, I've killed people. From what I understand, that's one of the big sins."

The Colonel chuckled. "Well, first of all, it does say, 'Thou shall not kill,' but that more pertains to murder. When you killed, pretty sure it was either in self-defense, or in defense of someone else."

"Yes."

"Okay. Having said that, sin, is sin, is sin, my man. Just because you sin differently than someone else, doesn't make it any less of a sin than another. Jesus paid the penalty for *all* sin. When He died, He took it all. Don't you understand what He did for you?"

"More than you know," Seth said, remembering when Nick ran out after the gunrunner so no one else on the team would, and he ended up in a coma.

"The story's not over though, brother."

"There's more?"

"Yeah. You mentioned earlier that you thought Jesus was still alive."

"Right."

"He is. Ya see, He did die on that cross that day so long ago. However, He wasn't done yet. He fought back from death and won. Three days later, just as He predicted, He was raised from the dead. And do you know what He did as one of the first things?"

"I'm curious. I would imagine it wasn't getting a steak dinner."

The Colonel chuckled. "Nope. It wasn't a steak dinner. As a matter of fact, He found Peter, and forgave him three times, therefore negating Peter's denial of Him. Ya see, Jesus knew how deeply that affected Peter, and Jesus wanted to make sure Peter knew how much he meant to Him."

"That's pretty cool."

"That's the heart of Jesus," the Colonel pointed out. "His heart is what makes Him who He is. He only wants your heart in return."

"What do you mean?"

"He wants you to accept His gift of salvation. He wants to show you a life of love and purpose. He can do great things with you and through you, all you have to do is ask."

Just then, their plane was called for boarding.

Looking from the gate, to the Colonel, he quickly said, "We have to board, but as soon as we find our seats, I want to pray and accept Jesus' gift. I want to ask Him to forgive me of my sins. I've heard enough over the last few years to know what I want…and I want Him."

"Perfect! See you on the plane." The Colonel got up and made his way over to the line.

Standing, Seth whispered, "Thank you," before he headed toward the gate.

Chapter 14

Endless Summer

The Colonel and Seth talked throughout most of the trip, only stopping to take power naps. Seth was like a sponge, soaking in as much information from this seasoned veteran Christian as he could. He knew he would need it to face the upcoming days.

"Look, man, I can honestly say that I've been where you are. I've walked this walk more times than I care to count," the Colonel said, as they stood to exit the plane. "What you're about to do, will bring a sense of peace to those who love Nick."

"I know. Despite what I'm about to do in delivering him to his family, Nick gave me a gift I can never thank him for."

"Yes, you can. When you see him again, you can thank him yourself."

"Right. I'll see him in Heaven."

"Don't think he won't be looking out for you wherever he is," the Colonel pointed out as they walked down the terminal.

"I know. This is going to break my heart, but I know he's in a much better place."

"You'll be stronger for having walked through this."

"Here's hoping."

*   *   *

The Colonel waited with him to get through customs, and for the casket. Once they were through all of the security checks, they headed out to the vehicle that contained Nick's casket.

"Thank you for walking with me through this," Seth said, appreciatively. "This is not easy, and I'm grateful you were with me."

"Oh, I'm not leaving you yet."

"What does that mean?"

"Colonel!" Danny Hawk yelled from the parking lot.

"There's our ride."

"What do you mean?" Seth asked, his heart racing.

"Do you really think God would make you walk this alone?" the Colonel asked, as two men walked toward them.

"Colonel?" Seth asked.

"Relax, Seth. These guys are A.N.G.E.L.s, like me."

"Welcome to 'Stralia." Danny Hawk hugged the Colonel. "Wish the circumstances were better, but things are gettin' interestin' t' say the least 'round here."

"I understand. Look, I can't be here for too much longer. I need to get back to The States. I'm going to leave this with you," the Colonel said, handing Danny a metal box about three feet in length, two feet wide, and two feet tall. "Guard this with your life. I have to get some things set up and get back here shortly. Mark and Derek are here with a charge of their own."

"Understood," Danny acknowledged. "Do you want to finish this portion off?"

"No. I trust you two will take care of Seth. He's now one of the Lord's."

"Of course!" Danny stuck his hand out, "Danny Hawk, an' this is Ethan Carson."

Seth reluctantly shook their hands, still not sure what was going on. "Seth Simmons."

The Colonel put his hands on Seth's shoulders, making sure Seth was looking at him. "Seth, you are young, and Satan would like nothing better than to get one of the Lord's who is still young. Trust these men."

"Can I? I am in a foreign country with people I don't know. I'm carrying the body of my best friend, and I have no idea where to go next, except to find his parents, who were supposed to meet me here."

"They're at the station," Danny explained. "We knew you were coming. They asked us to come an' escort you so ya won't get lost."

"I...thank you. I just don't know what's going on."

"That's where ya need t' learn t' trust in God. He's got a plan already in place."

"All right. I give."

"Good. Let's go. Have a safe trip, Colonel. See ya in a few days," Danny said to the Colonel before the Colonel went back into the airport.

"Ready for a long drive?" Ethan asked.

"Why not? I've just gotten off a long flight. What's a long drive on top of it?"

Ethan smirked. "No worries, mate," he said, resting his hand on Seth's shoulder, "I'm drivin' so ya can catch a kip."

"A kip?"

"A nap," Danny clarified. "Go with Ethan an' I'll be right behind you."

"Yeah. Sure. Ya betcha. Just go with the flow. I'm learning that I'm not the one in control anyway."

"None of us are, mate." Ethan chuckled. "And, I, for one, am grateful that I'm not."

"Believe it or not, me neither," Seth agreed as they got into their vehicle. He sighed. "I'm just along for the ride."

*   *   *

After hours of driving down the dusty roads, all the travel was starting to get to Seth. Doing his best to figure out how in the world these men expected Seth to sleep while they bounced down the rocky dirt roads was beyond him.

Pulling into a long dirt driveway, they went under a metal sign that identified the place as 'Serenity Wells Station.' Photos in Nick's apartment of the station flashed through Seth's mind as he saw the places in the photos now in living color.

Sighing, Seth admitted, "I can't believe I'm actually here. And, what's worse, I can't believe I am bringing my best friend's body here to rest."

"There's a family graveyard here on the station where his family is buried," Ethan explained, pulling up to the main house.

"I really hate that I'm here, but I wouldn't want anyone else to bring him home."

"I'm sure his family feels the same."

"About time you mates got here!" Nana reprimanded the men as they got out of the vehicle.

Danny hugged her. "Nana, always happy t' see ya, love."

When she caught sight of Seth, compassion filled her eyes. "Yer Seth, yeah?"

"Yes, ma'am."

"Well, I'm Nana. Welcome t' Serenity Wells Station."

"Thank you. I only wish it were under better circumstances."

"C'mon in, ya must be bushed. Lunch will be served in about an hour. In the meantime, you should come in outta the sun. The closer summer gets, the hotter it gets."

"Summer?" Seth questioned. "It's October."

"Right. Summer starts here shortly. Remember, yer down under, mate. Things around here are reversed. This is spring, an' we're headed into summer."

"Got it."

"Enough gum bumpin', let's get inside."

When they walked in, Seth couldn't help but think of the houses from the Old West. Made completely of wood, the main house had two stories. To his right when he walked in, was a staircase to the second story, to his left was a living room, which had an archway opening into a large dining room. From there, he could see another opening leading into the kitchen.

"Have a seat." Nana gestured. "I'll go get ya somethin' t' snack on. Those planes don't have any decent tucker on 'em."

"Tucker?"

"Food. No worries, mate, yer lookin' a bit confused. There's a lot we'll have t' teach ya here."

"No, the food wasn't the best," Seth agreed. "Um, shouldn't we take out –"

Nana waved him off. "We'll get t' that."

"Look, I know you're laid back down here, but this is blowing my mind," Seth objected. "I have your grandson's body out there, and you're acting like this is a social visit."

"It's *you* who doesn't understand," a brown-haired Nick said, coming out of the kitchen, with a drink of sun tea in his hand.

"Nick," Seth breathed out, as he stood in shock. "I don't understand."

"I see that. An', it's actually Nicolas Zachariah Sullivan now, but people call me Nico."

"I don't understand. If you're here, then who's in the casket?" Seth asked. He couldn't believe his eyes. "Please, tell me what's going on?" he begged, as he dropped onto the couch.

"Let's take a walk, mate," Nick said, helping him off the couch. "Looks like ya could use a cold one, but this'll have t' do." Passing the tea to Seth, Seth followed Nick out into the station to a bench near the barn.

When they sat down, Seth started, "So, you're really Nick? Not Nate?"

"Nate? No way! That's an insult! As Eugene would say, it's an insult of the highest offense."

Seth chuckled nervously. "Is this a dream? Is this a product of my lack of sleep?"

"No, brother, I'm real. Like I said, you're going t' have t' call me Nico here, though. According t' those in the area, I'm a cousin. Nana's trainin' me t' take over the station."

"What happened?"

"Well, that's a long story."

"Seems we have plenty of time." Seth gestured out toward the station. "I'm not going anywhere until I know what's going on. Start from where you guys drove off."

"Okay…"

*   *   *

"GO!" Seth roared before he fired off a couple more rounds. Changing the magazine, he shouted, "Don't make me tell you again! GO!"

Nick floored the vehicle, leaving Seth behind. "Katie, love, are you hit?"

"No," she said weakly.

"Can you come up here?"

As she made her way to the front of the Explorer, with blown out windows, her body was trembling. "I can't stop shaking."

"I know, just get your seat belt on," he said, fishing his cell phone out from his pocket. When she was settled, he asked, "Katie, do you love me?"

"Of course I do. Why would you ask?"

"Do you want to be with me for the rest of our lives?"

"For however long it is, yes."

"Do you trust me?"

"With my life."

"Then know that I've already got a plan in place that I need to activate."

"What does that mean?" Katie asked, her heart racing out of control.

"We need to go under. There's no escaping Lucca and Joey Rossi, unless we're dead."

"But –"

"Dial Sandy," he said into his phone, cutting her off.

"Hey, Nick! What's up, buttercup?" Sandy answered her phone.

"Sandy, do you have what I asked you to find about three weeks ago?"

Sandy's tone immediately shifted as she asked, "This isn't a social call, is it?"

"Did you do what I asked?"

"Yes."

"Can you meet me at the Cleveland Marriot?"

"The one near City Hall?"

"Yep."

"Yes."

"Bring the envelope I gave you from Damian, along with the little bag," he said before he hung up.

"What did Damian give you?" Katie asked, her nerves raw from the day's events.

"I had him get a hold of one of his contacts, who created fake paperwork for us."

"For *what*?" Katie asked, stunned by what she was hearing. "How did you know to plan this?"

"I've had this set up for some time. Actually, since I found out that Rossi was the one who was hunting you down. The only people I have included in the scheme are Sandy and Damian."

"And the bag?"

"It's hair color for me, along with some cash. I'll need to change my hair color to brown."

"Okay," Katie said, taking a deep breath. "And, what *exactly* is the plan?"

"Sandy's found a couple cadavers to represent both me and you. This took a bit, but she obviously was able to find them. In the meantime, I had Damian get our paperwork."

"What are our new names?"

"Well, I hope you don't mind that I took liberties with your name. Mine is going to be Nicolas Zachariah Sullivan, having people call me 'Nico' – using my dad's first name as my middle, and Nana's maiden name as our last name. Yours, I had changed to Kathryn Megan Sullivan. Megan is for your mother, and I used Kathryn, as a form of Katie."

Tears slowly crept down her cheeks, as she said, "That was very thoughtful. Thank you."

"Are you seriously okay with this?"

"Yes. You're right. We're never going to get away from them."

"No. And that was too close for me. I will *not* lose you."

Without another word, she reached over and grabbed his hand.

"I love you too," he said, pulling into the parking lot of the Marriot. They parked in an area where there were no cameras.

They only had to wait a few minutes, before Sandy pulled in, driving a van.

"Head over to Whiskey Island Marina," Nick said when Sandy handed him an 8x10 envelope.

"Is she okay?" Sandy asked, getting a good look at Katie.

"I think so. She's in shock, though. We just got out of a fire fight."

"I see that." She gestured to the shot out windows. "Is Seth okay?"

"He was when I left. I pray he still is."

"He will be. Mark is there," Katie said, absentmindedly.

"Who?" Nick asked, concerned.

"Mark English. He's another A.N.G.E.L. friend of Danny Hawk and Ethan Carson, from Australia. He's the one who brought me to you. He was taking out the shooters. He had me count to twenty before I ran."

"I see. When we're gone, please give Seth a call to make sure he's okay," Nick said to Sandy.

"Will do," she mentioned as she headed back to her van.

By the time they got to the marina, Katie was a nervous wreck. Worried about her friends and family getting hurt by her abrupt disappearance, she asked, "What will happen to everyone else when we disappear?"

"They'll be safe, for one. If you run, and the Rossi's think you're still alive, they're dead."

She gulped. "I see."

"Katie, I love you. I wouldn't be doing this if it wasn't necessary."

"I know."

"This is the only way I can think of to make sure everyone is safe."

"Okay. Then, let's do this," she said, as Sandy pulled next to them in an area in the marina, where there once again there were no cameras.

Nick moved the cadavers into the driver and passenger seats. While he put his watch on the male, Katie put her necklace on the female. Then he poured gasoline all over the interior before he looked to Katie, and asked, "Are you sure?"

"Light it up," Katie said, climbing into the back of the van.

Pulling out his throw away weapon, he shot each of the cadavers dead center in the chest before tossing his gun into Lake Erie. Afterward, he threw the match into the vehicle. There was a bright flash, quickly followed by the instant heat of flames swallowing the contents of Nick's Explorer. Nick sent a text and then deleted it before he threw it into the flaming Explorer.

"Okay, let's go to Burke Lakefront Airport. I've got a connection ready to take us to another airport, where we'll disappear using these," Nick said, holding up the envelope.

As Sandy pulled away, the Explorer exploded. She sighed. "I'll miss you guys. I understand why this has to be done, but you *do* know this will break Seth's heart."

"I do," Nick agreed, "and I know it's a lot to ask of you, so thank you."

"I'm going to have to lie to him."

"If he delivers my body to my family, I'll explain it then."

"You'd better. And, you'd better explain that you *made* me do this."

"I will. You just take care of your end of things."

"I already have the certificates and medical reports your friend got for me to replace with the real ones. I'll get my end done. Oh! Here, give her one of these, and then one for the next ten days."

"What's this?" he asked, giving Katie a pill and a bottle of water.

"It's Diazepam. You guys used it a while ago for her, and I had a feeling if you were calling me for your, um, we'll call them *friends*, that she was going to need them."

"I can't thank you enough. You're like the sister I never had."

"Unfortunately, I have many brothers," she countered. "But I could say that you're the brother I actually like," she said with a smirk. "Now, where are we going?" she asked, pulling into the airport.

"Over there," he directed her through the airport to a waiting plane. Once Katie hugged Sandy, and was on the plane, Nick hugged Sandy. "Really, thank you."

"I would do anything for you. Take care of her, or I will hunt you down and kill you for real."

Nick chuckled.

"No. Really. I will. Make sure to give those to her, or she's going to have a nervous breakdown," Sandy said, reminding him of the pills. "She'll sleep for quite a while with them. Give them to her once a day."

"I will. Thanks," Nick said, and climbed the staircase into the plane, and they were off.

*   *   *

"So, you're telling me that Sandy had full knowledge of this entire plan of yours?" Seth asked, stunned. "She *lied* to me?"

"I made her," Nico admitted.

"Nick, I mean Nico, I mean…I have to call you Nico?"

"Yep. An' ya have t' call Katie, Kit."

"You're serious?"

"Very much so. Ya can't call me Nick anymore."

"Fine," Seth sighed.

"I do have some good news, though."

"Please. I'll take what I can get at this point."

"Well, there's more t' the story."

"Go ahead. Let's hear it."

* * *

By the time they landed in Australia, Katie was beyond exhausted. They were greeted at the airport by Danny Hawk and Ethan Carson, who drove them directly to the station.

"Didn't expect t' see ya this soon," Nana greeted them with hugs. "What's with the brown hair?"

"I dyed it in the airport as a disguise."

"I see." Getting a good look at Katie, she shook her head. "Tsk! Tsk! What 'ave ya been doin' t' her? She looks like a dog's breakkie!"

"She's been through a lot," Nick acknowledged. "Both of us have."

"The boys have been sworn t' secrecy or they're dealin' with me," Nana explained. "We have the guest room set up for the two a' ya."

He shook his head. "We're not married yet."

"Already took that into consideration. If you two are t' have the same last name, ya should be married," Nana explained. "One a' Pete's tribe elders, George, is going t' marry you. He's inside, waiting for ya."

"We don't have a license, though, and I don't want it on record." Nick shook his head. "We need t' somehow do it so it's not on record."

"Look," Danny spoke up, "you have the same last name already. Let this be between you two an' the good Lord, with the witnesses currently here of Ethan, Nana, an' myself. Will that work for the two a' ya?"

"I don't want to be with anyone but you…ever," Katie said sternly as she took Nick's hand.

"Me neither," he agreed. Turning to Danny, he nodded. "Let's do it."

"Here, you can use my wedding ring," Nana said, taking her ring off. "I'll get another one when we're in town."

"I don't want to take your ring. That's too precious," Katie objected.

"It's a family heirloom," she explained. "It follows whoever owns the station. Nick's taking it over. It'll be yours anyway. Please, take it," she said, handing it to Nick.

Throwing his arms around Nana, Nick was at a loss for words.

"Thank you!" Katie grinned. "This means a lot."

"You mean a lot t' us as well. C'mon," she pushed Danny, "get this over with so they can get t' bed. She looks like she'll blow away in the wind."

Nick and Katie followed George's instructions, and repeated the vows before God, George, Danny, Nana, and Ethan, right there in the living room. Not quite the way she always dreamed of, but she was with the man of her dreams, so she didn't care how it was done, as long as it was right in the sight of the Lord.

When George asked Nick to put the ring on her finger and say his own vow, relief embraced his entire body. Tears of joy filled Nick's eyes when he placed the ring on her finger and said, "I didn't think I would ever be able to do this. The thought of not seeing that brilliant smile, or those beautiful eyes each day ripped me to shreds. I promise you that if it's in my power, I will do everything I can to protect you. I will keep you in my prayers, and every day I will find ways to make sure you know what you mean to me." When he looked into Katie's eyes, he saw her heart breaking. Using his thumb to wipe away her tears, he continued, "I promise to stand by you when the times are good, and when they're bad. There is nothing you can do to ever lose me again. I also promise not to keep any secrets from you, and to be by your side for as long as the good Lord allows. You are my love and have my heart."

"Kathryn?" George asked.

"I don't have a ring for you," Katie sniffed, wiping her tears.

"We'll get one next time Nana goes to town. Just say your vows, and we'll fix that issue later," Nick said, understanding her desire.

Nervously clearing her throat, she started, "Okay. Here it goes." Taking his hands in hers, she looked into his eyes. "Nick, same as you, I didn't think this was ever going to be possible, but God reminded me that love never fails. I trusted Him to bring you back to me. You have touched my heart and life more than I ever felt possible. I feel safe when I'm in your arms. Again, this is something I never thought possible. I know with Jesus and you by my side, there is nothing in this world that can ever hurt me. With your love, I see hope in the world. With your heart, I see the beauty of this planet. With your hands, I feel strength and protection. I pledge to you my honor and loyalty.

For as long as the Lord allows me to live on this planet, I will be yours. You are *my* love and have *my* heart."

When she looked to George to continue, he said, "With these vows before these people an' God, you have made yer intentions clear. By the power invested in me by the good Lord, I now pronounce ya husband an' wife. You may now kiss the bride," he barely got out before they leaned in for their first kiss since that night in the car.

As soon as their lips touched, electricity passed through them. Starting with their lips and fingertips, love flooded through them and between the two of them. Katie was sure sparks were flying as they pulled away and looked at each other.

"Perfect," Nana said, wiping the tears that slid down her cheeks. "Now, get t' bed with the two a' you!"

"Nana!" Nick blushed. "Could you be a little less blunt?"

"I meant because you were tired, not – oh!" she said, her faced flushed bright red.

Everyone burst out in laughter while Nana, for the first time she could remember, fumbled for words.

"It's okay. We're going," Nick assured her. "We're exhausted."

"Okay, Mr. an' Mrs. Sullivan. Take the room Katie used when she was here. It has a queen bed," Nana said, shoving them toward the stairs, while George headed toward the barn to see Pete before he left.

When they were out of earshot, Nana turned to Danny and Ethan. "What are ya going t' do about this?"

"Right now, Shawn O'Brien is still here, but only for another day. We do have a couple other things we have coming up, though, that are going t' get us sent out into the Outback," Danny explained. "We have t' borrow him, but onc we're done, we'll send him back until we feel that they're safe."

"When? Where?"

"We can't tell you that."

"I understand. If you pull him, are ya going t' send someone in his place?"

"He's only going t' be needed for a couple days. In that time, you can hold things together."

"That field makes me nervous." Nana shuffled her feet. "We've seen that horseman multiple times since Nick first saw him. There's something up there where the stations meet."

"We know. That's why he was here in the first place."

"With Nick here, though, isn't that gonna put a bigger target on this place?"

"It's not so much Nick as it is Katie," Danny admitted.

"What does Katie have t' do with the family curse?"

"She'll be the one t' carry your bloodline. In the process, she'll also be carrying future generations that will do great things for the Lord. There is another lady we need t' take care of who is in an equally scary position, only she's in imminent danger," Danny explained. "We have t' pick up Shawn tomorrow."

"Whatever ya need," Nana agreed. Then she admitted, "I don't pretend t' understand this God stuff, but if He's lookin' out for my grandson an' his new wife, then I will do what I can."

"Oh! He is," Ethan assured her. "He has some big plans for them."

"Go help that other young lady. Do you need t' bring her here?"

Danny shook his head. "Thank you for the offer, but she needs t' go deeper. Please have Nick pray for them, though. They have a tough road ahead."

"I will. Thank you for bringing them an' being here for their wedding," Nana said, giving the two A.N.G.E.L.s a hug before they left. As they pulled away, Nana looked toward the heavens and said aloud, "If You're really up there, please protect these men, as well as the young lady they're rescuing in the next couple of days. While You're at it, please protect us an' the land around us? That horseman terrifies me. They tell me that Yer the one in control. If You are, please show me."

*   *   *

Katie stood nervously in the middle of the room, as she waited for Nick to return from the bathroom. When she heard him come in, she tucked a piece of her hair behind her ear and cleared her throat. "I, um, am not sure what to do."

Nick looked from her, to the bed, and back again. "What are you talking about? Going to bed? Are you asking if I want the left or the right?"

"No, I..." she nervously glanced at the bed before looking back to Nick.

"Katie," he rested his hands on her shoulders, "I would love to show you how I feel about you, body and soul."

"I've never, um –"

"I know you haven't. What if we lie down and take things one moment at a time?"

Searching his eyes to see if he understood, she asked, "You know it's not that I don't want to, it's that I don't know how. I've never gone beyond kissing. I've been saving myself for my…" she corrected herself, "for *you.*"

Nick crawled into bed in his boxer shorts, and held the covers up for her to come in. "C'mon over. We'll sort this out one moment at a time. To be honest, I'm glad I can finally show you how I feel about you."

"Is it going to hurt?"

"I hope not! C'mon," he encouraged, "I want to kiss you."

Katie nervously crawled into bed with him. Taking a deep breath, she smoothed the covers.

"Tell you what, why don't we just cuddle in each other's arms and go to sleep. I want things to move at a natural pace."

"Okay," she agreed, cuddling into him. "This is weird actually sleeping with you."

Lifting her chin, he gently kissed her. Feeling tingles throughout her body, she maneuvered herself into a better position, and returned his kiss. This lasted for only a few brief moments, before the kiss seemed to take control of her entire body, and she found herself immediately lost in his arms and body.

*   *   *

The next morning Katie groaned when the sun pierced through the curtains, right into her eyes. With memories of the night before flooding her mind, she turned to her husband and brushed her fingers on his cheek. "Morning, sunshine," she said when his eyes fluttered open.

He grinned. "Morning, Mrs. Sullivan."

"I like that. Kathryn Sullivan," she said, dreamily. "It's pretty, but," she crinkled her nose, "I don't think I like being called Kathryn. It sounds so formal."

"What about Kit, for Kit-Kat? Like my favorite candy bar, since you're so sweet," he said, with a wink.

"I like Kit. That'll work. Not sure about the Nico thing either."

"It's as close as I dare go to my real name. I figured it was close enough to our real names that we'll be comfortable in using them. Also, if we happen to mess up, we can quickly fix it."

"Got it. That makes sense."

"Can you handle the name changes?"

"You gave me your heart, my mom's name, and your grandmother's name. Of course I can handle a name change. It'll just take a bit of getting used to."

"Your words touch my heart. You know that?"

"And your heart touches my soul."

He pulled her down to him, and they reignited the passion that started the night before. Showing each other how deeply they felt for the other, they enjoyed their time in the room, undisturbed.

*   *   *

"So," Seth said, as they still sat on the bench on the station, "you're telling me that you and Katie, I mean, Kit, are married?"

"Yep."

"And that you're about to take over this station?"

"Yep."

"And that I *shouldn't* kill you for putting me through this mess?"

Nico chuckled nervously, realizing how deeply it hurt Seth. "I know you're hurt, an' I get that, but I needed it t' look authentic. I know a lot of people were hurt because of this, but at least ya now have the knowledge that we're safe an' sound."

"What would have happened had I not brought your body here?"

"Sandy said she would make ya do it. I'm pretty sure she didn't give ya a choice in the matter."

"Not really."

Nico sighed. "I miss her. She had a way of putting things into perspective."

"Trust me. I know. What I *don't* know is what I'm going to do."

"What do you mean?"

"I have to go back, knowing you're alive. You're my best friend. How can I go back, supposedly after your funeral, and act like you're dead? How can I go back at all? You don't understand. Your desk just sits there, empty. We've been brothers for too long to leave here, knowing you're alive. I can't do it."

"Can't go back, or go back t' work?"

Dropping his head into his hands, he sighed. "I don't know."

"Just take some time here t' relax and breathe. My funeral is set for tomorrow."

"*What?*" Seth asked, stunned. "You're still going through with it?"

"Yep. According t' everyone here, I'm dead. I may look like me, but most of my family resembles everyone else, so I look like a cousin. As a matter of fact, anyone from here who introduces me t' anyone, calls me a cousin from the Sullivan side."

"I can't believe you colored your hair," Seth grumbled, ruffling Nico's now dark brown hair.

"That helps remind the guys t' call me Nico instead of Nick. Also, if Nate shows his ugly mug around here, they'll know which one is which."

"What are you going to do about that? What *if* Nate shows up? He could blow this wide open."

"Nope. I'm Nana's nephew. Nate doesn't know all of her brothers an' sisters. He didn't care t' find out about his family. He's too self-centered."

"Sounds like a nice guy," Seth quipped.

"Not so much. Anyway, Nana's moved us t' the master bedroom, an' she an' Pop have the guest room as theirs now. Since Mum an' Dad aren't here, yer welcome t' use their room while yer here. Otherwise, yer sharing a room with my cousin, where ya both have a twin bed."

"Either one works." Seth shrugged. "I'm still in a bit of shock that you pulled this off without me knowing."

"I'm sorry, but the fewer who knew, the better."

"When do I get to see Katie...I mean, Kit? Grr! This is going to be frustrating for a bit."

"No worries. We understand. Imagine what it's like for us."

"I can't. How is Kit handling this?"

"She's still on the sedative for a few more days, sleeping most of it off. By the time she wakes an' is coherent, the guys would have worked out the name thing."

"Did you guys change her appearance at all?"

"No need. Not many people know her. Besides, as long as her hair is, I was *not* about t' ask her t' cut it, let alone color it. She gave up more than enough."

"Got it."

"You'll probably see her t'night at dinner."

"Okay." He sighed. "This is a lot to take in. I've been mourning you two for the last week, and now here you are, sitting right in front of me. For the first time in my life, I don't know what to do. Can I really go back in the field without my partner? Can I go back to Cleveland at all without the two of you there, knowing you're here?"

"Tell ya what. Why don't ya just relax an' enjoy what Serenity Wells has t' offer, an' we'll talk about it when it gets closer t' the time for ya t' go. When are ya set t' leave?"

"I'm not…yet. I didn't want to put a timetable on it, but I do have to be in contact with Director Shaw. Speaking of which, does he know?"

"Nope."

Seth shook his head. "Sneaky."

"That was the plan."

Chapter 15

Forever Fall

Dominic Cook couldn't believe what he was reading on Katie's social media page about her. There were words of memorial and loss about her. Looking up on the internet about her, he discovered that she and Nick died in a car bomb, and Joey Rossi was wanted for questioning in regards to the incident.

"Katie," he breathed out, tears crawling down his cheeks. "I can't believe she's dead."

Going over to his desk, he pulled out his new identity papers that he got about a month into his move to Canada. Deciding against going to Oklahoma, because he was wanted in the United States, he decided to follow the photos of her trip in Australia as a memorial to her. He had always wanted to visit Australia, and this was a good reason. He felt it was a fitting way to say good-bye to her. After printing out the photos, he applied for his visa.

* * *

The day he got his visa to visit Australia, Dominic bought his ticket. Picking up the photos he printed out, along with his passport and bag, he said, "Well, Michael Esposito, looks like you're going to Australia."

Daniel 2:20-22:

20 "Praise be to the name of God for ever and ever; wisdom and power are his. **21** He changes times and seasons; He deposes kings and raises up others. He gives wisdom to the wise and knowledge to the discerning. **22** He reveals deep and hidden things; He knows what lies in darkness, and light dwells with Him.

Sneak Peek from Forever Fall

Grace Restored Series, Book 5

When they walked into the dining room for breakfast that morning, Seth looked up, stunned. "Kit? You look great! A little sleepy, but *much* better than I have seen you in a long time." When he hugged her, he said near her ear, "And, I forgive you for this ruse as well. As long as you guys are safe, I feel much better."

Hugging him one more time before letting him go, she said, "Thank you."

"So, you're Kit?" one of the ranch hands, Liam, asked, looking her up and down.

"Mind yerself," Nana cautioned. "She's his," she said, nodding toward Nico.

"I get that. Just a little admiration."

"If he doesn't rip yer arm off an' beat ya with the messy end, *she* will," Nana warned.

"She doesn't look like she could pull skin off a custard."

"Oh, she can beat you within an inch of your life," Seth spoke up. "I know who trained her."

"What are you goin' on about, ya bloody seppo?"

"That's enough!" Nico snapped. "You've offended my wife, me, *an'* my cousin's best friend, *an'* we haven't even sat down t' eat breakkie. I know y'er new here, so I'm cuttin' you a break…this time. I want everyone t' hear this: I *do not* want t' hear the term 'seppo' on this station again, *ever*! Have I made myself clear?"

"Crystal," Liam mumbled before picking up the plate of bread to pass around.

"Not so fast." Nico stopped him. "You owe both of them an apology."

"Technically he owes all three of ya an apology," Nana pointed out. "Unless ya wanna work with Pete in the barn all day shovelin' horse –?"

"Nana!" Nico cut her off.

"Pucky," Nana finished.

Nico took a deep breath before he explained, "We need t' clean some a' the language around here too. In the long term, if we have any ankle biters runnin' around here, I don't want 'em havin' mouths worse than dock workers."

"Seriously?" Liam shook his head. "We can't even talk normal? What kind of station is this?"

"One that takes care of their people like family," Barwon explained. "I don't mind watchin' my tongue t' get treated equal t' family. That don't happen on many stations."

"I know, but havin' rules on what we can say an' what we can't?"

Nico gestured. "You know where the door is."

"Y'er bloody serious?"

"Watch it, Liam," Nana warned. When he looked at her stunned, she said, "*He's* the boss."

"No, he's not. *You* are."

"Nope. He's been givin' the orders for quite some time. I've only been handin' 'em out. Y'er lookin' at his nibs over there. An' personally? I wouldn't wanna go against 'im. He's kinda big."

"I see that, but can he hold 'is own?"

Nico burst out in laughter. When Liam raised an eyebrow, Nico suggested, "We could go a couple a' rounds if ya think you can handle it?"

"No," Nana said sternly. "No fightin'."

Liam sighed. "Fine. I'll go along with yer rules."

"Right-oh," Nico said, sitting down at the table, as Kit sat down between him and Seth. "So, where am I t'day?" he asked Nana, changing the subject.

"Sheep," Nana said. "Cattle starts next week."

"Why is he doin' that? Has he never been on a station?" Liam asked.

"Wow, y'er really pushin' it, aren't ya?" Nana snapped.

"Well, if he's the boss, why is he doin' the circuit?"

"Because he wants input from all y'all," Kit explained.

"You don't have a say in any a' this," Liam scoffed. Then under his breath, he added, "Bloody seppo."

"That's it!" Nico growled as he stood, slamming his hands on the table. "You got one more shot an' y'er outta here!"

"Nico?" Nana questioned.

"He just slammed *my wife*! *No one* will slam her on this station…*ever*! This is hers just as much as it is mine."

"From what I hear, she can't even ride a horse. How is she supposed t' run a station?" Liam challenged.

Barwon leaned over and turned Liam by his chin so he was looking at him. "If ya got a problem with Kit, then ya can take it up with *me*. She is part a' the station. Whether she can ride or not, does not make or break whether it's hers. Now, ya got somethin' else t' add, *mate*?"

Liam looked at him wide-eyed. Barwon's size was intimidating at best. "Uh, no. I'm done."

"Good. If *I* hear one more objection from that big mouth a' yers, we're gonna take a walk t' the road and sort this out. At that point we'll be off the station, so Nana can't object," he said glancing at Nana. When Nana nodded, he said, "See?"

"I get it," Liam growled.

"Good. Now that that's settled, how about –" Nico was cut off by a flash of blinding light that lit up the entire house as the barn roof blew out. "Get t' the horses!" Nico shouted while a sudden rush of rain poured from the sky like a waterfall, and debris blew all over the ground from the strike.

"Good heavens!" Nana exclaimed, as everyone ran outside. "The barn's gonna burn t' the ground!"

See the rest in Forever Fall!

Books in the Grace Restored Series

Book 1   Book 2   Book 3

Book 4   Book 5

Also check out C.J. Peterson's other series –

The Holy Flame Trilogy

Divine Legacy Series

Connect with C.J. – CJPetersonWrites.com